THE ADVENTURES OF A SIMPLETON

Hans Jacob Christoffel
von Grimmelshausen

THE ADVENTURES

OF A SIMPLETON

(Simplicius Simplicissimus)

Translated by
WALTER WALLICH

A Frederick Ungar Book
CONTINUUM • NEW YORK

1990

The Continuum Publishing Company
370 Lexington Avenue
New York, NY 10017

Twelfth Printing, 1990

Printed in the United States of America

Library of Congress Catalog Card Number 63-21987

ISBN 0-8044-6229-1

THE ADVENTURES OF SIMPLICIUS SIMPLICISSIMUS

That is
An Account of the Life of

A STRANGE VAGABOND

called

MELCHIOR STERNFELS VON FUCHSHEIM

Very diverting and useful to read

BOOK I

CHAPTER I

Simplex tells of his peasant descent
And the upbringing he underwent.

IN recent years (when many people think we shall soon see the end of the world!) there has arisen a disease among humble folk which makes them claim noble birth and ancient lineage as soon as they have scraped together a little money to buy themselves fine clothes or, by some stroke of luck, have risen above the common herd. More often than not, their fathers were chimney-sweeps, day labourers, carters, and porters; their cousins donkey drivers, card sharpers, or mountebanks; their brothers jailers and executioners; their sisters sempstresses, washerwomen, and whores; their mothers bawds or even witches; and, in a word, their whole pedigree of thirty-two ancestors as soiled and stained as ever was the pastry-cooks' guild in Prague. Indeed, these newly hatched noblemen themselves are often as black as if they had been born and bred in Guinea.

Such fools I have no wish to emulate, although, to tell the truth, I have often thought I must surely be descended from some great lord or at least a knight—to judge by my inclination towards a gentleman's life of ease. If only I had the means for it! Joking apart, my birth and upbringing could well be compared with that of a prince—except for the differences. Did not my Dad have his palace in the forests of the Spessart mountains, as good as any other? Indeed, of so special a kind was it that no king could ever have built it with his own hands nor, in all likelihood, would ever have wanted to. It was daubed with clay and roofed with good rye straw rather than with sterile slate, cold lead, or red copper. To make a proper show of his wealth and nobility my Dad had the walls around his castle built—not, as great

1

lords do, of stones which you find lying by the wayside or dig out of the earth in barren places, much less of miserable bricks which you can make and bake in no time at all—but of oak, that useful and noble tree which takes a hundred years to grow to maturity. What monarch would have done the same? My Dad had his halls, rooms, and chambers thoroughly blackened with smoke, and for this reason only: that it is the most durable colour on earth and takes longer to reach true perfection than an artist devotes to his greatest master-piece. His tapestries were of the most delicate weave in the world, made for him by spiders. In lieu of pages, footmen, and grooms he had sheep, goats, and pigs, all neatly clad in their native liveries, who waited upon me often in the pastures until, weary of their company, I drove them home. His armoury was well stocked with ploughs, mattocks, axes, hoes, spades, and pitchforks, and with these weapons he exercised himself daily. For hoeing and digging were his military dis-ciplines, as they were of the ancient Romans in time of peace. The yoking of oxen was his generalship, the piling of dung his fortress-building; ploughing was his campaigning, wood-chopping his daily exercise, and cleaning out the stables his princely diversion. Thus did he master the whole wide world as far as he encompassed it, and at harvest-time won from it a rich reward.

My Dad's way of life being so truly noble, any man of sense will readily understand how my education matched it. By the age of ten I had mastered the rudiments of my Dad's aristocratic pursuits, but as far as learning was concerned I could barely count the fingers on my hand. Perhaps my Dad's mind dwelt above such things, like those of other noblemen of our day who can't be bothered with studies (or, as they would call it, 'bookishness'), which they prefer to leave to their hired pen-pushers. For the rest, I was an excellent performer on the bagpipe, from which I could conjure as sad a dirge as ever did Orpheus from his harp. But as for my knowledge of religion, nothing will convince me that I was not unique for my age in all Christendom; for I knew neither God nor man, heaven nor hell, angel nor devil; nor yet the difference between good and evil. It is easy to see, therefore,

2

that in this respect I lived like our first parents in Paradise, who in their innocence knew nothing of sickness, death, or resurrection. Indeed, so perfect was my ignorance that I was not even in the least aware of it.

But my Dad would not allow me to enjoy such bliss for long, thinking it proper that I should live in a style appropriate to my noble birth. He therefore began to train me for loftier pursuits and to set me harder tasks.

CHAPTER II

Simplex is a shepherd made
And sings the praises of his trade.

HE invested me with the highest dignity that could be bestowed, not only in his household but in the whole world: the office of shepherd. First he entrusted me with his pigs, next with his goats, and finally with his entire herd of sheep—to guard, graze, and, with the help of my bagpipe, protect them from the wolf. Thus I followed in the footsteps of David (except that he had a mere harp instead of a bagpipe), which was not a bad start. Indeed, it was a good omen that I might, in time and with luck, become a famous man. For since the beginning of time great men have started life as shepherds, as we may read in the Holy Bible of Abel, Abraham, Isaac, Jacob and his sons, and of Moses himself, who kept his father-in-law's sheep before he became the lawgiver and ruler over six-hundred thousand men in Israel.

To this it may be objected that these were saintly, godfearing men, and not peasant lads from the Spessart who knew nothing of God. I cannot deny it, but why should my childhood ignorance be held to blame? We find as many examples among the ancient heathens as we do among God's chosen people. Romulus and Remus themselves were shepherds, and so was Spartacus, who struck terror in the heart of mighty Rome herself. What, was not Paris, Priam's son, a shepherd and the Trojan prince Anchises, father of Aeneas? The beautiful Endymion, for whom chaste Luna pined, he, too, was a

3

shepherd. Yea, the gods themselves were not ashamed of this trade: Apollo kept the cows of Admetus, King of Thessaly; Mercury, his son Daphnis, Pan, and Proteus were all shepherds of great experience. Cyrus, the mighty King of the Persians, was not only reared by Mithridates, a shepherd, but kept cows himself, and Gyges was a shepherd before, by the power of his ring, he became a king. So that Philo, the Jew, speaks much to the point when he says, in his Life of Moses, that the office of shepherd is a preparation for government. As men are trained and exercised for war by hunting, so those who are intended for government should first be reared in the gentle and kindly duties of a shepherd. All this my Dad must have understood full well, and to this day it gives me no little hope for my future greatness.

But to return to my flock: I must tell you that I knew as little of wolves as I did of my own ignorance. My Dad, in consequence, was the more careful and explicit in the instructions he gave me. 'Lad,' he would say, 'watch out! Don't let the sheep stray too far, and play the bagpipe boldly, lest the wolf come and cause us loss; for he is a four-legged rogue and thief who eats man and beast. And if you are slack I will give you a hiding.' To which I replied: 'Tell me what the wolf looks like, Dad, for I've never seen one in my life.' 'You jackass,' he said, 'heaven knows what is to become of you! Big oaf that you are and don't know yet what kind of a four-legged rogue a wolf is!' He continued for a while in this strain, but finally made off, muttering to himself and thinking, no doubt, that my rough and uncouth wit could not grasp his lucid instructions.

CHAPTER III

Simplex plays his pipe indeed
But the soldiers take no heed.

So I began playing my bagpipe to such effect that it went near to killing off the toads in the orchard, which reassured me concerning my constant preoccupation—the wolf. And remembering that my Mum was in the habit of saying that one day I'd kill the chickens with my singing, I also sang, so as to strengthen my defences against the wolf. And the song I sang was one my Mum herself had taught me.

Oh peasant race, how much despised,
Yet greatly are you to be prized.
No man your praises can excel
If only he regard you well.

How little would the world now yield
If Adam had not tilled the field!
With spade and hoe he dug the earth
From which our princes have their worth.

The bounty of our native soil
We owe to your devoted toil,
And all that fruitful makes the land
Has passed through your industrious hands.

The emperor who rules our lives,
His own from your hard toil derives,
So does the soldier, though his trade
To your great loss and harm is made.

Meat for our feasts you do provide,
Our wine, too, is by you supplied.
Your plough can force the earth to give
The bread whereby we all must live.

All waste the earth, and desert, were,
Did you not ply your calling there,
And sad, indeed, the world would be
Were it to lose its peasantry.

All honour, then, to your employ
By which all men their lives enjoy.
Nature herself your labour loves
And God your handiwork approves.

Whoever yet on earth did hear
Of peasants who the gout did fear?
Yet noblemen it makes its slaves
And brings the wealthy to their graves.

From all vainglory you are free
(As in these days you well may be)
And to preserve you from its curse
The Lord has made your cross the worse.

Yea, e'en the soldier's evil ways
Serve to confirm your state of grace.
For, lest you should to pride incline,
'Your goods and house'—he says—'are mine.'

At this point in my song I found myself and my herd of sheep surrounded by a troop of heavy cavalry who had lost their way in the deep forest and whom my music and my calls to my flock had brought back on the right path.

'Aha,' I thought to myself, 'so here we are! These must be the four-legged rogues and thieves my Dad told me of.' For I mistook horse and rider (as the American natives did the Spanish cavalry) for a single creature, and was convinced that these must be wolves. I therefore sought to frighten these terrifying centaurs and to chase them away. But I had hardly blown up my bellows for the purpose when one of them seized me by the arm and threw me so roughly on to one of their looted farm-horses that I tumbled to the ground again on the other side, right on top of my cherished bagpipe, which set up a wail so pitiful as if it were crying to all the world for mercy. But to no avail: although it bemoaned my sad accident to its last breath, back I was dragged on to the horse no matter what my bagpipe sang or said. And to add to my anger, the horsemen pretended that the bagpipe had made so heathenish an outcry because I had hurt it in my fall. So away went my mare with me at a steady trot till we reached my Dad's farm. As we jogged along my brain seethed with the oddest and silliest fancies. I imagined that, sitting on one of these strange beasts, the likes of which I had never seen,

6

would soon turn me into a man of iron like the soldiers who surrounded me. But as no such change occurred, my imagination took another turn. I began to think that these odd creatures had been sent to help me drive home my flock, especially since none of them made as if to eat the sheep, but all, with one accord, hastened straight towards my Dad's farm. I therefore kept an eager look-out for my Dad, expecting him and my Mum to appear at any moment to bid us welcome. But in vain, for they and our Ursula—my Dad's only daughter—had slipped out by the back door, unwilling to wait for the arrival of our unholy guests.

CHAPTER IV

The soldiers plunder Simplex' farm,
And no one's there to stay their arm.

ALTHOUGH it was not my intention to invite the peaceable reader into my Dad's house and farm with these horsemen, who will wreak much havoc there, yet the course of my story demands that I should leave to posterity a picture of the horrifying and quite unheard-of cruelties sometimes perpetrated in this our German war—the more so since my own example proves that the Almighty in His wisdom often inflicted such evils on us for our profit. For who, kind reader, would have told me that there is a God in Heaven had not the soldiers destroyed my Dad's house and so forced me to wander among folk who could give me the necessary instruction? Until then I neither knew nor could imagine anything but that my Dad, my Mum, Ursula, I and our household were the only inhabitants of the universe, for never had I met any other human being, nor seen any house but the princely palace in which we lived and which I have already described. But soon hereafter I learned of the way of men's coming into this world, how they are here only for a little while and must often depart from it again unexpectedly. Only in my appearance was I human, and only in my name a Christian—for the rest, I was a beast of the field. But the Almighty in His mercy saw my innocence and decided to bring me to a knowledge of Him and of myself. And though a thousand ways to this were no doubt open to Him, He presumably intended to use one which would, as an example to others, punish my Dad and Mum for the careless way in which they had brought me up.

The first thing these troopers did in the blackened room of my Dad was to stable their mounts. Thereafter, each fell to his appointed task, fraught in every case with ruin and destruction. For although some began to slaughter, cook, and roast, as if for a merry banquet, others stormed through the house from top to bottom, ransacking even the privy, as though they thought the Golden Fleece might be hidden there. Some packed great bundles of cloth, apparel, and household goods, as if to set up a stall for a jumble sale, but what they had no use for they smashed and destroyed. Some thrust their swords into the hay and straw as if they had not enough sheep and pigs to slaughter. Others emptied the feather-beds and pillows of their down, filling them instead with meat and other provender, as if that would make them more comfortable to sleep on. Others again smashed stoves and windows as if to herald an everlasting summer. They flattened copper and pewter utensils and packed up the bent and useless pieces; chests, tables, chairs, and benches they burnt, though in the yard they could have found many cords of firewood. Finally, they broke every dish and saucepan, either because they preferred their food roasted or because they intended to have no more than a single meal there.

Our maid, for shame, was so man-handled in the stable that she lay there like dead. Our man they threw bound to the earth, thrust a wedge between his teeth, and poured a bucket of liquid dung down his throat. They called it Swedish Punch, but he did not seem to like it at all, pulling the oddest faces. By this method they forced him to lead some of their number to another place, where they captured more men and cattle and brought them to our farm. My Dad, my Mum, and our Ursula were among them.

And now they began to unscrew the flints from their pistols and to jam the peasants' thumbs into them, and to torture the poor lads as if they had been witches. Indeed, one

8

of the captives had already been pushed into the bread oven and a fire lit under him, although he had confessed nothing. They put a sling around the head of another, twisting it tight with a piece of wood until the blood spurted from his mouth, nose, and ears. In short, each had his own device for torturing the peasants, and each peasant received his individual torture. My Dad was of all of them the luckiest— as I then thought—for he confessed laughingly what was extracted from others with torment and pitiful moans. This honour was due, no doubt, to his position as head of the household. They put him near a fire, bound him so that he could move neither hand nor foot, rubbed the soles of his feet with damp salt, and then made our old goat lick it off, tickling him till he well-nigh split his sides with laughter. This seemed to me so diverting and engaging (never before having seen my Dad indulge in such prolonged laughter) that, to keep him company or because I knew no better, I joined in his merriment with all my heart. With shrieks of laughter he confessed his guilt and revealed his hidden treasure, which contained far more gold, pearls, and jewels than you would ever have looked for in a peasant's home. Of the captured women, girls, and maidservants I have nothing in particular to tell, for the warriors would not let me see what they did with them. But this I do know: that from time to time one could hear pitiful screams coming from different parts of the house, and I don't suppose my Mum or Ursula fared any better than the others. In the midst of all this misery I turned the spit unconcernedly, not realizing fully what was happening. In the afternoon I helped to water the horses, which brought me to the stables where our maid was lying so strangely dishevelled that I did not recognize her. She, however, called to me faintly, saying: 'Run away, boy, or the horsemen will take you with them. Try to get away, for you see how miserably . . .' and here her voice failed her.

CHAPTER V

Simplex shows the soldiers a clean pair of heels,
But now the forest its terrors reveals.

THEN did I begin to realize my unhappy position and to think of a means of escape. But where should I go? I had far too little sense to make a plan, but finally, towards evening, I ran to the woods, not forgetting to take my beloved bagpipe with me. Yet where would I go from here? Especially as the paths through the forest were as strange to me as the road to China. Pitch-dark night, indeed, protected me, but to my dim wits it was still not dark enough. I therefore hid in a thicket from which I could hear both the shrieks of tortured peasants and the singing of nightingales. And so I lay down composedly and went to sleep. But when the morning star began to glimmer in the East I saw my Dad's house in flames with no one there to try to quench the fire. I emerged from my hiding-place hoping to find some member of the household, but was quickly observed by half a dozen troopers who shouted to me to give myself up or they would shoot me dead.

I remained rooted to the ground and open-mouthed, not knowing what they meant. As I stood gaping at them like a cat at a new barn-door, with a bog—to their evident annoyance—preventing them from getting closer to me, one of them discharged his musket at me, the sudden flash and crack of which so frightened me that I fell flat to the ground, paralysed with terror. The troopers rode away, no doubt leaving me for dead, but all that day I could not pluck up enough courage to get to my feet. When night fell I finally stood up and wandered into the forest until I saw from afar the gleam of a rotting tree which gave me yet another fright. I turned tail and wandered in the opposite direction until there, too, I came upon a rotting tree which put me to flight. In this way I spent the night running from one rotting tree to another until at last blessed dawn came to my rescue, commanding the trees to leave me in peace. But little enough was gained,

10

for my heart was afflicted with dread and terror, my thighs with weariness, my empty belly with hunger, my mouth with thirst, my foolish brain with mad fancies, and my eyes with sleep. Nevertheless, I wandered on, though I knew not where, and the farther I walked, the deeper I penetrated into the forest, away from human habitation. It was then that I experienced and suffered (albeit unawares) the effects of ignorance and lack of learning. Any dumb beast in my position would have known better what to do for its protection than I did. Yet I did have sufficient wit, when darkness descended once more, to creep into a hollow tree, carefully pulling my beloved bagpipe after me, and there to settle down for the night.

CHAPTER VI

Simplex hears words of comfort and aid,
But the sight of the speaker makes him afraid.

HARDLY had I shut my eyes when I heard a voice exclaiming: 'O boundless love towards us ungrateful mortals! Oh my sole comfort, my hope, my riches, my God!' and more of the same sort which I could not understand or remember. Here, indeed, were words to comfort and encourage any Christian soul in my troubled state. Yet alas for my simplicity and ignorance! It was gibberish to me and a wholly incomprehensible language. Not only could I not grasp it but its strangeness also terrified me. Yet hearing the speaker asking for his hunger to be stilled and his thirst slaked, my own ravenous hunger prompted me to invite myself to the feast. So I plucked up courage, emerged from my hollow tree, and approached the voice. What I saw was a tall man with long, greying hair which fell untidily about his shoulders. He had a tangled beard, almost round in shape like a Swiss cheese, and his face, though pale and thin, was quite kindly. His long gown was a patchwork of rags sewn roughly together. Round his neck and body he had wound a heavy chain like St William of Aquitaine, and to my eyes he appeared so dreadful and frightening that I began to shiver like a wet dog. What greatly increased my terror was a huge crucifix, some six feet high, which he clasped to his breast. As I watched this strange apparition I had no other thought but that this must be the wolf of which my Dad had so recently told me. In my fear I whipped out my bagpipe—the only treasure I had saved from the soldiers—blew the bellows, tuned up, and began to play with all my might to drive away the fearful wolf. This sudden and strange music in so desolate a place at first caused the hermit no small shock. No doubt he thought it was some devilish apparition, come, as it had to St Antony of Padua, to try him and disturb his meditations. But presently recovering himself he mocked me as his 'tempter in the hollow tree' (whither I had retired again). Indeed, he became so confident that he advanced towards me to defy— as he thought—the enemy of mankind. 'And who,' he exclaimed, 'may you be to challenge the saints without God's leave?' I heard no more, for at his approach such terror seized me that my senses were overwhelmed and I fainted dead away.

CHAPTER VII

Simplex becomes the hermit's guest
Though the entertainment is frugal at best.

How long it was before I recovered I do not know, but I remember on waking that the old man was holding my head in his lap and had unbuttoned my blouse. Seeing the hermit so close, I yelled in terror as if he had been about to rip out my heart. But he replied: 'Do not fret, my son, I will not harm you. Be at peace!' Yet the more he comforted and soothed me, the more I screamed: 'You'll eat me, you'll eat me! You're the wolf and will tear me to pieces!' 'Good gracious, no, my boy,' he said, 'have no fear, I will not eat you.' This struggle and terrified screaming lasted a long time till finally I let him take me to his hut. Poverty was the housekeeper there, hunger the cook, and want the steward.

Here my body was regaled with vegetables and water, and my sadly confused mind comforted and steadied by the old man's kindness. So I soon surrendered to my tiredness and fell into a blissful sleep. The old man, perceiving my need of it, left me alone in his hut, for there was no room for more than one person to lie down. Some time around midnight I awoke and heard him singing this song, which I also later learned to sing:

> *Come, nightingale, thou joy of night,*
> *And let thy song for our delight*
> *Through woods and meadows ring.*
> *Come, come, praise thy Creator blest*
> *For other birds have gone to rest*
> *And care no more to sing.*
>
> *Loudly raise thy voice in praise*
> *For thou above all canst prove*
> *To God with song thy love.*
>
> *Although the sun has left the skies*
> *And all the earth in darkness lies*
> *Yet can we sing a hymn*
> *Of God His grace and God His might,*
> *Nor can the shadows of the night*
> *Hold back our praise of Him.*
>
> *So loudly raise thy voice in praise, etc.*
>
> *Echo takes up the glad refrain*
> *Merrily throws it back again*
> *And joins the song of praise.*
> *It drives the weariness away,*
> *To which we evermore are prey*
> *And mocks our sleepy ways.*
>
> *So loudly raise thy voice in praise, etc.*
>
> *The stars that shine in heaven above*
> *God's glory by their brightness prove*
> *And honour Him on high.*

13

The owls, too, though they cannot sing,
Do with hoarse cries their tribute bring
To God as they pass by.

So loudly raise thy voice in praise, etc.

Come then, sweet bird, and wake with me,
That we may never sluggards be
Who waste their time in sleep.
But rather, till the rosy dawn
Brings cheer back to these woods forlorn
A prayerful watch may keep.

And loudly raise thy voice in praise, etc.

As he sang it seemed to me as if I could indeed hear the nightingale, the owl, and the echo joining in his song. If I had known the song of the morning star and been able to play it on my bagpipe I would have slipped out of the hut to join in, so sweet did this harmony sound to my ears. But I fell asleep again and did not wake up till broad daylight. The hermit was standing over me, saying: 'Get up, child. I will give you something to eat and then show you the way through the forest so that before nightfall you can get to the village where there are people.' 'What is that,' I asked, 'village and people?' 'What!' he said, 'have you never seen a village and don't you know what people or humans are?' 'No,' I replied, 'I've never been anywhere except here. But tell me, please, what "people", "humans", and "village" are.' 'God bless my soul,' exclaimed the hermit, 'are you an imbecile or a wit?' 'I'm my Dad and Mum's boy, and my name is neither Imbecile nor Wit.' The hermit sighed in amazement, crossed himself, and said, 'Well, dear child, it seems I am compelled in God's name to instruct you better.' Whereupon there ensued the following conversation:

CHAPTER VIII

Questions and answers give the hermit a chance
Of perceiving the boy's total ignorance.

Hermit: 'What is your name?'

Simplex: 'I'm boy.'

H.: 'I can see that you are not a little girl. But what did your father and mother call you?'

S.: 'I have no father or mother.'

H.: 'Well, who gave you the blouse you are wearing?'

S.: 'My Mum, of course.'

H.: 'And what did your mum call you?'

S.: 'She called me boy; or rogue, jackass, oaf, nit-wit, and brat.'

H.: 'Who was your mum's husband?'

S.: 'Nobody.'

H.: 'Well, with whom did your mum sleep at night?'

S.: 'With my Dad.'

H.: 'And what did your dad call you?'

S.: 'He called me boy, too.'

H.: 'But what was your dad's name?'

S.: 'He's called Dad.'

H.: 'But what did your mum call him?'

S.: 'Dad, or sometimes master.'

H.: 'Did she never call him anything else?'

S.: 'She did that!'

H.: 'Well, what was it?'

S.: 'Oaf, coarse brute, drunken pig, old shit-pot, and a lot of other things when she was scolding.'

H.: 'What an ignorant ninny you are, not to know your parents' names nor your own!'

S.: 'Well, nor do you, neither!'

H.: 'And do you know how to pray?'

S.: 'Like a donkey?'

H.: 'No, no! Do you know the "Our Father"?'

S.: 'That I do.'

H.: 'Well, say it then.'

S.: 'Our Father, which arteven, hallowbename, they kingdom come, they willbedone 'n earth and is heaven, give us our trespasses as we give then that trespassus and leadest notinto temptation but deliverers from the kingdom the powerandtheglory everandever amen.'

H.: 'Good heavens! Do you know nothing then of our Lord?'

S.: 'That I do. He stood beside the door of our house where my Mum stuck him when she brought him back from the church feast.'

H.: 'Merciful God! Only now do I realize the grace and blessing Thou bestowest on us in granting us enlightenment, and how a man is but an empty shell if he has it not. Vouchsafe me, Lord, so to honour Thy holy name that I may become worthy to give due thanks for the gifts with which Thou hast so liberally endowed me! Hear me, Simplicius (for I can call you by no other name), when you say the Lord's prayer you must speak thus: "Our Father, which art in heaven, hallowed be thy name, thy kingdom come, thy will be done, on earth as it is in heaven, give us this day our daily bread. . . ."'

S.: 'And cheese, too, please!'

H.: 'O my child, be silent and learn; that will profit you far more than cheese. Your mum was no doubt right to call you a jackass. It is not seemly for such as you to interrupt their elders. They should hold their tongues, listen, and learn. If only I knew where your parents live I would gladly take you back and also give them some advice on how to bring up children.'

S.: 'I don't know where to go. Our house is burnt down, and my Mum ran away with Ursula and then came back, and my Dad, too, and our maid was lying in the stable, ill.'

H.: 'Who was it that burnt the house?'

S.: 'Well, there were some iron men who sat on sort of big things like oxen, but without horns; and they slaughtered sheep and cows and pigs, and so I ran away, too, and afterwards the house was burnt.'

H.: 'And where was your dad?'

S.: 'Well, the iron men tied him up, see? And then the old

16

goat licked his feet and he had to laugh a lot, and then he gave the iron men lots of pennies—big ones and little ones, and pretty yellow ones, too; and sort of pretty glittering things and strings of little white marbles.'

H.: 'When did all this happen?'

S.: 'When I was guarding the sheep, silly! They wanted to take my bagpipe away from me, too.'

H.: 'When was it that you were guarding your sheep?'

S.: 'I'm telling you! When the iron men came. And afterwards our shock-headed Anne said I was to run away, too, otherwise the soldiers would take me away with them. I knew she meant the iron men, so I ran away and came here.'

H.: 'And where would you like to go now?'

S.: 'I dunno. I think I'd like to stay here.'

H.: 'That would be suitable neither for you nor for me. Come and eat, and then I will take you back to where there are people.'

S.: 'You still haven't told me what "people" are.'

H.: 'People are human beings, like you and me; your dad, your mum, and your Anne are human beings, and when there are many of them together we call them "people". Now go and eat.'

This was our conversation, during which the hermit often gazed at me and then sighed profoundly. But whether this was out of pity for my extreme ignorance, or for other reasons which I only discovered some years later, I do not know.

CHAPTER IX

Simplex becomes a Christian child
Who erstwhile was a beast run wild.

I FELL to eating and stopped prattling, but only until my hunger was stilled and the old man told me to be gone. Then did I marshal the gentlest words my rough peasant upbringing gave me to command, in a great effort to persuade him to let me stay. Although it must have been a trial for him

17

to bear with my unwelcome presence, he finally consented—not so much because he thought I might be of use to him in his approaching old age, but rather to instruct me in the Christian religion. His greatest concern was that the hard life he led would soon prove too much for my tender years.

A time of some three weeks or so was set as my probationary period, and as it was about the time when gardeners look to their tools after the winter's rest, I was instructed in this profession also. I bore myself so well that the hermit took great pleasure in me. And this not because of the work I did, and to which I had always been accustomed, but because he saw that I was as attentive in listening to his instructions as the impressionable and hitherto perfectly blank mould of my mind was apt at receiving them. This made him the more determined to bring me to a knowledge of everything that was good. He began his instruction with the fall of Lucifer, continued with Paradise and how our parents were driven out from there, and finally passed on to the laws of Moses. By means of the Ten Commandments and their interpretation (which he called a true measure to know the will of God and to lead a holy and righteous life) he taught me to distinguish virtue from vice, and to do good and avoid evil. At last he came to the Gospel and told me the story of Christ's birth, suffering, death, and resurrection, concluding with the Day of Judgement and a picture of heaven and hell. All this he told me in sufficient detail, yet without wearisome embroidery, just as he thought I could best grasp and understand it. When he had finished with one subject he would start another, and was so patient and discreet in answering my many questions that I could have wished for no better teacher. His life and his instruction were for me a constant sermon which by God's grace bore such fruit in my understanding—less dull and cloddish than it might appear from this story—that in those three weeks I absorbed all that a good Christian ought to know of his religion. Moreover, I conceived such an affection for my teacher and his lessons that it often kept me awake at night.

But the reason why I grasped so quickly all that the pious hermit taught me was that the tablet of my soul had previously been quite empty and void of other impressions which might have obstructed the imprint of his teaching. And to this day I have retained, compared with other people, that certain simplicity which first prompted the man of God, not knowing my true name, to call me Simplicissimus.

The hermit also taught me to pray, and when he had tested, to his own satisfaction, my firm resolve to stay with him we built a hut for me like his own: of wood, twigs, and earth, shaped like a soldier's tent or like the potato clamps which peasants construct in some parts, and so low that I could barely sit up in it. My bed was of dry leaves and grass and filled the whole hut, so that I hardly know whether to call this dwelling a hole, a covered bedstead, or a hut.

CHAPTER X

A hermit's life is hard indeed,
Yet Nature supplies his every need.

SOME two years I stayed in this forest—until the hermit died and just over half a year thereafter. I think it right, therefore, to give the curious reader, who often wants to know even the smallest details, an account of how we lived and occupied our time.

Our food consisted of all kinds of vegetables, turnips, cabbage, beans, peas, lentils, buckwheat, and the like. Nor did we despise beech-nuts, wild apples, pears, and cherries. Our hunger often made us grateful even for acorns. Bread—or what we called 'cake'—we made of ground Italian rye and baked in ashes. In winter we caught birds with traps and snares; in spring and summer God ladled their fledglings out of their nests for our sustenance. Often we made do with snails or frogs, and one of our pleasures was to fish with rod or net in a well-stocked brook nearby. All this helped to make our crude vegetables palatable. Once we caught a wild piglet which we penned, fattened with acorns and beech-nuts, and finally ate. For my hermit knew that it could be no sin to enjoy what God had created for man's benefit. We used little salt and no spices whatever, for, having no cellar, we dared not arouse a desire for drink. What little salt we needed we got from a parson who lived some fifteen miles away, and of whom I shall have much to tell hereafter.

As for household tools, we had enough. There was a spade, a pick, an axe, a hatchet, and an iron pot for cooking which was not our own, but borrowed from the parson. Each of us had a blunt, worn knife as our sole personal possession. We needed no dishes, plates, spoons, forks, kettles, pans, grills, spits, salt-cellars, or other kitchen and table ware, for our pot served us as a dish and our hands as forks and spoons. If we wanted to drink we sucked water from the well through a reed or else lowered our mouths into it like Gideon's men. Of clothing, wool, silk, cotton or linen—either for our beds or our table and furnishings—we had none but what we stood up in, for we were content if it protected us from rain and cold. Otherwise we had no fixed rule or order in our household, except on Sundays and holy days, when we set out at midnight, in time for divine service at the parson's church, which stood some way apart from the village. Afterwards we returned home as secretly as we had come and, footsore and weary, sat down with a good appetite to a frugal meal. The rest of the day the hermit spent in prayer and in teaching me the word of God.

On working days we did whatever needed doing, according to the seasons and our condition. Sometimes we worked in the garden, at others we gathered mould from shady places and hollow trees and spread it on our soil in place of dung. Sometimes we wove baskets or fish-nets or otherwise busied ourselves. And during all these occupations the hermit never ceased instructing me in all that was godly. Meanwhile this hard life trained me to withstand hunger, thirst, heat, cold, hard work and, indeed, all kinds of tribulations. Above all, it taught me to know God and how best to serve Him. To tell the truth, my faithful hermit would let me know no more, for he held that prayer and hard work were enough for a Christian's salvation. That is why, although well versed in spiritual matters, knowing my Bible and speaking German like a book, I yet remained an utter simpleton and, when I left the forest, cut so sorry a figure in the world that you could not have tempted a dog from the fireside with me.

CHAPTER XI

The hermit here is laid to rest,
And buried by Simplex, at his behest.

I HAD spent two years or so in this manner and had barely grown accustomed to the hard hermit's life when my best friend on earth grasped his pick, gave me the spade, took me by the hand as usual, and led me into the garden where we were accustomed to say our prayers. 'Well, Simplici, dear child,' he said, 'by the grace of God the time has come for me to pay my debt to Nature and to leave this world. I am leaving you behind, certain that you will not tarry long in this wilderness. Foreseeing what awaits you in the world beyond, I have tried to set your feet in the paths of virtue and to teach you those things which, if you rule your life by them, will ensure your soul's salvation and make you worthy to dwell in the presence of God and His saints for ever and ever.'

These words brought tears to my eyes, and I said: 'My dearest father, will you then leave me alone in this wild forest? Am I then . . .' I could say no more, for my heart-ache and the great love I bore my faithful father quite overpowered me, and I fell fainting at his feet. He raised me up, comforted me as best he could, and, gently chiding, asked me if I would question the decree of the Almighty. 'Do you not know,' he said, 'that neither heaven nor hell can contend against it? Enough, my son. Would you heap more burdens on this weary body of mine, which longs but for eternal rest? Would you force me to tarry in this vale of tears? Ah, no, my son, let me depart, for neither with tears nor with lamentations, and least of all with my consent, shall you force me to continue this miserable life, since God wills it otherwise. Dry your idle tears and listen rather to my last words: The longer you live, the more you should try to know yourself. And if you grow as old as Methuselah, do not cease to strive after self-knowledge. For most men are damned because they do not know what they are, nor what they could and should be.' He also advised me earnestly to avoid bad company, for its damage—he said—was beyond measure; and he gave me this example: 'If you pour a drop of Malmsey into a bowl of vinegar it straightway turns to vinegar. But if you pour the same amount of vinegar into a bowl of Malmsey it will become absorbed in the wine. Dearest son,' he said, 'above all things remain steadfast, for blessed are those who endure unto the end. And if, against my hopes, human weakness should make you stumble, do not persevere in sin but raise yourself up again by sincere penitence.'

When he had spoken these words he began to dig his own grave with his pick. I helped him as best I could and as he instructed me, yet without realizing his purpose. As we worked he said: 'My dear and veritable son (for you are the only creature I have raised to God's glory), when my soul has departed to its rest, do your duty by my body and pay it the last honours. Cover me over with the earth we are now digging.' Thereupon he took me in his arms and kissed me and hugged me tighter than would have seemed possible for so weak and old a man. 'Dear child, I commend you to God's protection and die the happier because I believe He will grant my prayer.' I, meanwhile, could do nothing but weep and cry out, clutching the chains he wore about his neck as if to hold him and prevent him from leaving me. But he said: 'Let go of me, my son, so that I may see whether the grave is big enough.' Then he took off his chains and his gown and descended into the grave like one about to lie down to sleep, saying: 'Almighty God, take back now the soul thou gavest me, into thy hands I commend my spirit.' And with these words he gently closed his lips and eyes. But I stood there like an ox, unable to believe that his dear soul had indeed departed from his body, for I had often before seen him in such a trance.

As was my habit on such occasions, I stayed beside the grave for several hours, praying. But when I saw that my beloved hermit would not wake I descended into the grave and began to shake, kiss, and caress him. But there was no response; inexorable death had robbed poor Simplicius of his dear companion. I bedewed and embalmed his lifeless body with my tears, and after I had run up and down for some time crying and tearing my hair, I at last began to heap earth upon him, with more sighs than spadefuls. Yet when I had barely covered his face I went down into the grave to uncover it again, so that I might see and kiss it once more. So I went on all day administering the funeral service and requiem, for there was neither bier, coffin, pall, candles, nor pall bearers, mourners, or priests to sing him to his rest.

CHAPTER XII

Determined to leave his forest behind
Simplex is soon brought to change his mind.

A FEW days after my dearest and most worthy hermit's death I went to the village to tell the parson of my master's end and to ask him what I should do next. Although he strongly advised me not to stay in the forest, pointing out the palpable dangers by which I was surrounded, yet I decided on the path of courage, following in my master's footsteps and living throughout the summer in the forest like a pious monk. But time, which changes all things, gradually wore away what I felt for my hermit, and the bitter frosts of winter cooled the ardour of my good intentions. The more I began to falter, the more negligent I became in my prayers, and instead of devoting myself to divine and lofty thoughts, I allowed my mind to become obsessed with a desire to see something of the world. My stay in the forest having thus lost its purpose, I decided to visit the parson once more, to see if his advice would reinforce my inclination. As I approached the village I saw that it was in flames, a troop of horsemen having just sacked and set fire to it, killing some of the peasants, putting others to flight, and taking a few prisoners. Among these was the parson. Merciful God, how full of trouble and misfortune is life! Hardly has one disaster passed when the next is already upon us. No wonder the heathen philosopher Timon had gallows erected in Athens so that people could hang themselves from them and end the misery of their lives by a brief act of violence. The horsemen were getting ready to depart and leading the parson by a rope, like a poor sinner. Some cried: shoot him! others wanted his money. But he raised his hands in supplication and asked, in the name of the Last Judgement, for mercy and Christian compassion. In vain; one of the horsemen rode him down, simultaneously striking him such a blow on the head that the blood spurted forth and he fell heavily to the ground, commending his soul to God. The captured peasants fared no better.

But even as it seemed that the horsemen, in their bloodthirsty cruelty, had altogether lost their senses, a crowd of armed peasants emerged from the forest like a swarm of wasps whose nest has been stirred with a stick. They yelled so fiendishly and set upon the horsemen with such fury that my hair stood on end, for I had never seen such a clash. The horsemen took to their heels, abandoning not only the cattle they had stolen but also their bundles and baggage, forsaking all their loot lest they themselves should fall prey to the peasants. Nevertheless, some of them fell into their hands and were shown no mercy.

This incident bade fair to rid me of my desire to see the world, for I thought: if this is how the world goes, then I am far better off in my wilderness. But still I wanted to hear the parson's opinion. I found him faint and shaken from his blows, but he summoned the strength to tell me that he could neither help nor advise me, having himself been brought to such a pass that he would doubtless have to earn his bread by begging. Even if I decided to stay in the forest—he told me—I could expect no help from him, seeing that his church and parsonage were destroyed.

Sadly I returned to my home in the woods, and since this journey had given me little comfort but much cause for serious thought, I resolved never to leave the wilderness and, like my hermit, to pass the rest of my life in pious contemplation. Already I had pondered whether I could not make do without salt (for which I had hitherto depended on the parson) and thereby cut my last link with mankind.

CHAPTER XIII

The war on Simplex' homestead preys,
He dreams of warriors and their ways.

So, to confirm my resolve and become a true anchorite, I donned the hair shirt my hermit had left me and bound myself with his chains. Not that I required them to mortify my unruly flesh, but in order to resemble my forerunner in my habit as well as in my way of life, and also to protect myself the better from winter's bitter cold.

But the second day after the sacking and burning of the village, as I was sitting in my hut and praying while some swedes were frying on the fire for my evening meal, I was surrounded by thirty or forty musketeers. Although they marvelled at the strangeness of my person, they lost little time in contemplation, but at once ransacked my hut, seeking what was not there for them to find. For I had nothing but books, which they threw all in a heap because they had no use for them. At last, when they had taken a closer look at me, they realized from my feathers what manner of bird they had caught, and that they would have little profit from their enterprise. They then fell to wondering at my austere way of life and expressed much pity for my tender years—especially the officer who commanded them. He showed me every consideration and begged rather than ordered me to guide him and his party out of the forest in which—he said—they had been wandering for days. I was only too happy to oblige him, in order to be rid as quickly as possible of my unwelcome guests. I led them by the shortest way to the village where the poor parson had been so grievously maltreated, that being the only way I knew out of the wood.

But when I returned home I discovered that the soldiers

had not only destroyed my hearth and plundered what household goods I possessed but also carried off my store of provisions which I had grown and gathered during the summer to see me through the winter. What now? In this extremity I learned the true meaning of prayer. I gathered my poor wits together and racked my brains what to do next. But since my experience of the world was as unhappy as it was limited, I could find no way out. In the end I did what was best: commending myself to God and trusting in Him, without which I would undoubtedly have despaired and perished. Moreover, the wounded parson and the enraged peasants were constantly on my mind; I thought less about my food and survival than about the enmity which existed between soldiers and peasants. Yet in my simplicity I could come to no conclusion but that there must be two species of human being in the world, not both descended from Adam; one tame and one wild, like the beasts of the field, since they pursued each other so relentlessly.

With such thoughts, cold, miserable, and hungry, I fell asleep. And it seemed to me, as I dreamed, that all the trees around my hut suddenly changed and took on a different appearance. On every tree-top sat an officer and every branch was decked—not with leaves but with all sorts of men. Some bore lances, others muskets, pistols, halberds, pennants, drums, and fifes. It was a gay sight, for they were all tidily mustered and graded. The roots of the trees consisted of people of no account: peasants mostly, artisans and labourers, but who gave the tree its sap and renewed its strength whenever it had need of it. Indeed, they even replaced from among their number the fallen leaves, to their own great hurt. Meanwhile they complained bitterly of those that sat in the tree, and with good cause, for the whole weight of it pressed upon them so heavily that it squeezed all the money from their pockets and even from behind locked doors. If the money would not come of its own accord the commissaries combed them with brooms (which they called military requisition) to such purpose that they drew sighs from their breasts, tears from their eyes, blood from their finger-tips, and the marrow from their bones. Yet not all felt the oppression equally, some

26

being what people call flibbertigibbets, who cared about nothing, took it all with a shrug of their shoulders, and in their
affliction had empty-headed folly for their comfort.

CHAPTER XIV

Simplex dreams more of soldiers and war
And how rarely the humble exalted are.

So did the roots of these trees suffer misery and tribulation
and those on the lower branches even greater hardship
and toil—although merrier than the roots and also arrogant,
tyrannical, godless as a rule, and a perpetual and intolerable
burden to the roots. And around those on the lower branches
was written this verse:

> *Hungry or thirsty, cold or hot,*
> *Working or wanting, whatever our lot;*
> *Injustice, rape, and murder our trade;*
> *That is how mercenaries are made.*

This verse was a true and perfect mirror of their employment. For gluttony and drunkenness, hunger and thirst, whoring and sodomy, gambling and dicing, murdering and being
murdered, slaying and being slain, torturing and being tortured, pursuing and being pursued, frightening and being
frightened, robbing and being robbed, looting and being
looted, terrorizing and being terrorized, mortifying and being
mortified, beating and being beaten; in short, nothing but
hurting and harming and being, in their turn, hurt and
harmed, this was their whole purpose and existence. From
this nothing could divert them—not winter or summer, snow
or ice, heat or cold, wind or rain, mountain or valley, swamp
or desert, ditches, mountain-passes, oceans, walls, water,
fire, or ramparts. Neither father nor mother, sister nor
brother, no, nor the danger to their own lives, consciences,
and souls, and the very fear of eternal damnation itself, nor
anything that can be named could stay their purpose. They
laboured at their task until at last, in battles, sieges, assaults,

campaigns, yea, even in their winter-quarters (which are the soldier's paradise, especially when he is billeted on a well-to-do peasant) one by one they died, perished, and rotted. All but a few who, in their old age, unless they had spent their time prudently in looting and thieving, made the very best beggars and vagabonds.

Immediately above these toilers sat old henroost-robbers who had spent some years in great peril on the lowest branches, clawed their way upward, and now looked somewhat more mannerly and reputable than their inferiors. Above them were others yet higher, whose pretensions, too, were more lofty, since they gave orders to those beneath them. And now came a length of tree-trunk, smooth and branchless, so greased with the lard of favouritism and the soap of envy that no man, by whatever feats of courage, skill, or wisdom, could climb it unless he was of noble birth; for the trunk was more smoothly polished than a marble column or a steel mirror. Above this stretch sat those with pennants—some young, others grey-beards. The young ones had been pulled up by their cousins, but some of the grey-beards had got there by themselves, either up the silver ladder of bribery or by some other bridge with which good fortune and the want of better men had provided them.

Above these sat still others who also had their worries, troubles, and annoyances; but they had this advantage, that they were able to lard their pockets with fat which they cut from the roots by means of a knife called 'requisitioning'. They were best and most suitably served when a commissary bird passed by and emptied a basinful of coins over the tree for its nourishment. Being at the top, they caught most of what came down, letting little or nothing fall through to the lower branches. And this is why of the lower ones more used to die of hunger than were killed by the enemy, a risk to which those on the upper branches never seemed exposed.

Thus the tree teemed with an incessant scrabbling and clawing, for everyone wanted to occupy the highest seat of good fortune. Some there were, lazy, feckless rascals not worth their rations, who cared little about preferment and merely did their duty. But in general those on the lower branches hoped for the fall of those above them, so that they could take their places. Yet if out of ten thousand one achieved success, it came to him so late in life that he would have been better off toasting crumpets by the fireside than facing the enemy in the field. Yet if a man bore himself well and did his duty, as like as not the envy of his fellows or some other stroke of ill-fortune would lay him low, stripping him of his position and his life. Nowhere was the climb harder than at the slippery stretch I have mentioned, for whoever had a good corporal or sergeant was loath to lose him—as he must if the man was to become an ensign. Therefore the choice mostly fell—not on veterans, but on pen-pushers, valets, overgrown pages, noblemen in distress, poor relations, or other parasites and starvelings, who took the bread out of the mouths of men of greater merit and became ensigns.

CHAPTER XV

Simplex leaves the hermit's home
Nor heeds the troubles yet to come.

As I looked at the trees, which covered the entire country, I saw them swaying and clashing one against the other, which sent the men tumbling down in clusters and crashing to the ground. One moment they were on top of the world, the next they were dead. In the twinkling of an eye one lost an arm, another a leg, and a third his head. And as I watched it seemed to me as if all the trees I saw were but a single tree, at the top of which sat Mars, the god of war, and the tree's branches covered all Europe. Indeed, this tree could have overshadowed the whole world, but envy and hate, suspicion and jealousy, pride, arrogance, avarice, and other such pleasing virtues blew it about like a blistering north wind, so that it was quite thin and transparent.

The mighty roar of these bitter winds and the rending sound with which the tree seemed to be breaking up woke me from my sleep, and I found myself alone in my hut. Again I began to brood and turn over in my mind what I should do. To stay in the forest was impossible, for my possessions had vanished. All that remained were a few books scattered about here and there. As I gathered them up with tears in my eyes and in my heart, a fervent prayer to God to guide and lead me whither I should go, I chanced upon a letter which my hermit had written while he was still alive, and this was what it said: 'My dear Simplici, when you find this letter, leave the forest forthwith and save yourself and the parson from your present troubles, for he has done me much good. God, whom you must always have in your heart and to whom you must pray with all your might, will lead you to the place where you must go. But when you leave, remember to keep your eyes fixed on God and try diligently to serve Him always, just as if you were still with me in the forest. Remember always my last words which I spoke to you before I died, and you will prevail. Farewell!'

I smothered the letter and the hermit's grave with kisses and set out to look for human beings. For two days I walked straight through the forest, resting at night in hollow trees. Food I had none but beech-nuts which I gathered as I went. On the third day I came upon a large, open field where I feasted, as you might say, on grain from the sheaves of wheat which the peasants had abandoned in their flight after the famous Battle of Nördlingen. I made my bed in a stook, for it was cruelly cold, and ate my fill from the ears of wheat I rubbed between my hands—a meal the like of which I had not enjoyed for a long time.

CHAPTER XVI

Simplex arrives at Hanau's gates
Where the figure he cuts great wonder creates.

A T break of day I had another meal of raw wheat and then went across the fields until I came to a highway which brought me to the splendid fortress of Hanau. As soon as I saw the first sentries I tried to run away, but two musketeers seized me and took me to their guardroom.

Now before I continue with my story I must acquaint the reader with the peculiar figure I cut at that time. My dress and carriage were so altogether odd, astonishing and uncouth that the governor of Hanau had my portrait painted. In the first place, my hair had not been cut, curled, combed, or brushed for two years and a half. Impregnated with the dust of many seasons instead of powder, the thatch upon my head and about my pale face gave me the appearance of a ruffled owl in a bad temper. Since I went bare-headed and my hair was naturally curly, it looked as if I were wearing a Turkish turban. My dress matched my crowning glory, for I was wearing the hermit's coat—if such it could be called—of whose one-time texture nothing remained but the shape, held together by more than a thousand patches of every colour, sewn edge to edge or joined by darns. Over this decayed and much-mended coat I wore a hair shirt like a gown, having unstitched the sleeves which I used for breeches. Above the shirt my whole body was hung before and behind with chains, neatly laced as in the pictures of St William of Aquitaine. In short, I looked like one of those one-time prisoners of the Turks who wander about the countryside begging for the friends they have left behind in captivity. My shoes were of wood, the laces pleated from strips of bark, and my feet were as red as boiled lobsters, so that it seemed as if I wore stockings in the national colours of Spain or had dyed my skin with brazil. I truly believe that if a fair-ground mountebank or stall-holder had exhibited me as a Samoyed or an Eskimo he would have found many a fool to pay the entrance fee.

Now though any man of sense could have told from my thin and starved appearance and wretched clothes that I had not escaped either from a cook-house or a lady's boudoir, still less from the court of some great nobleman, I was nevertheless closely questioned in the guardroom. And just as the soldiers could not take their eyes off me, so I, for my part, gazed in wonder at the mad apparel of their officer who examined me. I could not decide whether it was a He or a She, for he wore his hair and beard after the French fashion. Plats hung down either side of his face like horse-tails, and his beard had been so pitifully plucked and mutilated that between nose and mouth only a few short and almost invisible hairs remained. His wide breeches added to my confusion concerning his sex, looking, as they did, more like a woman's skirt than like a pair of men's trousers. I thought to myself: If this is a man, then he ought to have a proper beard, for the fop is not as young as he pretends. But if he is a woman, why has the old whore so much stubble around her mouth? Surely it must be a woman, I thought, for no honest man would ever let such indignity be inflicted on his beard, seeing that even billy-goats, when their beards have been cut, are ashamed to show themselves among the herd. As I could reach no firm conclusions and did not know that this was the present fashion, I finally took him to be half man and half woman.

This mannish woman or womanish man, as I thought him, had me searched from head to foot, but found nothing on me but a little book of birch-bark in which I had written my daily prayers and which also contained the letter which my pious hermit had left me as a farewell. This he took, and as I was afraid of losing it, I fell down before him, clasped his knees, and said: 'Please, dear hermaphrodite, let me keep my prayer-book!' 'You fool,' he answered, 'who the devil told you that my name was Hermann?' Then he ordered two soldiers to lead me to the Governor, giving them the prayer-book to take with them, since the dandy himself, as I had already noted, could neither read nor write.

So they led me through the town, where crowds gathered as if a sea-monster were on show; and all who saw me had their own ideas about my odd appearance. Some thought me a spy, others a lunatic, some swore I was a wolf-child, others again said that I must be a ghost or apparition portending some strange event. Some also there were who merely considered me a fool, and these would no doubt have been nearest the mark had I not had a knowledge of our Lord.

CHAPTER XVII

Simplex is carried off to jail,
But yet the Lord protects him well.

WHEN I was brought before the Governor he asked me
whence I came. I replied that I did not know. He then
asked: 'And where do you want to go?' Again I answered: 'I
do not know.' 'What the devil *do* you know, then?' he asked.
'What is your trade?' As before, I said I did not know. He
asked: 'Where is your home?' and when once more I said I
did not know the expression on his face changed, but whether
from anger or astonishment I could not tell. However, since
most people are inclined to expect the worst, and with the
enemy, moreover, not far away, he agreed with those who
thought me a traitor or a spy and ordered me to be searched.
When my escort told him that this had already been done and
nothing found on me but the little book they handed him, he
scanned the pages and asked me who had given me it. I
replied that I had always had it, having made it myself and
written what was in it. He asked: 'But why of birch-bark?'
I answered: 'Because the bark of other trees is not suitable.'
'You clown,' he said, 'I am asking you why you did not write
on paper?' 'Because,' I said, 'we had run out of paper in the
forest.' 'What forest? Where?' But to this I once again gave
my usual answer that I did not know.

Then the Governor turned to some of the officers of his
retinue and said: 'This boy is either an arch-rogue or a fool.
Yet he cannot be altogether a fool if he can write like this.'
And to show them the excellence of my handwriting he turned
the leaves of the book so briskly that my hermit's letter fell
out. As he ordered it to be picked up my face turned pale, for
I considered it my greatest treasure and relic. This did not
escape the Governor, and sharpened his suspicion of treason,
especially when he had opened and read the letter. He said: 'I
know this handwriting and that it belongs to an officer I know
well, though I cannot remember who he is.' At the same time
the contents struck him as strange and incomprehensible, for

he said: 'This is undoubtedly a code which no one can understand save he to whom it is addressed.' Then he asked me my name, and when I answered 'Simplicius' he said: 'Yes, indeed, and a very suitable name, too! Take him away and put him in irons, perhaps that will make him talk.'

So my two escorts went with me to what was to be my next lodging—the lock-up—and handed me over to the jailer who carried out his orders by chaining me hand and foot, as if I had not been wearing enough chains as it was.

This was but the beginning of the welcome the world held in store for me. Hangmen and their attendants soon arrived with instruments of torture, and though I took comfort from the knowledge of my innocence, my situation now seemed to me cruelly desperate. 'Oh God,' I said, 'how rightly am I served! Simplicius left the service of God and went out into the world in order to receive the just reward of his fecklessness. Oh unfortunate Simplici! Where has your ingratitude brought you? Behold, hardly had God made Himself known to you and accepted you as His servant when you turned your back on Him! Could you not have continued to eat acorns and beans in order to serve your Creator in peace? Did you not know that your faithful hermit and teacher fled the world and chose the wilderness for his home? Oh you blind fool, to leave it for the satisfaction of your base desire to see the world!'

Thus I accused myself, prayed to God for forgiveness and commended my soul to Him. Meanwhile we were approaching the prison, and when the peril was greatest God's help was nearest. For as, surrounded by hangmen and a great multitude of people, I stood in front of the gate waiting for it to open and let me in, it happened that the parson whose village had recently been sacked and burned also wanted to see what was afoot (he himself also being under arrest). When he looked out of the window and saw me he cried aloud: 'Is it you, Simplici?'

Hearing and seeing him, I could only raise both my hands to him, crying: 'Oh father, father, father!' He asked me what I had done. I replied that I did not know, but that I had assuredly been brought here because I had run away out of the forest. But when he heard that they took me for a spy he begged them to stay their hand, since he, knowing me better than anyone else, wanted to tell the Governor the truth about me, which could—he said—serve both his cause and mine and persuade the Governor not to lay hands on me.

CHAPTER XVIII

Simplex is saved from troubles sore
And Fortune smiles on him once more.

HE was granted permission to see the Governor, and about half an hour later I, too, was taken from the jail and brought to the servants' parlour, where I found two tailors, a cobbler with shoes, a shopkeeper with stockings and hats, and another man with other garments waiting to dress me. They took off my patchwork coat, my hair shirt, and my chains to allow the tailors to measure me for a suit. Then a barber came with lather and strong soap, but as he was about to demonstrate his skill on me, another order arrived which frightened me horribly, to the effect that I should at once resume my former clothes. Yet this was not as ominous as I had feared, for now there arrived a painter with his paints and brushes. He scrutinized me closely, sketched me, painted in the background, hung his head on one side to compare his subject with his painting, altered an eye here and a nostril there, until he had made so exact a copy of Simplicius that I was quite horrified when I saw myself. Only then was the barber given his head, who spent an hour and a half or more on my hair, cutting some of it off, in accordance with the fashion, for I had plenty to spare. Then he put me in a bath tub and cleaned the dirt of three or fours years from my thin, starved body. As soon as he had finished they brought me a white shirt, shoes, stockings, a collar, and even a plumed hat. The trousers, too, were very handsome and braided all over. The only thing missing was the jerkin, which the tailors had not yet finished. Meanwhile the cook appeared with nourishing broth and the maid with a cup of wine. And there sat Master Simplicius like a young lord, mightily pleased. Though I had no idea what they planned with me, I ate a hearty meal, never having heard of a condemned man's breakfast. All this agreed with me so well that it is impossible to describe, and I do not think I ever enjoyed myself more in my whole life than at that moment. When the jerkin was ready I put that on, too, and found myself looking like a coat-rack or a scare-crow, for the tailors had purposely made all my clothes too large, in the hope that I would soon put on weight, in which I did not disappoint them. My forest garb, together with the chains, they put in a museum with other rarities and antiques, and my life-size portrait beside them.

After supper his lordship—meaning me—was conducted to a bed the like of which he had never seen either in his Dad's house or with the hermit. But my belly growled and grumbled all night, keeping me awake, ignorant, no doubt, of what was good for it, or astonished at the splendid and unaccustomed fare with which it had been regaled. Nevertheless, I stayed in bed until the sun had risen (for it was cold), pondering the strange adventures of the last few days and how faithfully God had helped me and brought me to so comfortable a place.

CHAPTER XIX

Simplex hears the parson tell
Who was the man who taught him so well.

THE same morning the Governor's chamberlain ordered me to go to the parson to learn what the Governor had told him concerning me. An orderly was detailed to escort me. The parson took me to his study, seated himself, bade me sit down, too, and began: 'My dear Simplici, the hermit with whom you stayed in the forest was not only this Governor's brother-in-law but also his protector in war and his closest friend. According to the Governor, his brother-in-law was, from his earliest youth, as brave a soldier as he was godly and devout, though these two virtues do not often go hand-

36

in-hand. In the end, his religious bent and various unhappy experiences checked the course of his worldly ambition, causing him to relinquish his title and the sizeable estates he owned in Scotland; for he came to consider all mundane affairs vain, foolish, and contemptible. In a word, he hoped to exchange his present high rank for a greater glory hereafter, his noble mind having become disgusted with all worldly pomp. From that time on all his hopes and desires were directed to the hard life which you saw him lead in the forest and which you in some way shared with him until his death.

'Nor will I withhold from you how he came to our forest and to the austere hermit's existence that he craved, so that you may hereafter be able to tell the story to others. Two nights after the bloody Battle of Höchst was lost he arrived alone and unescorted at my parsonage in the early hours of the morning, just as my wife, my children and I had gone to sleep—for what with the noise of flight and pursuit all over the country which always follows a battle, we had been kept awake the whole of the previous night and most of this one. At first he knocked gently, then more violently until he had roused me and my weary household. At his request and after a short exchange of words—most civil on both sides—I opened the door and saw a Cavalier dismount from a splendid horse. His costly apparel was splashed with his enemies' blood as liberally as it was decorated with gold and silver braid, and in his hand he still gripped his naked sword, which gave me a bad fright. But he quickly sheathed it and treated me with the utmost courtesy, making me wonder why so fine a gentleman should ask a poor village parson so humbly for shelter. Handsome of person and splendidly attired as he was, I addressed him as the Count of Mansfeld himself, but he assured me that he was comparable to the count only in their common misfortune, and that in this, indeed, he thought himself the other's superior. For he lamented three sorrows: the loss of his wife, whose time was almost upon her, the loss of the battle, and his ill-luck in not having given his life, like other brave soldiers, for his Protestant faith. I tried to comfort him, but soon perceived that his noble spirit was not in need of comfort, so I set before him what the house could

37

afford and had a soldier's bed of clean straw prepared for him, for he refused to lie on any other, much though he was in need of rest. The following morning he made me a present of his horse, and divided his money (of which he had a considerable sum in gold) together with several precious rings, among my wife, my children, and my household. I did not know what to make of him, for soldiers are more apt to take than to give. So I hesitated to accept these magnificent gifts, objecting that I had done nothing to deserve them, nor could I hope to earn so great a reward at any time in the future. Moreover, if such riches—and especially the horse, which could not be hidden—were found with me and my household, we would certainly be suspected of having helped to rob or even murder him. But he told me to set my mind at rest; he would protect me from such dangers by a letter in his own hand. Indeed—he said—he did not want to take away with him so much as his shirt, let alone his other clothes; and then he acquainted me with his desire to become a hermit. I opposed his plan with might and main, for I thought it smacked of popery, and reminded him that he could serve the Protestant cause better with his sword. But in vain: he argued so sincerely and persuasively that in the end I agreed to everything and equipped him with those books, pictures, and household goods which you know, although the only thing he asked in return for all he had given us was the woollen blanket under which he had slept that night, and of which he had a coat made. Finally, I had to give him my wagon chains (those that he always wore) in exchange for a golden one from which hung a miniature portrait of his wife, so that he kept neither money nor money's worth. My servant led him to the densest part of the forest and there helped him to build his hut. How he lived there and how I helped him from time to time you know, in parts, better than I.

'Now when of late the Battle of Nördlingen was lost, and I, as you know, stripped of all I had and badly hurt to boot, I fled for safety to this town, where in any case my most valuable possessions were stored. When I began to run out of money I chose three rings—one of them a signet—and the golden chain with the miniature, all of which I had from the hermit, and took them to the Jew to turn them into cash. But he, seeing how valuable they were and of what fine workmanship, offered them for sale to the Governor himself, who at once recognized the coat-of-arms and the portrait, sent for me, and asked me how I came by these jewels. I told him the truth, showed him the hermit's handwriting or deed of gift and gave him an account of the whole story, including the hermit's life and death in the forest. But he did not believe me and placed me under arrest until the truth were known. Then, as he was about to send a detachment of troopers to search for the hermit's hut and to have you brought here, I happened to see you being taken to the prison. The Governor no longer has any reason to doubt my word, since I can call to witness not only you and the hermit's hut but also my sexton, who often let the hermit and you into the church before daybreak. Moreover, the letter he found in your prayer-book is eloquent proof, not only of the truth of my story but also of the hermit's saintliness. And that is why the Governor now wants to show us favour for his late brother-in-law's sake. You have only to decide what you want him to do for you. If you want to study he will pay for it; if you want to learn a trade he will have you apprenticed; and if you want to stay with him he will treat you like his own son, for he said that any dog that came to him from his departed brother-in-law would be welcome in his house.'

But I said I did not care. Whatever the Governor wanted to do with me would please me and be for the best.

CHAPTER XX

The Governor tells of the hermit's wife
Simplicius starts a page's life.

THE parson kept me at his lodgings until ten o'clock before taking me to the Governor to tell him of my decision. He did this so that we might be invited for dinner, for Hanau was blockaded, food was scarce for humble folk, and the Governor kept open house.

He succeeded so well that he found himself sitting at the head of the table next to the Governor, while I waited on the guests, plate in hand, as the chamberlain instructed me, at which I proved as apt as a donkey at the chess-board. But the parson made amends with his tongue for the clumsiness of my behaviour. He said I had been brought up in the wilderness, had never met people and could therefore easily be excused if I did not know how to comport myself. The fidelity I had shown the hermit and the hard life I had shared with him were worthy of admiration and sufficient not only to excuse my awkwardness but to set me above the noblest and most accomplished page. Then he told how the hermit had found in me his only joy because, as he often remarked, I so much resembled his wife, and how he had never ceased to marvel at my steadfastness and firm determination to stay with him, as well as at many other virtues he discovered in me. In short, the parson could not say enough of the passionate sincerity with which the hermit, shortly before his death, had commended me to him, saying that he loved me like his own child.

The Governor asked if his brother-in-law had not known that he was at that time in command of the fortress of Hanau. 'Indeed he did,' said the parson, 'it was I who told him. But although his face lit up and a smile flickered around his lips, he received the news as coolly as if he had never heard the name of Ramsay. When I think back on it I still wonder at the constancy and iron resolution of this man, who had so utterly renounced the world that he even put out of his mind his best friend, knowing that he was so near.' Though the Governor was no weakling but a brave and seasoned soldier, his eyes filled with tears. He said: 'Had I known he was still alive and where to find him, I would assuredly have brought him here even against his will, so that I might have repaid his kindness. But since fortune has denied me this, I will show my gratitude by caring for his Simplicius in his stead. Ah,' he continued, 'the good cavalier had much cause to lament his wife, for she was captured by a party of Imperial troopers during the pursuit, and in the same forest. Learning of this, and believing my brother-in-law killed in the Battle of Höchst,

40

I straightaway sent a trumpeter to the enemy to ask for my sister and ransom her. But all I could find out was that the party of troopers had been scattered by peasants and had lost my sister during the skirmish. I do not know to this day what became of her.'

Thus the Governor and the parson talked about my hermit and his wife, and those that listened pitied the couple the more because they had been married only a year. And so I became the Governor's page.

CHAPTER XXI

Simplex is taught the value of ink
But ends the lesson by making a stink.

MY Lord's favours towards me increased daily, and the longer the greater, for I resembled not only his sister —the hermit's wife—but also the Governor himself. And this more markedly every day, as good food and idle living made me sleek and handsome. Others, too, extended their favours to me, for whoever had dealings with the Governor took care to treat me well. My Lord's secretary took a special liking to me. He had been given the task of teaching me arithmetic, and derived much amusement from my simplicity and ignorance. He had but recently finished his studies, and his mind was still so full of students' pranks that at times I doubted his sanity. He often tried to convince me that black was white and white black, with the result that at first I believed everything he said and in the end nothing. Once I criticized his filthy ink-well, but he replied that it was the most valuable piece of furniture in his office. From it— he said—he extracted whatever he desired: money, clothes or trinkets. In short, everything he had achieved he had fished out of it. I could not believe that so small and insignificant an object could produce such splendid things. But he said that this power came from the Spiritus Papyri (as he called the ink), and that the ink-well was called a well because its bottom held unexpected treasures. I asked how these

41

could be extracted, seeing that one could barely insert two fingers in it. But to this he replied that he had an arm in his head which could perform this miracle, and hoped soon to fish out a rich and beautiful wife for himself, and, with luck, some land and servants of his own as well. Nor would he be the first to do so, since it had been done many times in the past. I marvelled at the dexterity he claimed and asked whether there were others equally skilful. 'Of course,' he said, 'all chancellors, doctors, secretaries, lawyers, notaries, commissaries, and merchants, as well as numberless others who, if they fish diligently and with an eye to their own profit, usually end up as men of wealth.' To which I replied: 'Then do peasants and other hard-working folk show little wit if they eat their bread in the sweat of their brow instead of learning this art, too.' He said: 'Some do not know the uses of the art and therefore have no desire to learn it; some would like to learn it, but lack the arm in their heads; others know the art and have the arm, but not the tricks by which it enriches them, and finally there are some who have all the knowledge and skill but who live on the wrong side of the road and lack my opportunity of practising the art.'

As we were discussing the ink-well (which now appeared to me like Aladdin's lamp) my hand chanced to alight on the book of titles, in which I discovered—as I then thought—more follies than I had ever seen before. I said to the secretary: 'All these are children of Adam, fashioned from a common clay. Why, then, all these distinctions? His Holiness, His Omnipotence, His Serene Highness! Are these not the attributes of God? Here is one called "His Grace", another "His Worship". And why always "well-born"? We know that no man falls from the sky, rises from the sea, or grows from the earth like a head of cabbage.' This made the secretary laugh, and he took the trouble to explain some of the titles and all the terms to me, but I still insisted that the titles did not do their holders justice. It would be more flattering to a man to be called merciful than worshipful. As for the term 'well-born', it was in any case a lie, as any knight's mother would vouch for if asked how she felt during her son's birth.

42

As I was laughing about these things there escaped from me by accident so dreadful a smell that it shocked both the secretary and me. 'Away with you, you pig,' he cried, 'be off to the pigsty where you belong, rather than in the company of honest men.' And in this way I lost all the goodwill I had previously acquired. Nor was this all, or even the worst. Heavier blows were yet in store for me because of my ignorance and innocence. For my Lord had besides me a thoroughgoing rascal of a page who had already served him several years. To this lad I gave my heart, for he was of my own age. He—I thought—is Jonathan and I am David. But he was jealous of me because of the great favour my Lord showed me, which increased daily. He feared that I might in the end supplant him, and so he bore me secret malice and planned how he could trip me and lower me in my Lord's esteem. But I was starry-eyed and of a different nature, and confided to him all my secrets which, innocent as they were, gave him no opportunity for mischief.

CHAPTER XXII

Simplex the theft of a calf's eye should rue
But instead is given the other one, too.

For the following day my Lord had prepared a sumptuous banquet for his officers and friends, having received the good news that his forces had captured the castle of Braunfels without the loss of a single man. My duties were to carry dishes from the kitchen to the banqueting hall, pour wine, and serve at table. The first day of the feast I was handed a big, fat calf's head (of which they say that no poor man may eat) to carry upstairs. It was well boiled and tender, and one of its eyes with the surrounding meat was almost falling away from the bone—a sight that delighted and tempted me. The smell of the gravy and of the ginger with which the head was spiced whetted my appetite and made my mouth water. In short, the calf's eye smiled into my eyes, mouth and nose, beckoning me, so to speak, to guide it into the embraces of

43

my stomach. I did not need much persuading, but followed my inclinations. With a spoon given me that very day I scooped out the eye as I went and dispatched it to its destination so deftly that no one noticed it until the dish was placed on the table, betraying itself and me. For when it was to be carved and one of the daintiest morsels was missing, my Lord quickly perceived what made the carver hesitate. Nor was he prepared to suffer the mockery that a one-eyed calf's head should be served at his table. The cook was called and questioned, and so were the servers. Then it all came out: how poor Simplicius had been given a head with two eyes to carry, but how nobody could say what had happened thereafter. My Lord, with a face like a thunder-cloud, asked me what I had done with the calf's eye. But I, unabashed, whipped my spoon from my pocket once more, turned the calf's head the other way and showed him just what he had asked; that is to say, I scooped out the other eye and swallowed it as I had the first. 'By God,' said my Lord, 'this trick is worth ten calves!' The company applauded him and called my action, committed in all ignorance, wonderfully clever and a promise of future boldness and presence of mind. Thus, by repeating the offence, I escaped the punishment I had deserved for first committing it, and also earned the praise of several jokers and flatterers at table who said I had done well to bring both eyes together again as Nature intended them to be. But my Lord warned me not to play any more such tricks.

CHAPTER XXIII

His first sight of drunkards makes Simplex think
There is more madness than health in drink.

At this banquet (and I suppose at others, too) all came to table soberly and said Grace quietly and with apparent devotion. This solemn and, as it were, monastic mood lasted as long as the soup and the opening courses. But after the first three or four drinks 'to your health' things got livelier. The way in which the noise gradually increased can be described only by comparing the whole company to a public orator who begins quietly and ends by bellowing.

I watched the guests eat like pigs, drink like cattle, behave like asses, and finally throw up like sick dogs. The noble wines of Hochheim, Bacharach and Klingenberg they poured into their stomachs by the bucketful, which soon showed its effect higher up—in their heads. And to my astonishment I saw a great change come over them. Sensible men, who a moment before had had all their wits about them, suddenly seemed to go mad, talked the most arrant nonsense, and behaved like clowns. No wonder I was amazed at their capers, for I had no knowledge of the effects of wine and drunkenness. I saw their strange behaviour, but did not realize its cause. Up till now everybody had emptied his plate and glass with a good appetite, but once their bellies were full they found the going as hard as a coachman whose horses have drawn him easily along the flat but cannot be made to quicken the pace uphill. Yet if their capacity failed them other means prevailed: one had imbibed thirst with the very wine he drank, another could not decline a toast to a friend's good health, a third was kept at it by that Teutonic probity which insists on a man matching his neighbour glass for glass. When in the end even these efforts were of no avail, each challenged the other to guzzle wine in buckets to the health of princes, friends and sweethearts. Whereat many broke out in a cold sweat, their eyes starting from their sockets; yet still the drinking must go on. Indeed, in the end they began beating drums, blowing fifes, and even letting off cannon—no doubt to let the wine take their bellies by assault. I wondered where they put it all, not realizing that before the wine had properly warmed inside them they brought it all up again, with much distress, by the very route down which they had just poured it with the greatest danger to their health.

My parson was also at the banquet and, being human like the rest, was constrained to leave the room awhile. I followed him and said: 'Parson, why do they reel about so? They all seem to have lost their wits. They have eaten and drunk their fill and swear the devil may take them if they can down another drop; yet they go on swilling. Are they driven to it

45

or do they indulge in this waste wilfully and to offend the Lord?' 'Dear child,' the parson replied, 'where wine goes in, wit flies out. This is nothing to what is to come. Even at daybreak tomorrow they will still be at it. Though they have stuffed their bellies they still have not made merry enough.' 'But don't their bellies burst if they stuff them so fiercely? Can their souls, which are God's image, abide in the hog's bodies in which they lie imprisoned in dark cells, as it were, and verminous dungeons—far from any contact with Our Lord? How can their immortal souls stand such torture? Are not their senses, which should serve their souls, buried as in the bowels of unreasoning beasts?' 'Hold your tongue,' said the parson, 'or you'll get a thrashing you won't easily forget. This is neither the time nor the place for preaching, else I would do it better than you.'

So I looked on in silence as they wantonly wasted food and drink, heedless of poor Lazarus, who stood at the door in the persons of several hundred homeless peasants, hunger staring from their eyes, who would have been glad of it. For there was famine in the town.

CHAPTER XXIV

The man of God is put to flight
The others drink throughout the night.

MY parson, when he returned to the table, was urged to continue drinking with the rest, but having no stomach for it, he said he did not want to lower himself to the level of the beasts. To this a sturdy toper replied that it was the parson who drank like a beast and the others like human beings. 'For,' he said, 'animals drink only to quench their thirst, they do not appreciate the pleasures of life and have no taste for wine. We humans, on the other hand, use wine for our enjoyment and have been soaking up the noble juice of the grape since time began.' 'Perhaps so,' replied the parson, 'but my cloth enjoins discretion.' 'Very well,' said the other, 'drink discreetly then and be as good as your word.'

And he fetched a tankard with a lid, filled to the brim. But by the time he had staggered back with it to the parson the latter had made his escape and left the toper standing with his flagon.

Once they were rid of the parson, all restraint was abandoned. It was as if the feast provided an opportunity for them to settle old scores with each other, intoxicating their neighbours and disgracing and shaming them. For when one had been dispatched under the table the other would exclaim: 'We're quits! You did the same to me before, now you have a taste of your own medicine!'

He who could last longest and drink deepest boasted of it and thought himself a splendid fellow. In the end they were all staggering about as if they had taken henbane. It was a truly marvellous spectacle, but there was no one to marvel at it save me. One sang, one wept; one laughed, another groaned; one cursed, one prayed; one shouted boasts, another was speechless; one was quiet and peaceful, the other tried to exorcise the devil by picking quarrels; one slept and was silent, one babbled at such a rate that none could interrupt him. One told of his love affairs, another of his prowess in war. Some talked of the Church and religion, others of politics and public affairs; some could not stand still but must keep walking up and down, others were prostrate and could not move so much as a finger, let alone stand on their feet; some were still shovelling food into themselves, others were throwing up all they had eaten that day.

In the end fighting broke out at the bottom of the table, glasses, cups, dishes and plates flew about, and the revellers belaboured each other not only with their fists, but with chairs, chair-legs, and even swords, until the blood began to flow. But my Lord soon put a stop to that.

CHAPTER XXV

The Governor himself succumbs
Simplex receives some of the crumbs.

WHEN peace had been restored those who could still walk took the musicians and womenfolk off to another house where a big hall had been prepared for a different sort of folly. My master, however, lay down on his couch because he was in pain—either from anger or over-eating. I let him lie so that he could rest and sleep, but had hardly reached the door when he tried to whistle to me, but his lips failed him. So he called out, but could only utter, 'Simpli'. I ran to him and found his eyes turned up like a stuck pig's. I stood rooted to the ground, not knowing what to do, but he pointed to the wash-stand and gasped: 'Br-bra-bring me that there, you clot —the ba-ba-basin; I mu-mu-must shoot a fox.' I hurriedly fetched the basin, and when I came back he had a pair of cheeks like a trumpeter's. He grabbed my arm, pulled me forward so that the basin was right under his nose, and then up it came, with a painful retching. Such an appalling mess cascaded into the basin that I nearly fainted with the stench, especially as some of the pieces hit me in the face. I very nearly kept him company, but when I saw how pale he turned, anxiety made me forget about it, for I feared he would throw up his soul with his vomit. He broke into a cold sweat and his face looked as if he were about to die. But he recovered quickly and ordered me to bring fresh water with which to sluice out his wine-sodden guts.

Then he told me to remove the 'fox', which, reposing in a silver basin, seemed to me far from contemptible, but rather a dainty portion for about four persons—certainly not to be thrown away. Moreover, I knew that my Lord had gathered nothing inferior in his stomach, but delicious pasties, venison, game-birds and veal, much of which was still quite recogniz-able. It revolted me, but I did not know what to do with it, and this seemed no time to ask my Lord. So I went to the chamberlain, showed him the delicate dish, and asked him what to do with the 'fox'. He replied: 'Go take it to the tanner for skinning, you fool!' I asked where I could find the tanner and he, seeing my simplicity, said: 'No, better take it to the doctor so that he can see the state of his master's health.' And on this fool's errand I would have gone had not the chamberlain had second thoughts. So he told me to take the revolting mess to the kitchen with orders for the cook to have it served with seasoning. This I passed on in all good faith, and the women there gave me a sound drubbing for my pains.

CHAPTER XXVI

Simplex tries his hand at a dance,
But is not given a second chance.

MY master was just leaving when I had got rid of the basin. I followed him to a large house where I saw men and women twirling and swirling around so fast that it made my head spin. I thought they must be demented, stamping and bawling as they did, for I could not imagine what the raging tumult signified. So terrifying did they seem to me that my hair stood on end and I was convinced they had lost their reason. As we approached I recognized them as our guests, who only that same morning had been as sane and sober as judges. My God, I thought, what has happened to these poor people? They seem to be moon-struck! Then it occurred to me that they might be hellish apparitions in disguise, come to mock mankind with capers and monkey-tricks, for if they possessed human souls in God's image, surely—I thought— they would not behave like this. As my Lord made to enter the room the tumult ceased, save for some jerking and bobbing of heads and curtseying, and shuffling of feet, as if they were trying to obliterate the footmarks they had stamped into the ground in their frenzy. By the sweat that poured from them, and their stertorous breathing, I perceived that they had been working hard, but their cheerful faces indicated that their labours had not been disagreeable.

Eager to know the purpose of this mad behaviour, I asked my fellow page, whom I loved and trusted, to enlighten me. With great solemnity he told me that, as a matter of fact, the assembled company had made a vow to break through the floor of the room by brute force. 'Why else do you imagine,' he said, 'they should so exert themselves? Look, they have already smashed all the windows for fun. In a little while they will have done the same with the floor.' 'Good heavens,' I replied, 'but then we shall all crash to the floor beneath and break our necks!' 'Yes, indeed,' said my companion, 'that is their purpose and the devil they care about the consequences. Just watch: when they start off again risking their necks, each grabs a pretty woman or girl, for it is said that couples who fall clasped in each others' arms usually escape injury.' But I, believing all this, was seized by such fear of imminent death that I knew not where to turn. Then the musicians, whom I had not noticed before, struck up again, the men ran towards the women like soldiers to their arms at the sound of the alarm, seizing them by the hand, and I, in my terror, fancied I saw the floor already disintegrating and us all plunging to our deaths. But when they began jumping up and down so that the whole building shook (for the band was playing a rollicking peasant dance) I thought my last hour had struck and that the house would suddenly collapse. So, in my overwhelming terror, I suddenly seized a lady of the highest rank and virtue—who was deep in conversation with my Lord —by the arm, like a bear, and clung to her for dear life. And as she started back and struggled, unaware of the mad fancies that assailed me, I became quite desperate and began to yell as if I was being murdered. The music stopped abruptly, so did the dancers, and the good lady to whom I was still clinging freed herself and went off deeply offended, thinking my Lord had arranged this on purpose to insult her. Then my Lord gave orders for me to be whipped and locked up, for he said this was not the first time I had played him tricks that day. But the grooms who were entrusted with the task had pity on me, spared me the whipping, and locked me up in the goose-shed under the stairs.

BOOK II

CHAPTER I

Two lovers come to Simplex' shed,
He leaves them to their reeking bed.

IN my goose-shed I pursued those reflections on drinking
and dancing which I have already described in the first
book, so I need say no more about them here. But I must
confess that I was still in two minds over the dancers: whether
they had indeed tried to stamp through the floor or whether
I had been fooled.

And now I will tell how I escaped from the goose-shed.
For three long hours—that is, until the *Praeludium Veneris*
(or should I call it the respectable dance?) had ended—I sat
in darkness, until someone came creeping to the door and
fumbled with the bolt. As I listened with bated breath the
door opened and a man slipped into the shed as eagerly as
I would gladly have slipped out, dragging with him a girl
whom he held as I had seen them doing at the dance. I did
not know what to expect, but so many strange adventures
had befallen me that day that I was resigned to bearing
patiently whatever else fate might have in store for me. So
I hugged the wall closest to the door and waited in fear and
trembling for what might happen next. The man and the girl
began to whisper, but I understood nothing of what they said
save that she complained of the evil smell of the place and he
comforted her, saying: 'Indeed, fair lady, I bitterly deplore
the envious fate that denies us a better place to enjoy the
fruits of love, but by my honour: your adorable presence
makes this stinking hole more agreeable to me than paradise
itself.' Then I heard kisses and observed strange postures;
not knowing their meaning I stayed as quiet as a mouse. But
when the noises grew stranger, and the goose-shed—which
was no more than some boards nailed together under the

stairs—began to creak and groan, and the girl to moan as if in pain, I thought: these are two of those maniacs who helped stamp through the floor and have come here to do likewise and let you perish. At this thought I seized the door and leaped out, uttering a yell as blood-curdling as that which had brought me to this place. But still I had the presence of mind to bolt the door behind me before making my way to the house. And this was the first wedding I ever attended, albeit uninvited and without bringing a wedding present.

Gentle reader, I tell this tale not to make you laugh, but so that my story may be complete, and to make you realize what seemly fruits are to be expected from dancing. For of this I am sure: many a wanton bargain is struck at these dances of which afterwards the whole company has cause to be ashamed.

CHAPTER II

Tells how the Governor decreed
To make this fool a fool indeed.

THE following morning my Lord summoned the parson to his presence early, to talk with him about me before the guests reassembled. He questioned him closely whether he thought me sane or mad—a simpleton or a mischief-maker, and told him of my doings of the previous day, which had in part been taken amiss by his guests, who suspected that they had been arranged designedly and to insult them. All his life —he said—no one had played him such tricks as I had done in the presence of so many respectable people; he was at a loss what to do with me except have me soundly whipped and, since I showed so little sense, send me to the devil.

When he had ended the parson replied that if the Governor would listen to him patiently awhile he would tell such droll tales of Simplicius and his lack of all worldly knowledge that all would be persuaded of his ignorance, and those who had thought themselves insulted lose all suspicion of deliberate offence. This he did when the company had again assembled at table, and the chamberlain, too, gave instances of my childish credulity, so that the whole meal long there was nothing but talk and laughter about me. In the end they conceived a plan which was to settle my fate: they would confuse me yet more than hitherto, so that at last I would become such a court fool as would do honour to a prince, and make even the dying laugh.

CHAPTER III

Simplex is put in uniform
From which the foe takes little harm.

THEY were just beginning to carouse and make merry as on the previous day, when the sentry brought a letter for my Lord. It was from a Commissary waiting at the gate with orders from the war council of the Crown of Sweden to inspect the fortress and review the garrison. This news turned the vine to vinegar in their mouths and their jollity collapsed like the bellows of a bagpipe when the air escapes. Musicians and guests vanished like tobacco smoke, leaving only the smell. My Lord, accompanied by the adjutant with the keys and a detachment of the main guard, went in person to welcome the pen-pusher, as he called him. He wished—he said—the devil had broken his neck in a thousand pieces before he ever reached the town. But as soon as he had let him in and welcomed him on the inner draw-bridge, he all but held his stirrup to show his devotion. Indeed, their mutual respect was such that the Commissary dismounted and walked with my Lord towards his lodgings, and each insisted that the other should walk on his right.

In this manner we approached the main guard, and the sentry called out: 'Halt, who goes there!' although he could see it was my Lord. But the Governor was reluctant to answer, intending to leave the honour to the other. The sentry, getting no reply, repeated his challenge more loudly than before. At last the Commissary replied: 'He who pays the piper.' As we passed the sentry, with me trailing behind, I heard the man—a new recruit who had previously been a prosperous young peasant—mutter to himself: 'You lying bastard! "He who pays the piper," forsooth! A skin-flint who robs others, that's what you are. So much money have you squeezed out of me that I would a hailstorm struck you dead before you left the town again.' From then on I became convinced that this strange gentleman in the velvet beret must be one of God's elect, for not only did curses seem to have no power over him, but those who hated him did him every kind of honour and service. That very night he was entertained like a prince, made blind drunk, and then put in a most luxurious bed.

The following day, during the inspection, all was at sixes and sevens. Even I, poor simpleton, was able to fool the wise Commissary and lead him by the nose—and it took me less than an hour to learn to do it. The whole art consisted in beating the time on a drum, for I was too small to impersonate a musketeer. I was dressed for the occasion in borrowed clothes (for my page's breeches would not have done at all) and my drum, too, was borrowed (as, indeed, was I). And so I slipped through the inspection. But since they did not trust my puny brains to memorize a strange name to which I must answer and step forward from the ranks, I had to remain Simplicius. The Governor himself chose my surname, having me entered in the roll as Simplicius Simplicissimus; making me, like a whore's son, the first of my line, although, as he himself was wont to say, I resembled his own sister. This name I was to keep until I discovered my proper one, and under it I served the Governor well and did the Crown of Sweden no harm. For this was all the war service I ever did for the Crown of Sweden, and its enemies, too, have little cause, therefore, to reproach me with it.

CHAPTER IV

Simplex is taken off to hell,
But Parson has prepared him well.

WHEN the Commissary had gone, the parson called me
secretly to his lodgings and said: 'Simplicius, I pity
your youth, and the unhappiness that lies in store for you
moves me to compassion. Listen, my child, and understand
that your Lord has decided to rob you of your senses and turn
you into a fool, and for this purpose has already ordered a
suit to be made for you. Tomorrow they will begin the enterprise, and they will surely give you such a harrowing as will
make you a lunatic, unless with God's help and by some
practical means it can be prevented. Since their intention is
evil and dangerous I, charitable Christian that I am, have
decided, in memory of the pious hermit and for your innocence's sake, to help you with my counsel and give you some
medicines. Therefore take my advice and this powder, which
will so strengthen your brain and memory that you will be
able to withstand all their efforts unharmed. Here, too, is an
ointment which you must rub on your temples, the nape of
your neck, and your nostrils. Use both these medicines before you go to sleep at night, for you will never be sure when
they may drag you out of bed. But see to it that no one comes
to know of these my warnings or of the medicines, or it may go
ill with both of us. And when they start their devilish treatment, do not believe everything of which they try to persuade
you, but only pretend that you do. Talk little, lest those in
charge of you become aware that they are threshing empty
straw, or they will prolong your torments (although I do not
know how they will deal with you). And when at last you
have donned your fool's cap and coat, come to me again so
that I may advise you further. Meanwhile I will pray to God
that He may preserve your brain and your health.' With that
he gave me the powder and the ointment and I made my
way back home.

As the parson had said, so it happened. In my first sleep

came four fellows with frightening devils' masks into my room, stood round my bed, and then performed a weird dance. One had a red-hot hook in his hand, another a blazing torch. The two others fell upon me, dragged me out of bed, danced around with me awhile, and then forced me to dress. But I pretended to take them for real devils, wailing pitifully and expressing terror in my every gesture. They told me that I must go with them and tied a towel round my head so that I could neither hear, see, nor cry out. Then they led the poor, shivering heap of misery that I was along many devious ways, up and down, and at last to a cellar where a big fire was blazing. When they had removed the towel they began pledging me in Sack and Malmsey. They had a happy time persuading me that I was dead and descended into hell, for I took care to pretend that I believed their every lie. 'Go on, drink up!' they said, 'for you will be staying here for ever, and if you won't be a good sport and join in our frolics, into the fire you go!' The poor devils were trying to disguise their voices and accents so that I should not recognize them, yet I perceived at once that they were my Lord's grooms. But I gave nothing away, while laughing up my sleeve that they who were trying to fool me were themselves being fooled. I drank my share of Sack, but they drank more than I (such heavenly Nectar rarely coming their humble way) and I would have wagered that I could have drunk them under the table. However, when I thought the time was ripe I began to reel and stagger as I had seen my Lord's guests do at the banquet, and in the end pretended that all I wanted was to sleep. But they chased and pushed me with their hooks—which they kept red-hot—from one end of the cellar to the other as if they themselves had gone mad, in order to make me drink or at least prevent me from sleeping. If I fell down, as I often did on purpose, they set me on my feet again and made as if to throw me into the fire. I was treated, in fact, like a falcon in training, and very disagreeable I found it. True, I could have outlasted every one of them in drink and wakefulness if they had all worked on me at the same time. But they took their turns, so that in the end I must have lost the game. I spent three days and two nights in that smoky cellar, lit only by the fire. My head began to throb as if it would burst, and at last I knew I must think of some trick to rid myself of my torment and my tormentors at one blow. This I did by imitating the fox, who, when he can no longer elude the hounds, makes water in their faces; but I improved somewhat on his device. At the same time as I obeyed the call of nature I stuck two fingers down my throat to make myself vomit, and altogether produced such a fiendish stench and mess that even the devils could not abide it. So they rolled me in a blanket and gave me such an unmerciful beating that my inward parts and my very soul seemed like to leave me. What they did to me after that I do not know, for I had quite lost consciousness.

CHAPTER V

Simplex finds angels by his bed,
But soon is back in his goose-shed.

WHEN I recovered my senses I was no longer in the dungeon with the devils, but in a fine, large room, attended by three of the most hideous old hags that ever blemished the face of the earth. At first, opening my eyes a little, I took them for veritable spirits from hell. One had a pair of eyes like will-o-the-wisps, and between them a long, bony hawk's nose whose tip or point curved to her lower lip. Her mouth held only two teeth, but these so enormous, round, and thick that each resembled in size and shape a ring finger, and was the colour of a ring, to boot. In short, there was enough to furnish a whole mouthful of teeth, but badly distributed. Her face was like Spanish leather and her white hair tumbled about her head monstrously dishevelled, for she had only just been fetched out of bed. Her lean dugs resembled nothing so much as a pair of empty cow's bladders, with two blackish-brown teats two inches long hanging from them. In short, a fearful sight, enough to daunt even the rank lust of a lecherous goat. The other two were no better looking, except that they had snub monkeys' noses and were a little more tidily

dressed. When I had recovered somewhat I saw that one of
them was our dish washer and the others the wives of two
of our grooms. I pretended that I could not move a limb (and
indeed, I did not feel like dancing) while these honest old souls
stripped me stark naked and cleansed me from my filth like a
small child. It did me good, for they tended me with great
patience and compassion, so that I came near to revealing to
them how sane I still was. But I thought: No, Simplici!
Trust no old woman, but consider it victory enough if, young
as you are, you can outwit three crafty old hags who could
catch the devil himself in the open. From such beginnings
you may take hope that in your old age you will do even
better.

When they had finished with me they put me in a splendid
bed in which I fell asleep at once. I think I must have slept
more than twenty-four hours at a stretch, and when I woke
again two beautiful boys stood by my bed, clad in white
night-shirts and silk ribbons and bedizened with pearls, jewels,
gold chains, and other dazzling trinkets. One carried a gilt
dish full of cakes, shortbread, marchpane and other sweets;
the other held a gilt goblet in his hands. These would-be
angels tried to convince me that I was now in heaven, having
safely passed through purgatory and escaped the devil and his
dam. So (they said) I was free to ask for all my heart desired, confident that all I could wish for was either at hand
or at least at their beck and call. I was parched with thirst,
and seeing the goblet before me asked only for a drink, which
was most willingly served. But the goblet contained no wine
but a gentle sleeping-draught, which I drank in one gulp and
fell asleep again as soon as it had warmed inside me.

The following day I awoke again, though no longer in my
fine bed in the large room, nor with the angels, much less in
heaven, but instead in my old goose-shed. It was pitch-dark
and I was dressed in a suit of calf-skins, the hairy side outward. The breeches were cut after the Polish or Swabian
fashion, and the doublet even more oddly. At the neck it was
fitted with a hood like a monk's cowl, which was pulled over
my head and adorned with a fine pair of ass's ears. I could
not help laughing at my own misfortunes, seeing by the nest

and the feathers what manner of bird I was to be. At that time I first began to take counsel with myself and to think what was best to do; and I decided there and then to play the fool to the utmost, and otherwise to wait patiently for what fate might yet have in store for me.

CHAPTER VI

Simplex, in his calf skin dress,
Plays his new part with success.

IT would have been easy for me to escape from my goose-shed, yet because I was supposed to be a fool I not only acted like a fool who lacks enough sense to free himself, but also pretended to be a hungry calf, lowing for its mother. My bleats were soon heard by those appointed to watch me. Two soldiers came to the goose-shed and asked who was inside. I answered: 'You fools, can you not hear that it is a calf?' They opened the door, let me out, and pretended to be amazed to hear a calf talk. Their play-acting was as painful as that of a strolling player performing a part he has not learned, and I often felt tempted to help them out with their jests. They discussed what to do with me and agreed to present me to the Governor, who would give them more for a speaking calf than would the butcher. They asked me how things were with me, and I answered: 'Pretty disorderly.' 'Why?' they asked. I said: 'Because it seems the custom hereabouts to lock up honest calves in goose-sheds. You fellows should know that if I am to become a proper ox I must be treated as befits a self-respecting steer.' Then they led me across the street to the Governor's house and a great swarm of boys followed us, all bleating like calves. A blind man might have thought us a herd of calves from the sound, but to those with eyes to see we appeared a crowd of fools, old and young.

The soldiers presented me to the Governor for all the world as if they had captured me on a foray. He gave them some money for their pains, and to me he promised the best I could ask for. 'That's all very well, sir,' I said, 'but you

59

must not have me locked up in a goose-shed. We calves cannot stand such treatment if we are to grow up into fine cattle.' The Governor promised me better treatment for the future and thought himself very clever to have made so presentable a fool out of me. But I thought to myself: Patience, my Lord, I have come through an ordeal by fire and it has hardened me. We shall soon see who will lead the other a dance.

Just then I saw a peasant driving his cattle to drink. I hurried outside, bleating, and made for the cows as if to suck them. But they panicked at my approach, worse than if I had been a wolf, although I wore their skin. They shied and stampeded as if a nest of hornets had got among them, so that their master lost control of them altogether. This proved splendid entertainment for the crowd which had quickly gathered, and my Lord laughed fit to burst, saying: 'One fool makes a hundred others.' But I thought to myself: And that goes for you, too, my Lord!

From then on everybody called me 'calf'; so I, too, had nick-names for them all. Many of these seemed most apt to the court, and especially to my Lord, for I christened each according to his foibles. In short, everybody thought me a witless fool and I considered them foolish wits; and as I see it, this is still the way of the world: that each is satisfied with his own wit and believes himself cleverer than his fellows.

The prank I played with the cattle made a short morning still shorter, for it was the time of the winter solstice. At dinner I waited at table as before, but introduced several droll diversions. When I sat down to eat nobody could persuade me to take the food and drink of humans. I refused everything but grass, which at that season was impossible to come by. So my Lord ordered a pair of fresh calves' skins to be fetched from the butcher's in which he dressed two young pages. These he placed beside me at table, gave us winter salad for our first course and encouraged us to fall to. He even had a live calf brought and enticed it with salt to eat the salad. I stared at it, as if in surprise, but the company urged me to join in. Seeing my reluctance, they said: 'To be sure, it is not so unusual as you think to see calves eat meat, fish, cheese, or butter. They even get drunk now and again.

Animals nowadays know what is good; indeed, things have come to such a pass that there is but little difference between them and human beings. Why, then, should you be the only one to refuse?'

I allowed myself to be persuaded, though by my hunger rather than their arguments, having already discovered for myself that some human beings are more swinish than pigs, more savage than lions, more lecherous than goats, more jealous than dogs, more stubborn than asses, thirstier than cattle, more cunning than foxes, greedier than wolves, vainer than monkeys, and more poisonous than snakes or toads—differing from brutes only in their shape, and withal lacking the innocence of a calf. So I ate with my fellow-calves as my appetite prompted me, and a stranger who had come upon us unexpectedly at this meal would doubtless have thought that old Circe had risen from the dead, who could turn humans into animals—an art now practised by my Lord. As I ate my dinner so was I served at supper. Then, as my fellow guests and parasites had again eaten with me (to encourage me to take my food), I insisted that they must also go to bed with me unless my Lord would have me sleep in the cow-shed. This I did in order to make the greater fools of those who would make a fool of me, and from it all I concluded that a merciful God has given every man as much wit as he needs to maintain himself in his station in life. Many may think they have a monopoly of wisdom, yet are there as good fish in the sea as ever came out of it.

CHAPTER VII

A morning with the ladies spent
Gives my Lord cause for merriment.

NEXT morning, as soon as I entered the house, I was ordered to the parlour, where my Lord was entertaining several noble ladies who wanted to see and hear this new fool. I entered and stood stock-still without opening my mouth, which caused the lady whom I had seized at the dance to remark that she had been told this calf could speak, but that evidently it was not true. I replied: 'I, on the other hand, supposed that monkeys could *not* speak, yet now I hear that I, too, am mistaken.' 'How now,' said my Lord, 'why do you think these ladies are monkeys?' 'If they are not, they soon will be. Who knows what the future holds. I, too, did not expect to turn into a calf, yet here I am.' My Lord asked how I could tell that these ladies would turn into monkeys and I replied: 'Our monkey has a bare arse and these ladies have already bared their breasts, which decent girls are wont to cover.' 'You rogue,' said my Lord. 'You are a foolish calf and talk like one! These ladies purposely reveal what delights men's eyes, whereas our monkey goes naked for want of clothing. Come now, say something quickly to atone for your offence, or I shall have you whipped and set the dogs on you to chase you back to your shed, as is the fate of calves which do not know their manners. Let us hear whether you can praise a lady as she deserves.'

Whereupon I scrutinized the lady from top to bottom and back again, gazing at her lovingly as if I would have married her. At last I said: 'My Lord, I see now where the mistake lies. The knavish tailor is to blame. He has left the cloth he should have used to cover her breasts at the bottom of her dress, where it now trails on the ground. The bungler should have his hands cut off if he cannot tailor better than that. Lady,' I said, turning to her, 'get rid of him before he ruins your appearance. You should try to get my Dad's tailor— Master Paul, they called him—who made such pretty pleated skirts for my Mum and Anne and Ursula, cut evenly all round the hem. Those skirts never trailed in the mud like yours. And you should have seen the beautiful dresses he made for the whores! They were a fine sight.' My Lord asked whether our Anne and our Ursula had been more beautiful than this lady. 'Oh dear me no, my Lord,' I said, 'this lady has hair as brown as rich dung and a parting so smooth and white as if she had hog's leather on her head. Her hair is prettily curled and twisted, like hollow pipes or loops of little sausages draped over her ears. Behold her beautiful brow, smooth and rounded like a fat baby's arse, and whiter than a weatherbeaten skull. A pity only that her tender skin is so stained with hair powder. People who saw it and did not understand these matters might think she was suffering from dandruff. Look at her sparkling eyes, blacker than the soot in my Dad's chimney, which gleamed so fiercely when our Anne held a straw mat in front of it to make the fire leap. Her cheeks are rosy, yet not so red as the new braces the carters from Ulm wear to hold up their trousers. But the red of her lips is far redder than the braces, and when she laughs or speaks (as my Lord can see) she shows two rows of teeth as even and white as if they had been carved whole out of a chunk of turnip. (Oh, you lovely creature! I cannot believe it would hurt to be bitten by those teeth!) Behold her neck! It is as white as curdled milk, and so are her little breasts, and doubtless as hard as the udders of a goat in need of milking. To be sure, they are not as flaccid as those of the old hags who washed my bottom the other day when I went to heaven. And look, my Lord, at her hands and fingers! As long, strong and agile as those of the gipsies who picked our pockets the other day. But what is all this compared with her body—though I cannot see all of it —which is as delicate, slender, and graceful as if she had just recovered from eight weeks of the flux.' This caused such laughter that I could spare myself the remainder of my speech. So I took French leave and went my way to let others fool me at my leisure.

CHAPTER VIII

An argument whether the wise and brave,
Should carry their honours to the grave.

At the midday meal that followed I continued to play my new part with a will. For I was resolved to discourse on every folly and berate every vanity, seeing how favourable an opportunity my new status afforded me for it. There was no one at table, however eminent, whose vices I would not expose, and if any took offence he must either suffer the mockery of his fellows into the bargain or else my Lord would remind him that a wise man does not quarrel with a fool. But the secretary, at my Lord's prompting, countered my sallies with reasoned argument. When I called him a title-smith, mocked him about his honours, and asked what titles man's first ancestor bore he replied: 'You speak like an unreasoning calf, not knowing that after our first parents came men of differing quality. Some of them so ennobled themselves and their descendants by rare virtues—such as wisdom, deeds of great valour, or the invention of useful arts—that their contemporaries honoured their names above all others and counted them the very equals of the gods. If you were human, or had, like a human, read the story of mankind, you would understand how greatly one man may differ from another, and would readily allow each the honour of his title. But being a calf, and neither capable nor worthy of any human honour, you talk about the matter like the foolish calf you are, begrudging mankind the merit which is one of its glories.'

To this I replied: 'Yet was I once as good a human being as you, and not ill-read, and therefore I answer that either you have an imperfect understanding of the matter, or your self-interest prevents you from speaking the truth as you know it. Tell me now, what great deeds have been done and useful arts invented that warrant the ennobling of an entire house, for centuries after the hero or the sage has died? Has not the hero's strength and the sage's wisdom died with him? If you fail to grasp this, and still maintain that the fathers' virtues are inherited by the children, then I must conclude that your father was a stockfish and your mother a flounder.' 'Ho,' said the secretary, 'if we are to settle this argument by personal abuse, then I might well say that your father was a coarse Spessart peasant and that, oafish as is the race your native country breeds, you have descended even from that level and turned into a brutish calf.' 'Nor did you ever speak a truer word to prove my point,' I replied. 'For this is the very thing I maintain: that the virtues of the parents do not always descend to the children and that the children are therefore not always worthy of their parents' titles of honour. As for myself, it is no disgrace to have turned into a calf, for in this I have the honour of following in the footsteps of the mighty king Nebuchadnezzar; besides, who knows: perhaps it will please God one day to turn me into a human being again, and a worthier one, too, than my Dad was. But for my part I will honour only those who are ennobled by their own virtues.'

CHAPTER IX

*Simplex tells the Governor straight
That he does not envy his fate.*

MY Lord, too, wanted to divert himself at my expense and said: 'You cannot fool me: lacking the courage to seek nobility you affect to despise the honours nobility brings with it.' I replied: 'My Lord, even if I were at this moment offered the chance of stepping into your shoes I would refuse it.' My master laughed: 'I can well believe it! The bullock is content with his straw. But if you had a noble mind you would be eager for high honour and dignity. I, for my part, do not consider it a trifle that Fortune has raised me above my fellows.' I sighed and said: 'Ah, what hard-won felicity! I assure you, my Lord, that you are the most miserable person in Hanau.' 'How come, calf?' replied my Lord, 'how come? Tell me the reason, for I do not find it so.' I answered: 'If you do not know and feel the cares and burdens with which you are beset as Governor of Hanau, then you are either dazzled by excessive pride in the honour of your position or you are made of iron and utterly without feeling. True, you give orders and those who serve you must obey. But do they do it for nothing? Are you not, in fact, the servant of them all? Look beyond the walls. Your fortress is surrounded by enemies, and its safety is your responsibility alone. You must scheme to foil your foes and at the same time take care that your schemes are not discovered. Do you not often feel that the town would be safer if you yourself kept watch, like a common soldier?

'Moreover, you must see to it that there is never any lack of money, ammunition, supplies, or troops. For this, you must

65

hold the surrounding countryside to ransom. When you send your men out for this purpose their usual course is robbery, pillage, theft, arson, and murder. Within the last few days they have plundered the village of Orb, sacked Braunfels, and laid Staden in ashes. They have their booty, but you bear a heavy responsibility before God. I do not count that, with the honour, you enjoy the material benefits of such sorties. But you do not know who, in the end, will profit from the treasures you may be hoarding. Even if you succeed in keeping these riches—which is doubtful—you cannot take them with you when you die. Only the sins with which you have burdened yourself in amassing them will accompany you on your last journey. And if you are fortunate enough to thrive on your plunder it is the sweat and blood of the Poor from which you profit—those who are now suffering hardship and want, and, maybe, dying of hunger.

'Do I not often see you distrait and absent-minded because of the burdens of your office? Yet I and my fellow calves sleep peacefully and without a care. If you, on the other hand, cast care aside it may cost you your head if something is forgotten for the security of your fortress and your men. See now how I am spared such cares. Since I know that I owe Nature but a single death, I do not fret about who might assault my stable or that I might have to fend for my life. If I die young I am at least spared the burdens of an ox in harness. You, however, are beset by a thousand intrigues, and your life, in consequence, is one of eternal care and wakefulness. For you must fear friend and foe alike, who seek to strip you of your life, your money, your reputation, your command, or whatever else—just as you seek to strip them of theirs. Your enemies defy you openly, and your so-called friends secretly envy you your good fortune. Even your subordinates you cannot trust completely, not to speak of the ambition which constantly consumes you, driving you here and there in search of more fame, higher office, greater fortune, how to outwit and master your enemies or take a garrison by surprise. Seeking, in fact, to do all those things which will injure others, harm your soul, and displease God.

'Worst of all, you are so spoiled by your courtiers that you do not even know yourself. They have so possessed and poisoned you that you no longer see the dangerous path you tread; for everything that you do they praise, and all your vices they declare and proclaim virtues. They call your fury justice, and when you devastate the countryside and bring ruin to its people they say you are a good soldier. Thus to the people's misfortune do they egg you on, in order to retain your favour and to line their pockets.'

'You runt! You impertinent little snot-nose!' burst out my Lord, 'who taught you to preach like this?' I replied: 'My dearest Lord, are you not proving me right when I say your flatterers and idle courtiers have so spoiled you that you are beyond help? Others, however, are quick to see your faults, and this not only in great and important matters but also in small things of little concern. Do you not know of enough examples from olden times? The Spartans criticized Lycurgus because he went about with his head bowed; the Romans took it ill that Scipio snored in his sleep and that Pompey used only one finger to scratch himself; Julius Caesar they mocked because of the way he wore his belt. The people of Utica spoke ill of Cato because he ate too greedily, and the Carthagenians murmured against Hannibal because he walked about barechested.

'Well, then, my dear Lord, do you still maintain that I should change places with one who—beside a dozen or so drinking companions, flatterers, and hangers-on—has a hundred or more likely ten thousand open or secret enemies, slanderers, and envious rivals? Moreover, what sort of joy or happiness can a man have who bears responsibility for the safety and comfort of so many people? Must you not watch and care for all your subjects, listen to all their complaints and worries? Would this in itself not be burdensome enough —even without enemies and rivals? Well do I see what a hard life you lead and what a burden it must be to you.

'And what, my dearest Lord, will be your reward? What, I ask you, will you gain from it? If you do not know, let Demosthenes, the Athenian, tell you who after defending and protecting his country was unjustly and miserably banished like a common criminal. To Socrates they gave poison, and Moses and other holy men, too, experienced the violence and fury of the mob.

'Therefore keep your Command and whatever joy it may bring you. I want no part of it, for even if all goes well with you it will profit you nothing but a bad conscience. If, on the other hand, you want to keep your conscience clear it will not be long before you are removed from your Command just as if, like me, you had become a foolish calf.'

CHAPTER X

Simplex shows how the good sense of beasts
May equal that of humans at least.

THIS my speech caused the assembled company to stare at me in some astonishment, for they said it would have done honour to a man of sense, spontaneously delivered as it was and unprepared. But I concluded by saying: 'Therefore, my Lord, I would not change places with you. Nor have I need, for the springs of the forest give me drink more wholesome than your noble wines, and He whose pleasure it was that I should become a calf will also know how to bless the fruits of the field so that they may serve me (as they did Nebuchadnezzar) for food and sustenance. You, on the other hand, often find the best of food unpalatable, and the wine splits your head and plunges you into one sickness after another.'

My Lord replied: 'I do not know what to make of you. For a calf you have too much sense. Could it be that under your calf's skin you conceal the hide of a jester?' I pretended to be angry and said: 'Why do you humans always think us animals fools? Never believe it! I swear that if animals older than I could speak they would answer you better than I can. If you think us so stupid, who, think you, taught the wood-pigeons, jays, blackbirds, and partridges to purge themselves with laurel leaves, and the doves and chickens with dandelions? Who taught dogs and cats to eat grass with the dew fresh on it if they want to void their bellies? Who

68

taught the tortoise to heal a bite with hemlock, the wounded stag to seek the aid of calamint, or the weasel to use rue when it fights a bat or a snake? Who shows the wild boar ivy or the bear mandrake and tells them that it is good medicine for them? Who instructs the swallow to use swallow-wort for her fledglings' dim eyes? Who teaches the snake to eat fennel when it wants to slough its skin, or the stork to purge itself with water, the pelican to bleed itself, and the bear to have itself cupped by bees? Indeed, it might almost be said that you humans have learned your arts and sciences from us animals! You eat and drink yourselves to death—a thing we animals never do. A lion or a wolf, if he is growing fat, fasts until he is lean, alert, and fit again. Who, then, acts more wisely? Look also, I pray you, at the birds of the air; behold the varied and ingenious structure of their delicate nests! No one can emulate their work, from which it follows, as you must admit, that they are cleverer and more skilful than humans. Who tells our summer birds when to migrate in spring and hatch their young and, in autumn, when to leave us again and fly to warmer lands? Who teaches them that they must have a place of assembly for their migrations? Who leads them and shows them the way? Is it you humans who lend them compasses so that they do not go astray? No, my friends, they know the way without you, how long it takes and in what stages to fly it, needing neither your compasses nor your calendars. Next, look at the toiling spider, whose web is almost a miracle. See whether you can find so much as a single knot in all her work. What hunter or fisherman taught her how to spread her net and, according to the kind of web she weaves, to stalk her prey from an obscure corner or from the centre? You humans marvel at the raven who, as Plutarch tells, dropped stones into a basin half full of water, until the level had risen enough to let him drink in comfort. Yet how much more would you marvel if you could live with and among animals and study all their other actions and behaviour! Then, indeed, would you have to admit that all animals appear to have something of a special, natural and individual virtue in their actions and inclinations; in their caution, strength, gentleness, fierceness, and in the teaching and instruction of their young. Each knows the other, although all are distinct. They pursue what they prey on, avoid what is harmful, flee from danger, gather what they need for their nourishment, and even, now and again, lead you humans by the nose. Wherefore many wise men of old have seriously considered these matters and not been ashamed to question and discuss whether unreasoning beasts do not, after all, have understanding. But I wish to talk no more about this. Go to the bees and see how they make honey and wax, and then come again and tell me your opinion.'

CHAPTER XI

The Governor and the parson debate
How best to settle Simplicius' fate.

BY now the company was divided in its views about me. The secretary held that I must be considered mad, since I imagined myself to be an unreasoning animal, and because people who had a screw or two loose and yet prided themselves on their wisdom commonly made the best and most spectacular fools of all. Others said that if only I could be cured of my fancy of being a calf and persuaded that I was human again I would be considered intelligent and sensible enough. My Lord said: 'I think him a fool because he tells everybody the truth so bluntly, yet his discourse is by no means that of a fool.' All this they said in Latin so that I should not understand it. Then he asked me whether I had studied in my human state, to which I replied that I did not know what the word meant. Then he asked whether, now that I was a calf, I still prayed as humans did and hoped to go to heaven one day. 'Indeed I do,' I said, 'for I still have my immortal human soul which, as you may imagine, would not like to go to hell, where I was so roughly handled on my recent visit. I am merely changed, like Nebuchadnezzar long ago, and perhaps one day will turn into a man again.' 'Amen to that!' said my Lord with something of a sigh, from which I could see that he repented of having made me mad. 'But

70

let us see,' he continued, 'how you pray.' So I knelt down and raised my eyes and hands to heaven in best hermit fashion. And as my Lord's repentance, which I had noticed, touched my heart and comforted me, tears came to my eyes and I prayed to all appearances with the deepest devotion—first, the Lord's prayer and then for all Christendom, for my friends and enemies, and that God in this life would grant me so to live that I might be worthy to praise Him in the life to come. This was a prayer my hermit had taught me to say in reverently chosen words, and it brought some of the softer-hearted guests near to tears. My Lord's eyes, too, brimmed over, of which he seemed ashamed and explained his emotion by saying that the sight of so sorry a figure, so closely resembling his lost sister, almost broke his heart.

After dinner my Lord sent for the parson and told him all I had said, giving him to understand that he feared something had gone wrong, and that perhaps the devil had taken a hand in the matter; for heretofore I had shown myself simple and ignorant, but now could utter words to make men marvel. The parson, who knew my condition better than anyone, replied that this should have been considered before it was decided to turn me into a fool. Man was the image of God, he said, and it was dangerous to play tricks with the soul, especially in one so young. But he would never believe that the Evil One had been allowed to take a hand, because I had always commended myself most fervently to God. But if, contrary to all expectations, this had indeed been decreed and permitted, then those responsible bore a heavy load of guilt before God, for it was undoubtedly a grievous sin for a man to rob another of his reason and thus of his powers to praise and serve God, the purpose for which he was created. 'I have asserted before now,' he continued, 'that the boy had wit enough. The reason why he bore himself badly in company was that he had been brought up in great simplicity by his father, a coarse peasant, and by your brother-in-law in the wilderness. Given a little patience at first, he would no doubt have improved in time. He was, in fact, a pious, simple child, ignorant of the world's malice, but I have no doubt he can be set to rights again if only he can be cured of his fantasy

71

and made to abandon his belief that he is a calf. I have read of a man who firmly believed that he had turned into an earthenware jug and kept asking his family to keep him somewhere high up on a shelf, so that he might not get broken. Another imagined he was a cockerel and crowed night and day as long as his sickness lasted. Yet another thought that he was dead and a spirit, wherefore he refused all nourishment until at last a wise doctor got two men to pretend that they, too, were ghosts, but also ate and drank to their hearts' content. They persuaded the patient that nowadays ghosts were in the habit of eating and drinking, and in the end he was cured. I myself had a sick peasant in my parish who, when I visited him, complained that he had three or four barrels of water in his belly. If this could be removed he was sure that he would mend, and he asked me to have him either slit open to drain the water or else hung up in the chimney to dry him out. So I persuaded him to let me remove the water in another way. I took a tap such as you use in wine or beer barrels, fastened a tube to it and the other end of the tube to the bung-hole of a large vat full of water. I pretended to fix the tap in his belly, which I had swathed in rags to prevent it from bursting, and then let the water in the vat run off through the tap, whereat the ninny was delighted, discarded his rags, and in a few days was cured. In the same way another man was helped who imagined his belly to be full of bits and bridles. His doctor gave him a purge and then put all manner of saddlery into his privy so that the man thought he had got rid of it through his motions. It is also told of a lunatic who thought that his nose was so long that it trailed on the ground, that they fixed a sausage to it and cut it away bit by bit until the knife touched his nose, whereupon he cried "enough!" and averred that his nose was now its proper length again. So, perhaps, Simplicius can also be cured of his fancy even as these were.'

'All this may well be,' said my Lord, 'but what troubles me is that heretofore he was quite ignorant, whereas now he can talk and tell of matters which are beyond the knowledge of many an older, more experienced, and better-read man. He has expounded the habits of many animals and described my own person as perfectly as if he had a life-time's experience behind him, which has amazed me and almost made me consider his words as an oracle or a divine warning.'

'My Lord,' replied the parson, 'there may be a perfectly natural explanation for all this. That he is well-read I know, for he and the hermit went through all my books, of which there were many. And as the boy has a good memory and his mind is now idle and has forgotten his own personality, he can reproduce all that his brain has absorbed. I am sure that in time he can be cured.' In this way the parson held the Governor between fear and hope, defended me and my cause most ably, brought me happy days and for himself free access to my Lord. In the end they decided that they would keep me under observation a little longer, which the parson arranged more for his own sake than for mine, since by his comings and goings and his pretence to be deeply occupied and concerned with my fate he gained favour with my Lord, who finally took him into his service and appointed him chaplain to the garrison. In those hard times this was no small favour and one which greatly pleased me for his sake.

CHAPTER XII

Simplex leads a life of ease,
Till Fate a sudden change decrees.

FROM this time on I can boast that I possessed in full my Lord's favour, grace and love. All that marred my happiness was a surfeit of calf's skin and a lack of years, but at the time I did not know it. Moreover, my parson did not want me to recover my wits yet, thinking it too soon and also not in his own best interest. My Lord, meanwhile, seeing that I delighted in music, had me taught, and also apprenticed me to an excellent lute player whose art I quickly mastered and thereafter excelled him because I sang more tunefully than he to the accompaniment. In this way I served my Lord for his pleasure, diversion and admiration. The officers, too, regarded me kindly, the richest citizens treated me with respect, and the servants and soldiers were well disposed towards me because they all saw how my Lord favoured me. They gave me presents as occasion offered, knowing that jesters often have more of their master's ear than counsellors; and their presents, of course, always had a purpose. One rewarded me so that I should tell no tales about him, another in order that I should. In this way I earned a fair sum of money, most of which I handed to my parson, since I did not yet know its uses. As I had no cause to envy anyone, so also was I untroubled by jealousies, cares, and sorrows. All I thought about was my music and how I could point out their faults to men without giving offence. In fact, I grew up like a pig in clover and waxed strong and fat. It was easy to see that I no longer mortified my flesh with water, acorns, beech-nuts, roots, and herbs, but throve on good morsels and Rhenish wine or strong Hanau beer. In those miserable times this could be accounted a great blessing of God, for all Germany was ravaged by war, famine, and pestilence, and the town of Hanau itself besieged by the enemy—none of which concerned me in the least.

When the siege had been lifted, my Lord intended to send me as a gift to either Cardinal Richelieu or Duke Bernhard of Weimar, for, on the one hand, he expected much thanks for the present and, on the other, maintained that he could no longer bear the daily presence, in fool's clothing, of one who more and more resembled his lost sister. The parson advised against this, for he had in mind that the time was at hand when he would perform a miracle and turn me again into a reasoning human being. He therefore suggested to the Governor that he should have two other suits of calf's skin made and two boys dressed up in them. Then he should get someone to impersonate a doctor, prophet, or sooth-sayer who would undress us three with strange rites, pretending that he could turn animals into humans, and vice versa. In this way, he said, I could doubtless be set to rights again and quite easily turned into a human being. The Governor approved the plan, and the parson let me know what had been agreed and easily persuaded me to consent to it. But envious Fate would not allow me to escape so lightly from my fool's clothing, or to continue to enjoy my lush life. Even while the

74

tanners and tailors were preparing the clothes required for the
comedy, I was playing with several other boys on the ice outside the fortress. Suddenly, I know not how, we were surrounded by a detachment of Croats, who seized us, put us on
some farm-horses they had stolen, and rode off with us. So
I went once more on horseback and had occasion to see how
a single instant of misfortune can set at naught all settled
comfort, and so part a man from his happiness and salvation
that he bears the scars of it for the rest of his life.

CHAPTER XIII

*The Croats' way of life is rough
And Simplex finds it hard enough.*

THOUGH the people of Hanau raised the alarm, made a
sortie on horseback, and for a while detained and har-
assed the Croats with a skirmish, yet they could not make
them part with their booty. For we were no great impediment
to our captors, who made their way to Büdingen, where they
fed their beasts and gave the citizens the rich young Hanau
boys to be ransomed and also sold them the stolen horses and
other loot. Then they set out again and overnight rode through
Büdingen forest to the abbey of Fulda, taking with them
whatever they found by the wayside. Robbing and looting
did not in the least impede their rapid progress, for they
were like the devil, of whom it is said that he can make love
while running and yet miss nothing along the way. So that
same evening we reached the abbey of Hirschfeld, where
they had their quarters, laden with booty. This they divided
among themselves, and I was allotted to one Colonel Corpes.
   In the service of this master all seemed to me disagreeable,
not to say barbarous. The fat morsels of Hanau were replaced
by coarse black bread and tough beef, or, if I was lucky, a
piece of stolen lard. Wine and beer turned to water, and in
lieu of a bed I had to make do with the straw in the horses'
stable. Instead of playing the lute, with which I had been
accustomed to entertain the company at dinner, I was made

to crawl under the table with other boys of my age, howl like a dog, and let myself be pricked by their spurs, which seemed a poor sort of entertainment to me. Instead of my leisurely Hanau walks I rode out on foraging parties, groomed horses, and cleaned out stables. Foraging, however, meant simply this: a party set out with much trouble and sweat—and often at great risk to life and limb—to roam the surrounding villages, threshing, grinding, baking, stealing, and taking what it found; maltreating and ruining the peasants and raping their womenfolk (although for this task I was still too young). Yet if, by chance, the poor peasant was displeased and dared to rap a forager over the knuckles if he found him at his work alone (there being many such unwelcome guests around Hanau at that time), he was knocked on the head if he was caught, and if not, at least his house was burned to the ground. My master had no wife (and, indeed, few warriors of this sort have, for any woman they find will serve their purpose as well), no page, no valet, and no cook; but instead a horde of grooms and stable-lads who waited indifferently on him and his horses. Nor was he ashamed to saddle and feed his own horse. He never slept anywhere but on straw or on the bare ground and used a fur coat as a blanket. So it came about that you could often see fleas disporting themselves on his clothes, of which he was not in the least ashamed, but thought it a great joke if someone picked a few off. He wore his hair close cropped and had a broad peasant's beard which served him well when, as he often did, he disguised himself in peasant clothes to go on patrol. Though, as I have said, he did not eat in state, yet he was loved, honoured, and feared by his men and by others who knew him. His detachment was never at rest, but always ranging far and wide. One day we would raid the enemy, the next we ourselves were raided. Never did we cease doing damage to the Hessian forces, nor did they spare us in their turn, but cut off many a trooper and sent him prisoner to Cassel.

This restless life was by no means to my liking, and I often vainly wished myself back in Hanau. My greatest cross was that I could not rightly talk with the fellows and must let myself be pushed, plagued, beaten, and harried by one and all. My colonel's chief pastime was to have me sing in German and blow out my cheeks for him to bang, like the other stable-lads. This did not happen often, but when it did the blows he dealt me were so hard that he soon drew blood and I bore the marks for days.

In the end, and because I was of little use as yet as a forager, I busied myself with the cooking and with cleaning my master's musket, of which he was very proud. In these tasks I succeeded so well that I gained my master's favour, which he showed by having a new fool's suit made for me of calf's skin with far larger asses' ears than the one I had before.

As my master was not particular about his food, I needed little skill for my cooking. But I often lacked salt, fat, and seasoning, and so soon wearied of my new trade and thought day and night how I might escape, the more so now that it was spring-time. In the end I offered to gather up the offals of slaughtered animals which surrounded our camp and remove them to a more distant place because of the stench. My colonel gave me permission, and I busied myself with this task outside the camp until nightfall, when I escaped to the nearest wood.

CHAPTER XIV

*Simplex finds a purse of gold
And lives in the forest as of old.*

BUT instead of mending, my condition worsened apace, so that I thought I had been born only to misfortune. For within a few hours of my escape from the Croats I was caught by some highwaymen. Unable to see my fool's dress in the dark, they doubtless thought they had made a famous catch, for they detailed two of their number to take me to a certain part of the forest. When we got there it became clear that what they wanted from me was money. One of them laid aside his musket and gauntlets and began searching me, asking: 'Who are you? Have you any money?' But as soon as he became aware of my hairy clothing and the long asses' ears on my cap (which he took for horns), and also saw the sparks which usually fly from the hides of animals when they are stroked in the dark, he was seized with terror. Perceiving this, I gave him no time to recover his wits, but began stroking my suit with both hands until it glittered as if I had been stuffed with burning sulphur. Then—in a terrible voice—I answered his question: 'I am the Devil and have come to wring you and your fellow's necks!' At which the two took such fright that they ran off through the undergrowth as if pursued by hell-fire. In the darkness they stumbled over roots and stones, ran into trees, and fell over each other, but away they went as fast as their legs would carry them, until the sound of their retreat faded into the distance. During all this time I had kept up a fiendish laughter which reverberated through the forest and must have been a ghastly sound in that wilderness.

As I was about to leave that place myself I stumbled over a musket. This I took, having learned with the Croats how to handle one. A little farther on I came upon a knapsack which, like my suit, was made of calf's skin. I picked this up, too, and found that it had attached to it a cartridge-pouch complete with powder, lead, and all other equipment. I slung this round me, shouldered the musket like a soldier, and made my way into the thicket to sleep awhile.

At break of day, however, the whole party of highwaymen came back to the place, searching for the lost musket and knapsack. I pricked up my ears and kept as quiet as a mouse. When they found nothing they began to laugh at the two who had run away from me saying: 'For shame, you cowards, to let yourselves be frightened and put to flight by a single man and lose your musket into the bargain!' But one of them said the devil should take him if it hadn't been the devil himself. Had he not, with his own hands, felt his horns and rough skin? The other one was very angry and said he did not care whether it had been the devil or his dam, if only he could recover his knapsack. One of the party, who seemed their leader, said to him: 'And what do you think the devil would want with your musket and knapsack? I would wager my neck that the fellow whom you so shamefully let escape took both.' But another suggested that a party of peasants might well have passed that way since, found the things, and taken them. In the end this explanation was accepted by all and the whole party firmly believed that they had laid hands on the devil himself—the more so as the fellow who had tried to search me in the dark asserted it with fearful oaths and gave a most vivid description of the rough, glittering skin and the two horns—all of which were well-known attributes of the devil.

At last, when their search had revealed nothing, they went their way again. But I opened the knapsack to find something for my breakfast, and the first thing I pulled out was a purse containing some 360 ducats. No need to ask whether I was delighted. Yet I can assure the reader that I was far more delighted to find the knapsack well stocked with provisions than I was about the money. And since ducats are far too rare birds among common soldiers to be carried on a sortie, the thought occurred to me that the fellow must have seized the money secretly on that very patrol and slipped it quietly into the knapsack in order not to have to share it with the others.

After this discovery I ate a cheerful breakfast, found a merry little spring at which I refreshed myself, and counted my beautiful ducats. For the life of me I could not have told what country or district I was in. I stayed in the forest as long as my provisions, which I husbanded, lasted. Then, when my knapsack was empty, hunger drove me to the farmers' houses, where at night I climbed into their kitchens and cellars and stole what food I could find and carry. This I took back with me into the depth of the forest, where I lived once again the life of a hermit—except that I stole much and prayed little and also had no fixed abode, but wandered hither and thither. It was much to my advantage that summer had now begun, although I could also light a fire with my musket if need be.

CHAPTER XV

Simplex arouses the peasants' fears.
And finds a use for his asses' ears.

IN the course of my wanderings I sometimes came across peasants in the woods, but they always fled at my approach. I do not know whether this was because the war had made them wary, hunted, and never truly settled in their homes, or because the highwaymen had spread abroad their adventures with me, so that those who saw me thereafter also believed that Beelzebub in person stalked the countryside. Once I lost my way in the forest and wandered about for several days until my supplies threatened to run out and leave me starving, for I was no longer accustomed to eating roots and herbs. As I pondered gloomily on this prospect I heard a woodman's axe and followed the sound with rising spirits. When I came upon the two men who were wielding the axe I drew a handful of ducats from my pouch before approaching them cautiously. Using my glittering coins as a lure, I said: 'My masters, if you will help me I will make you a present of this handful of ducats.' But they, as soon as they saw me and my gold, took to their heels, leaving their axes and wedges behind, together with a bag full of bread and cheese. This I put in my knapsack, went back into the forest, and almost began to despair of ever making contact with human beings again.

After much thought I reasoned thus: Who knows what is yet to come. As long as I have money and can entrust it to someone for safekeeping I can live comfortably for some time. So in order to hide the money away safely somewhere I hit upon the idea of turning my two asses' ears, which so frightened people away, into two armlets which I filled with the money I still had from Hanau as well as the highwayman's ducats, and tied them securely around my arms above the elbow. Then I continued my raids on the peasants and took from them whatever I needed and could lay my hands on. And though I was still a simpleton, I had sense enough never to visit the same place twice for thieving, so that I was fortunate in my raids and never caught.

CHAPTER XVI

Simplex becomes a fool once more
And acts the part as he did before.

ONCE, however, contrary to my habit, I slept the night in an open field and was aroused about nine o'clock by some foragers, who took me with them, first to some windmills where they ground their corn, and then to the Camp before Magdeburg, where I fell to the share of an infantry colonel. He asked me where I came from and who my master had been. I gave him a full account of myself, and since I could not name the Croats, described their clothing and gave some examples of their speech, telling him how I had escaped from them. But about my ducats I said nothing.

Meanwhile a crowd had gathered, and among them was one who had been a prisoner in Hanau the previous year and taken service there, but later rejoined the Imperial Army. This man knew me at once and said: 'Hoho! that's the calf of the Commandant of Hanau!' The colonel questioned him about me, but he could tell him little except that I played the lute well, that the Croats of Colonel Corpes' regiment had captured me outside the fortress of Hanau, and that the Commandant there had been sorry to lose me because I was an excellent jester. Thereupon the colonel's wife sent to a friend of hers—also a colonel's wife—who played the lute passably and therefore always carried one with her, asking her for the loan of it. When it arrived I was ordered to play, but I maintained that they should first feed me, since an empty belly was a bad match for the round belly of the lute. To this they agreed, and when I had eaten a hearty meal washed down with a draught of good Zerbst beer I showed my prowess with the lute and with song. In between I talked much ill-assorted nonsense—whatever first entered my head—so that I had little trouble in persuading my audience that my dress accorded

81

well with my wits. The colonel asked me what I proposed to do next, and when I told him that it was all the same to me, we soon came to an agreement that I should stay with him as his squire. He also wanted to know what had become of my asses' ears. 'Indeed,' I thought to myself, 'if you knew where they were they would fit you well enough!' But I took good care to reveal nothing of their whereabouts and condition, for they contained all my wealth.

I soon became known to all the officers of rank in both the Imperial and the Elector of Saxony's camps, and more especially to their wives, who trimmed my hood, my sleeves, and my docked ears with silk ribbons of every hue, so that I verily believe it set the fashion for some of our present-day fops. But any money I received from the officers I soon put into circulation again, for I spent it all, down to the last farthing, with good companions on Zerbst and Hamburg beer, to both of which I became much addicted. And this despite the fact that wherever I went I could have all I wanted for the asking.

However, when my colonel, who thought I would stay with him for ever, got me a lute of my own I was no longer allowed to roam from camp to camp. Instead, he put me in the charge of a tutor, who was a man after my own heart: quiet, sensible, and learned, with good but not superfluous conversation and, above all, God-fearing, well-read and versed in many arts and sciences. At night I slept in his tent and in the daytime, too, he kept a watchful eye on me. He had been counsellor and official to a noble Prince, and very rich. But the Swedes had ruined him utterly, his wife had died, and his son, unable to continue his studies for want of money, had been compelled to take employment as a clerk in the Saxon Army. So he himself took service with the colonel as his equerry, to wait until the vicissitudes of war along the River Elbe abated and the sun of his former happiness might shine on him once more.

CHAPTER XVII

The tutor listens in the night
And discovers Simplex' plight.

M Y tutor, being well advanced in years, was a light sleeper, and so, before a week was out, had discovered my secret and assured himself that I was not such a fool as I pretended. He had already guessed as much from my features, being a student of physiognomy, but proof came to him one night around midnight, when I awoke and reflected on my life and strange adventures. Finally I arose and recounted to the Almighty, by way of thanksgiving, all the blessings He had vouchsafed me and the dangers from which He had preserved me, asking Him to forgive me all the sins I had committed in my office of jester, and that it would please Him soon to deliver me from my fool's clothing. Then I lay down again with a deep sigh and slept until the morning.

My tutor had heard all, but pretended to be a deep sleeper. The same thing occurred several nights in a row, giving him ample evidence that I had more sense than many an older man who prided himself on his wit. But he did not talk to me about this in the tent with its thin walls, because for certain reasons of his own he did not want anyone else to know my secret until he was assured of my innocence. So when one day I strolled outside the camp he did not call me back, for it gave him a welcome opportunity to search for me and speak to me in private. He found me, as he intended, in some lonely spot where I had gone to think aloud and said: 'My dear young friend, I am glad to be able to speak to you here alone, because I have your welfare at heart. I know you are no fool as you pretend, and that you have no wish to remain in the miserable and contemptible state in which you are. If you want help and will trust an honest man, tell me your story, and I will see if I can assist you, by word or deed, to rid yourself of your fool's clothing.'

Then I threw my arms around his neck and showed such joy as if he had been an angel or at the very least a prophet come to deliver me from my fool's cap, and when we had sat down on the ground I told him the story of my life. He examined the palms of my hands and wondered at both my past adventures and what was still to come. But on no account would he advise me to take off my fool's clothing just yet, for he said that his knowledge of chiromancy showed him that I was likely soon to be imprisoned, with great danger to life and limb. I thanked him for his kindness and good advice, prayed God to reward him, and begged him, since all the world had abandoned me, to be for ever my faithful friend and father.

CHAPTER XVIII

*Through friendship with the tutor's son
Is courage, aid, and comfort won.*

As the days went by, my tutor became ever fonder of me and I of him, but we kept our friendship very secret. I continued to play the fool, but without bawdiness and buffoonery, so that my performances, though simple enough, turned out witty rather than idiotic. My colonel, who was extremely fond of the chase, took me with him one day when he went out to catch partridges with a draw-net, an invention which I found most diverting. But the dog we had with us was so eager that he pounced before we could pull the strings, and so we caught little. Then I advised the colonel to have the bitch mated with a falcon or an osprey, as is done with horses and donkeys to produce mules, when her whelps would have wings and could catch the partridges in the air. I also suggested, since our siege of the city of Magdeburg proceeded so leisurely, that we should have an enormous rope made, as thick as a wine barrel, encircle the city with it, harness to it all the men and beasts in both camps and have the city pulled down in a single day. Such foolish ideas and jokes I invented daily by the score, as this was my trade, and always kept a plentiful stock of them. My master's clerk, moreover, an unpleasant customer and hardened rogue, provided me with much material to pursue my fool's calling, for whatever tall tales this downy bird told me I not only believed but also used in discussion whenever opportunity offered.

When once I asked him what our regimental chaplain was, who dressed so differently from other people, he replied: 'He is Master *dicis et non facis*; that is, in good German, a fellow who gives wives to others but does not take one for himself. He hates thieves like poison because they do not talk about what they do, whereas he talks about what he does *not* do. Nor can the thieves, for their part, be very fond of him, for as a rule they are hanged when they become too friendly with his sort.' When, later, I described the good, honest priest after this fashion I raised a good laugh at his expense, but I was suspected of malice and roguery and soundly thrashed for it.

My tutor, on the other hand, entertained me with very different discourse when we were alone. He also acquainted me with his son, who, as I have already told, was a clerk in the Elector's Army and of a very different mettle from my colonel's clerk. For this reason my colonel liked him well and tried to get his captain to release him, so that he could make him his regimental secretary, a post which his own clerk also coveted.

With this young man, who, like his father, was called Ulrich Heartsbrother, I formed a close friendship, and we swore eternal brotherhood, never to forsake each other in good fortune or ill, in happiness or in sorrow. Since this was done with the knowledge of his father, our bond was the stronger and firmer, and thereafter our chief thought was how I might be rid with honour of my fool's clothing and we could serve each other faithfully. But the older Heartsbrother, whom I honoured and obeyed like a father, did not approve of this, saying very earnestly that if I altered my state too quickly I would suffer rigorous imprisonment with great peril to life and limb. Since he also foresaw, for himself and his son, some imminent great disgrace, and consequently much need for caution and discretion in their behaviour, he did not want to become involved in another's danger as well. For he feared that if I revealed myself he might have to share my misfortune, having long known my secret but kept it from the colonel.

Soon afterwards I had even stronger proof of the mad jealousy my colonel's clerk felt for my new brother, fearing that he might be appointed to the secretary's post over his head. I noticed how he fretted, how his envy riled him, and how he sighed darkly whenever he saw the old or the young Heartsbrother. From this I concluded for certain that he was plotting how he could trip and overthrow him. I faithfully told my brother of my suspicions so that he might beware of this Judas, but he made light of it, knowing that he was the other's match with the pen as well as the sword, and that, moreover, he enjoyed the colonel's grace and favour.

CHAPTER XIX

Simplex sees a knave's trick played
Whereby a good man is betrayed.

IT is the practice in war to promote old and tried soldiers to the post of provost, and we had one of these in our regiment. He was an out-and-out rascal, and so crafty a rogue that it might with justice be said that half his experience would have fitted him better for the task. He was, in fact, a sorcerer, magician, and practitioner of the black arts, completely bullet-proof not only in his own person but able to make others so and to conjure whole squadrons of cavalry out of the ground. In appearance he resembled closely the portrait painters draw of Saturn, except for the stilts and scythe. Though hapless soldiers under arrest who fell into his merciless clutches cursed their luck, there were those who enjoyed this blackguard's company, and chief among his friends was Olivier, our clerk. The more his envy of young Heartsbrother (who was of a happy disposition) grew, the closer became the intimacy between him and the provost. It needed but little arithmetic on my part to put two and two together and to realize that this conjunction of Saturn and Mercury boded the honest Heartsbrother no good.

Just at this time my colonel's wife was blessed with the birth of a son, and a princely christening feast took place at which young Heartsbrother, because of his obliging nature, was asked to serve. This gave Olivier his chance to commit a piece of roguery which he had long been hatching. When the feast was over my colonel's large gilt goblet was missing, which he resented the more, as it had still been there when all the guests had departed. True, the page said he had last seen it in Olivier's hands, but he would not swear to it. So the provost was called for his advice. If, by his arts, he could produce the goblet, he was ordered so to arrange matters that only the colonel should know who the thief was, for some officers of his regiment had still been present when it disappeared, and if one of them had so far forgotten himself as to take it he did not wish to ruin him.

Now as we all knew ourselves to be innocent, we entered the colonel's large tent, where the magician was to show his tricks, happily enough. Each looked at his neighbour, wanting to know when the performance would start and where the goblet would reappear. The provost mumbled a few words, and all of a sudden there jumped out of everyone's pockets, sleeves, boots, flies, and wherever else there was an opening in his clothing one, two, three, or more puppies. They frisked around the tent, all exceedingly pretty and distinctly marked, so that it was a most diverting spectacle. As for me, my tight Croat calf-skin breeches were spirited so full of pups that I was forced to pull them off; and as my shirt had long ago rotted away on my body in the forest, there I was, naked, and exhibiting front and rear, for all to see, that with which Nature had favoured me. At last a puppy jumped out of Heartsbrother's breeches which was the most active of all and wore a golden collar. This dog devoured all the others, though there were so many of them gambolling about that one could hardly put one's foot to the ground. When it had finished them all off it gradually became smaller and smaller, whereas the collar grew and grew until in the end it turned into the colonel's goblet.

Then the colonel and everyone else present could not but assume that Heartsbrother had stolen the goblet, and the colonel said: 'How now, you ungrateful guest! Did the favours I showed you deserve this piece of thieving, of which

87

I would never have thought you capable? Behold, tomorrow I intended to make you my secretary. But now you deserve that I should have you strung up this very day. And this I would most assuredly do if I did not regard your honest old father so highly. Quick, begone out of my camp, and never let me set eyes on you again!'

Heartsbrother tried to justify himself, but no one would listen, since his guilt was so manifest; as he left, old Heartsbrother fell into a swoon, giving us all enough to do to revive him, and the colonel himself to comfort him, saying that a pious father should not be made to suffer for his prodigal son. So Olivier, with the help of the Devil, achieved what he would never have got by honest means.

CHAPTER XX

The asses' ears reveal their treasure
To help his friend is Simplex' pleasure.

As soon as Heartsbrother's captain heard this tale he dismissed him from his clerk's post and made him a common pikeman; after which he was so much despised by one and all that even the dogs would not piss on him and he often wished himself dead. His father, meanwhile, was so deeply affected that he fell into a decline and prepared himself for death. But as he had in any case foretold that he would stand in great danger of life and limb on 26 July (which was approaching) he obtained permission from the colonel for one last visit from his son, to talk to him about his estate and acquaint him with his last will. I was present at their meeting as a fellow-mourner, and soon saw that the son had no need to justify himself before his father, who knew his breeding and was therefore convinced of his innocence. Wise, sensible, and clear-sighted as he was, he easily surmised from the circumstances of the case that Olivier had made use of the provost to confound his son. Yet what could he do against a sorcerer, from whom he might expect even rougher treatment if he dared to avenge himself? Anticipating his own impending death, he grieved at the thought of leaving his son behind in such disgrace. The latter, for his part, felt the less able to bear his present state, as he would in any case gladly have preceded his father to the grave. Their common grief was so pitiful to behold that I wept bitterly.

In the end both decided to commend their cause to God, and that the son should consider ways and means of obtaining his discharge from his company and seek his fortune elsewhere. But when they regarded the matter more closely they found that they lacked the money with which Heartsbrother could buy his freedom from the captain. As they discussed this and lamented the misery in which their poverty kept them prisoners, cutting them off from all hope, I remembered my ducats, which I still had sewn up in my asses' ears. I asked how much money they needed for their purpose. Young Heartsbrother replied: 'If someone came and brought us a hundred rixdollars I would undertake to solve all my problems with them.' 'Brother,' I said, 'if that is all you need, be of good cheer, for I will give you a hundred ducats.' 'Ah, brother,' he exclaimed, 'what are you saying! Are you a fool indeed or so wanton that you would make a jest of our deepest sorrow?' 'No, no,' I said, 'I truly mean to let you have the money.' And with that I pulled off my jerkin, untied one of the asses' ears from my arm, opened it, and let him count out the ducats for himself and take them. The rest I kept and said: 'This I will use to help your ailing father if ever he needs it.'

Then they fell upon my neck, kissed me, and did not know how to contain themselves for joy. They wanted to give me a warrant in writing that I should be joint heir to old Heartsbrother with his son, or that they would return the money to me with interest and thanks if ever God helped them again to their own, but I would not accept anything, commending myself only to their continuing friendship. Then young Heartsbrother wanted to swear an oath that he would be avenged of Olivier or die in the attempt, but his father forbade him, saying that whoever killed Olivier would in his turn be slain by me. 'Yet am I certain,' he said, 'that you two will not kill each other, for neither of you will die a violent death.' Then he made us swear that we would love each other even unto death, and help each other in every adversity.

Young Heartsbrother bought himself off with thirty rix-dollars, for which his captain gave him an honourable discharge; and, commending his father to my care, set out, with the rest of the money and a favourable opportunity, for Hamburg, where he equipped himself with two horses and joined the Swedish Army as a volunteer trooper.

CHAPTER XXI

Two prophesies are here revealed,
The first, alas, is soon fulfilled.

NONE of my colonel's men was better fitted than I to tend old Heartsbrother in his sickness, and as he was well content with me, the colonel, who showed him much kindness, entrusted me with the task. What with the care I lavished on him and the relief at seeing his son's fortunes restored, he mended visibly, so that even before 26 July he had almost completely recovered. But he preferred to keep to his bed and feign weakness until this day, of which he went in evident dread, should have passed. Meanwhile many officers of both armies called on him to have their fortunes told, for he was a good mathematician and reader of horoscopes as well as an excellent physiognomist and chiromancer, and his prophesies were rarely false. He even foretold the day on which the Battle of Wittstock was subsequently fought, and therefore many came to him who had been warned that they would meet a violent death at about that time. He assured the colonel's wife that she would have her lying-in in camp, because Magdeburg would not fall to our forces in less than six weeks. The treacherous Olivier, who tried hard to curry favour with him, he told to his face that he would die a violent death and that, happen when and where it might, I would avenge it and slay his murderer—whereafter Olivier held me in high esteem. To me he told my entire future in such detail that it seemed

90

as if it had already happened and he had been my constant companion. But I paid little heed at the time, though later I remembered many things he told me when they were already past or had come true.

When 26 July dawned he entreated me and a musketeer (whom the colonel had given him this day at his request) most earnestly not to let anyone into his tent. He lay there alone, spending his time in prayer. In the afternoon a lieutenant arrived on horseback from the cavalry lines and asked for the colonel's equerry. He was directed to our tent, but we told him that he could not be admitted. He would not take 'no' for an answer, but begged and wheedled the musketeer to let him see the equerry, with whom, he said, he must at all costs have a word before nightfall. When he saw that this also would not avail he began to curse and roar hail and thunder, saying that he had come many times before to see the equerry and never found him at home. Was he to be denied yet again, even when the man he sought was in? He dismounted and began to undo the flap of the tent. I sank my teeth into his hand, but got a stinging box on the ear for my pains. As soon as he saw the old man he said: 'Sir, I beg you to forgive my insolence in requesting a word with you.' 'Very well,' replied the equerry, 'what is it you wish?' 'Only to ask you, sir, if you would be graciously pleased to read my horoscope for me?' The equerry answered: 'I most earnestly hope you will forgive me, honoured sir, if for this time and on account of my sickness I must refuse your request. The work requires much calculation, of which my dull brain is at present incapable. But if you will have patience until tomorrow I hope to satisfy you in everything.' 'Sir,' retorted the lieutenant, 'if you would meanwhile but read something of my fortune from my hand!' 'The art, sir,' said old Heartsbrother, 'is most fallible and deceptive. Therefore I beg you to excuse me until tomorrow, when I will gladly fulfil your every wish.'

The lieutenant, however, would not be denied, but approached my father's bed, held out his hand and said: 'Sir, I implore you! Only a word concerning my end, and I assure you that if it is ill-omened I will accept it as a warning from

91

God and take the greatest care. For God's sake, sir, do not hide the truth from me!' So then the honest old man said very curtly: 'Very well, sir; take care that you do not hang within the hour!' 'What, you old rascal!' cried the lieutenant, who was fighting drunk, 'do you dare speak like that to a cavalier?' With that he drew his sword and ran my dear old Heartsbrother through as he lay on his bed.

The musketeer and I raised the alarm with such fury that all around leapt to their arms. But the lieutenant hurriedly mounted his charger and would undoubtedly have escaped if the Elector of Saxony himself had not happened to pass with a large retinue and have him arrested. When he heard what had happened he turned to our general, von Hatzfeld, and observed mildly that discipline seemed pretty lax in the Imperial camp if even a sick man in bed was not safe from murderers. It was a sharp rebuke, and enough to cost the lieutenant his life. Our general had him strung up there and then by his precious neck and let him spend the remainder of his arrest with his toes two feet from the ground.

CHAPTER XXII

Simplex, as a maid disguised,
Finds himself too greatly prized.

FROM this true story it may be seen that not all prophecies are to be spurned, as some coxcombs do who refuse to believe anything. We may also conclude that a man will not easily exceed his allotted span, even though his fate has been revealed to him by such sooth-saying. To the question—which may well be asked—whether it is necessary, useful, or proper for a man to have his future foretold and his horoscope read, I can only reply that old Heartsbrother told me so much that I have often wished, and still do, that he had kept silent. I have never in the past been able to avoid the misfortunes he foretold me, and those still to come cause me needless grey hairs, because I fear that they, too, will come to pass—guard myself as I may. As for the strokes of good fortune that are foretold, it is my belief that more often than not they are a disappointment, or at any rate do not turn out as true as do the evil prophecies. What did it profit me that old Heartsbrother swore by high heaven that I was born and reared by noble parents, when I knew only of my Dad and Mum, who were rude Spessart peasants? But let others cudgel their brains over this; I must return to my story.

To have lost both my Heartsbrothers in this manner disgusted me utterly with the camp before Magdeburg, which even before then I used to call a town of canvas and straw, surrounded by walls of mud. I was so tired and weary of my jester's role that the very thought of it made me sick. I was resolved, once and for all, to stop being every man's butt and to rid myself of my fool's clothing, even at the risk of my life. The way I set about it was as follows—and very clumsy it was, since no better opportunity offered.

Olivier, the secretary, who had become my tutor after old Heartsbrother's death, often allowed me to go on foraging raids with the stable-lads. One day we rode to a large village where some of the troopers had their baggage stored, and they all went in and out of the houses searching for loot. So I, too, made off, in search of some cast-off peasant clothing with which to replace my fool's garb. But I could not find what I wanted, and had to make do with a woman's dress. There being no one about, I put it on and threw my calf-skin suit into a privy, confident that all my troubles would now be over. In this attire I went into the street, walking in the direction of some officers' wives with such mincing steps as Achilles might have used when his mother commended him to the care of Licomedes. But I had hardly emerged from the house when some foragers caught sight of me and taught me to mend my pace. They cried out for me to stop, but I only ran the faster, reaching the officers' wives just ahead of them. I fell on my knees at their feet and begged them, in the name of all honest and virtuous women, to save my maidenhood from these lewd knaves. The ladies took me under their wings; one of them, the wife of a captain, even kept me as her maid, and I made my home with her until our troops had taken Magdeburg and all the surrounding fortifications.

This captain's wife, though still young, was no innocent maid, and became so enamoured of my smooth face and straight body that she began to pursue me with sidelong glances and amorous sighs and at last, meeting with no response, gave me to understand in no uncertain terms where the shoe pinched her. But I, at that time, was still unspoilt; I pretended not to understand her and permitted myself no word or gesture which did not accord with the bearing of a pious maiden. The captain and his servant were smitten with the same sickness, and the former commanded his wife to have me better dressed, so that she might not be shamed by my rough peasant skirt. She, for her part, did more than she was bid and dressed me up like a French doll, whereby the passions of the three of them were still further inflamed. So there were master and servant eagerly seeking from me what I could not give them and what, with much courtesy, I denied the mistress. In the end the captain resolved to seize an opportunity to have me by force; but his wife guessed his intention, and hoping yet to overcome my resistance, balked and thwarted him at every turn so that he thought he would go mad with frustration.

Of the three of them it was the servant, poor lad, whom I pitied most. For whereas master and mistress could quench their lechery with each other, he had no such solace. One night, when the captain and his wife were asleep, he came to the cart in which I had my bed, confessed his love to me with many hot tears, and begged me on his knees to have pity on him. But I remained as hard as a rock and gave him to understand that I intended to preserve my chastity until my wedding night. He pressed his suit the harder, swearing a thousand oaths that he would marry me. When he got nothing for his pains but my assurance that it was impossible for me to marry him, he finally gave way to despair—or at least pretended to—drew his sword, placed the point against his breast and the hilt against the cart, and made for all the world as if to run himself through. I thought to myself: the devil take it all!, spoke fairly to him, and promised that I would let him have my final answer in the morning. With that he was content and went to sleep, but I stayed awake the longer, brooding over my predicament. I saw that the business must assuredly come to a bad end, for the captain's wife was growing ever more importunate with her advances, the captain bolder with his demands, and the servant more desperate in his constant love. Yet though I saw it all quite clearly, I could think of no way out of this maze.

I often had to catch fleas on my mistress in broad daylight, and that for no other reason than to give me ample opportunity to see her snow-white breasts and touch her lithe body. Being made of flesh and blood, I found this more and more difficult to bear. When the wife left me in peace the husband molested me, and when I was rid of the two of them during the night the servant came to torment me. All in all, I was finding my woman's dress a far greater burden than my fool's cap had been. Too late I recalled my dear departed Heartsbrother's prophecy and warning, thinking that this must be the prison of which he had spoken, in which I was to lie in danger of life and limb. The woman's dress made a prisoner of me, since I could not escape in it, and the captain would have had the hide off me had he discovered my secret and found me searching his beautiful wife for fleas. But what to do? In the end I decided to reveal myself to the servant the next day. This would dampen his ardour, and if I gave him a few of my ducats he would surely help me to some men's clothing, and so out of all my difficulties. The idea was sound enough, if only luck had favoured me. But fortune was against me.

For my impatient Johnny the day dawned at midnight, at which time he came to get my consent. He rapped on the cart just as I had sunk into my first and deepest sleep. A little too loudly he called out: 'Sabina, Sabina my love! Get up and keep your promise!' Before his voice succeeded in rousing me it woke the captain, who had his tent near the cart. No doubt he saw red, for he was a jealous man at best, but he did not leave his tent to interrupt our business, preferring to observe unseen what was about to happen. At last the servant's importunate pleading woke me, too, and forced me to choose whether to join him outside or let him come into the cart with me. I scolded him and asked him if he thought me a

95

whore. My promise of the night before was founded on matrimony, without which he should never possess me. He said I ought to get up anyway, to make an early breakfast for the servants; he would fetch wood and water and kindle the fire for me. I retorted: 'In that case I can sleep the longer. Go and do as you say, and I will be with you soon.' But as the fool persisted I got up—to do my work rather than to dally much with him, especially as I saw that his former desperate madness seemed to have subsided. I could well pass for a maidservant in the field, for I had learned cooking, baking, and laundering with the Croats, and soldiers' wives rarely spin during a campaign. Whatever else of woman's work I could not do, such as combing and pleating hair, the captain's wife readily overlooked, knowing full well that I had not learned it.

When I descended from the cart with my sleeves turned back poor, love-sick Johnny was so violently inflamed by my white arms that he could not forbear to kiss me; and as I did not put up much resistance, the captain, who was looking on, could also no longer contain himself, but leaped from his tent sword in hand to take vengeance on my unfortunate lover, who made off hastily and forgot to return. To me the captain said: 'You whoring bitch . . .' and then words failed him in his fury, and he belaboured me with the flat of his sword as if he had lost his senses. I began to scream, which made him leave off for fear of rousing the camp, for both armies—the Emperor's and the Elector's—lay close together in expectation of the Swedes, who were approaching under Count Banér.

CHAPTER XXIII

Lewd striplings for the false maid fight
And quickly bring the truth to light.

At daylight, when the two armies struck camp, my master handed me over to the stable-lads, a seething rabble of lewd urchins, who hunted me fiercely and without mercy.

They dragged me to a thicket to satisfy their bestial lust with me, as is their custom when a woman is delivered into their hands in this manner. A crowd of other lads followed them, all eager to see this miserable sport. Among them was my Johnny, who did not let me out of his sight, and when he saw that they would have their will of me he tried, at the risk of his life, to rescue me by force. When he said that I was his promised bride he gained supporters who felt pity for me and him and joined the struggle on his side. But this did not suit those rascals who thought they had a better title to me and were determined not to let me out of their clutches. So force met force and blows fell thick and fast on both sides. The tumult quickly grew and soon resembled a tournament where each man strives his hardest for the sake of a beautiful lady. The uproar reached the ears of the provost-marshal, who arrived on the scene at the very moment when they had stripped me of my clothes and discovered that I was not a woman. His presence put a quick end to the riot, for he was feared more than the Devil himself, and those who had been fighting rapidly melted away. He informed himself briefly of the affair, but instead of rescuing me, as I had hoped, he had me arrested, for it was unusual—not to say suspicious—for a man to be found in the army disguised in women's clothes. Then he and his men took me along the ranks of the Army, which was drawn up in column of route ready to march off, intending to hand me over to the judge-advocate-general or some other official. But when we passed my colonel's regiment I was recognized and hailed. The colonel had me clothed after a fashion, and I was put in the charge of our old provost, who chained me hand and foot.

I found marching in irons mighty hard work, and would have suffered the pangs of hunger as well had not Olivier, the secretary, provided for me. For I dared not reveal my ducats—which I had rescued through all my adventures—for fear of losing them and exposing myself to even greater danger. That very evening Olivier brought me news of the reasons for my close imprisonment and why the regimental clerk had orders to examine me at once, so that my deposition could be dispatched to the judge-advocate-general as soon as possible: I was suspected not only of being an agent and a spy but also of witchcraft. For soon after I had run away from my regiment some witches had been burned who confessed that I had conspired with them to dry up the River Elbe, in order to speed the fall of the city of Magdeburg.

Next morning there came orders from the judge-advocate-general to our provost to guard me closely, for he intended to examine me in person as soon as the armies came to rest after their march. In that case I would undoubtedly have been put to the torture, had God not willed it otherwise. In my imprisonment I thought constantly of the old parson of Hanau and of my dear departed Heartsbrother, who had both foretold how it would go with me if I divested myself of my fool's clothing. I also reflected how difficult and well-nigh impossible it was for a poor virgin to preserve her maidenhood in times of war.

CHAPTER XXIV

A battle graver ills averts,
The provost gets his just deserts.

THAT same evening, as soon as we had made camp, I was brought before the judge-advocate-general, who had my deposition before him as well as pens and paper, and began to examine me more searchingly. I told my tale as best I could, but he did not believe me. Nor could he determine whether he had a fool to deal with or a hardened malefactor, for all my answers were neatly to the point and the affair itself exceedingly strange. He ordered me to take a quill and write, to see if perchance my handwriting were known or if at least something might be deduced from it. I took pen and paper as if to the manner born and asked what I should write. The judge, vexed perhaps because the interrogation was dragging on till late into the night, exclaimed: 'Heigh-ho, write your mother is a whore!' I put down the words for him, and when he read them my affairs were not improved, for he said angrily that he knew my kind and how to deal with them. He asked the provost whether I had been searched and if anything in writing had been found on me. The provost replied: 'No, to what purpose would we have searched him seeing that the provost-marshal brought him to us almost naked?'

But the answer, alas, did not satisfy them. In the presence of the whole court the provost had to search me, and as he did it thoroughly he found the two asses' ears with the ducats tied to my arms. Then they all exclaimed: 'What further proof do we need? This traitor has doubtless engaged himself to commit some great villainy. Why else would a man of sense disguise himself as a fool, or a man in women's clothing? For what other reason would he be supplied with so great a sum of money than for some major treachery? Does he not say himself that he learned to play the lute at the Court of the Governor of Hanau, the craftiest soldier alive? What other tricks may he not have learned from that wily warrior and his henchmen! There is only one thing to be done with him: tomorrow he shall be put to the torture and afterwards, no doubt, sent to the stake as he deserves, having consorted with witches and being worthy of no better fate.' The gentle reader may imagine my feelings at that moment. Though I knew myself to be innocent and trusted steadfastly in God, I saw my imminent danger and lamented the loss of my beautiful ducats, which the judge put in his own pocket.

But before they could carry out their desperate design the Swedes under Count Banér closed with our forces. A sharp skirmish ensued, and then a struggle for the heavy artillery, which our armies incontinently lost. Though our precious provost, who could make such pretty dogs, stayed well behind the battle with his men and his prisoners, we were yet close enough to our brigade to recognize each man from behind by his clothes. Then a Swedish squadron bore down on them, and we found ourselves in as mortal peril as the combatants themselves, for in a trice the air was so full of whistling bullets that the salvoes seemed to have been aimed at us personally. The timorous ducked as if to hide, but the braver ones and those who had seen such sport before let the fusillade pass over them without flinching. In the line of battle, however, each man sought to prevent his own execution by striking down whoever came within reach. The crackle of musketry, clangour of cuirasses, clash of pikes, and yells of attackers and wounded provided a dreadful accompaniment to the trumpets, drums, and fifes. A thick blanket of smoke and dust blotted out the horror of mutilation and death, but through it came the pitiful groans of the dying and the lusty shouts of those still full of courage. The very horses seemed to gather strength for the protection of their masters, so wildly did they disport themselves in the performance of their duty. Some fell dead beneath their riders, laid low by the wounds which rewarded their faithful services. Others, from the same cause, fell on top of their masters, and so in death had the honour of being borne by those whom they bore while they lived. Others again, relieved of the burden which had spurred them on, forsook mankind and its raging madness, making for the open fields and their first taste of freedom.

The earth which commonly covers the dead was here in its turn covered by them, and all in the most diverse states of confusion and disorder. Heads there were which had lost their bodies, and elsewhere bodies which lacked their heads. Some lay gruesomely with their entrails spilled on the ground, others had their skulls crushed and their brains spattered about them. Corpses were waxen from loss of blood and the living red with the blood of those they had slain. Severed arms there were with fingers still twitching as if eager to rejoin the fray, while fellows who had not suffered a scratch took to their heels; torn off legs lays on the ground heavier than when they had borne the body's burden. Mutilated soldiers begged for a quick dispatch, while others implored their conquerors to have pity on them and spare their lives. All in all, it was a wretched and miserable sight to behold.

The Swedish victors drove our vanquished troops from the battlefield on which they had fought with such ill luck and scattered them in quick pursuit. My worthy provost with his prisoners also took to his heels, though the scant resistance we had offered had earned us no harm at the victors' hands. Just when he had forced us by threats of death and torture to join him in his flight young Heartsbrother came charging up with five other horsemen and saluted him at the point of a pistol. 'How now, you dog,' he said, 'what price the puppies you make so well! I'll pay you back for your pains.' But his bullet did the provost no more harm than if he had been an anvil of steel. 'Oho,' said Heartsbrother. 'So you are bullet-proof! No matter; I will see to it that I have not come to call on you in vain, you spawner of pups! Die you must, even if your soul be grafted to your body.' Then he commanded one of the provost's own men, on pain of instant death, to split his skull with an axe. So the provost got his reward. As for me, when Heartsbrother saw me he had my chains removed, mounted me on a horse, and ordered his servant to take me to safety.

CHAPTER XXV

Simplex meets a subtle foe
Whom no musket can lay low.

BUT while the servant was removing me from further danger, the master, fired by greed for glory and plunder, rode on into the thick of the fray until at last he was cut off and captured. When the victors came to divide the spoils and bury their dead and Heartsbrother could not be found, I, together with his servant and his horses, fell to the lot of his captain, who would give me no better employment than as a stable-lad —with the promise that if I proved myself he would make me a trooper when I grew somewhat older. With that, for the time being, I had to be content.

Soon after, my captain was promoted to the rank of lieutenant-colonel, and I performed for him the duties which David discharged for Saul in times gone by. In camp I played the lute, and on the march I carried his cuirass, which I found a troublesome task. For although this armour was invented to protect its wearer from hostile blows, I found by contrast that the creatures I hatched on my body persecuted me the more securely under its shield. There they found free passage and ample space to disport themselves, so that one might have thought I carried the cuirass for their protection rather than for mine. Try as I might, I could not reach beneath it with my arms to fight them.

I thought of many stratagems by which I might annihilate this armada, but lacked both time and opportunity to exterminate them either by fire (as is done in baking ovens), by water, or by poison (for I knew well what quicksilver could do). Still less could I get rid of them by putting on a new suit or clean shirt, but had to bear with them and nourish them with my flesh and blood. When they tormented and plagued me beneath my cuirass beyond endurance I drew my pistol as if to exchange bullets with them, but took only the ramrod and pushed them away from their feed. In the end I devised a method of winding a scrap of fur round its end dipped in bird-lime. When I poked beneath my harness with this louse-trap I fished them out by the dozen from their hide-outs and cast them from the saddle to the ground to break their necks. But it availed me little.

One day my lieutenant-colonel was ordered to make a raid into Westphalia with a strong force, and if he had been as well provided with troopers as I was with lice he could have set the world by the ears. But as he was not, he had to proceed cautiously and conceal himself in a forest between Hamm and Soest which is called the Gemmer Mark. Just at that time my relations with my personal enemies had reached a climax. They so tormented me with their burrowing that I feared they would end by lodging under my skin. No wonder the Brazilians eat their lice out of sheer fury and revenge because they plague them so! I, at any rate, felt that I could not bear my torment another moment, and when the troopers were busy feeding their horses, sleeping, or standing guard I went some way apart under a tree to give battle to my foes. For this purpose I removed my cuirass—though it is more usual to put it on when going to war—and began such a massacre among them that the two swords on my thumbs were soon dripping with blood and smothered in corpses—or rather skins. Those which I could not kill I banished into exile and let them walk about beneath the tree.

To this day, when I think of that encounter, my skin itches all over as if I were in the very thick of the battle. The thought occurred to me that I ought not to rage so furiously against my own blood and such faithful retainers, who did not forsake a man even on the rack or the gallows, and on whose multitude I had often lain comfortably on the unyielding earth under open skies. Nevertheless, I continued my merciless slaughter so single-mindedly that I did not notice that Imperial troops had overrun our patrol until they reached my tree, relieved the poor lice, and took me prisoner. They seemed in no wise impressed by my manhood, which had just slain so many thousands and far excelled the feat of the tailor who killed seven at one stroke.

I fell to the lot of a dragoon, and the best bargain he had of me was my lieutenant-colonel's cuirass. He sold it in Soest, where he had his quarters, to the commandant for a fair price. So he became my sixth master in this war, and I his stable-lad.

CHAPTER XXVI

For soldiers who require a rest
A nunnery is doubly blest.

THE mistress of our billet now must needs rid me of my enemies, unless she wanted to see them invade her whole house. She gave them short shrift, stuffing all my rags into the baking oven and burning them as clean as an old pipe. As for me, I lived in a garden of roses without my vermin, relieved beyond measure to be rid of the torment in which I had spent the past few months as if in an ant-heap. But I soon discovered that I had a new cross to bear, for my new master was one of those soldiers who hope to go to Heaven. He was frankly content with his pay and would not have hurt a fly. His entire fortune consisted of what he earned by going on extra watch and what he saved from his wages. Though it was little enough, he prized it more than other men do pearls. He sewed every ha'pence into his clothes, and I and his poor horse had to help him increase his supply of them. So I exercised my jaws furiously on hard black bread and made do with water or, when we were well off, small beer, which I relished the less, as my throat was quite sore from dry bread and I was growing visibly thinner. If I wanted better fare I could go stealing, but with strict orders that he was to know nothing about it. Had all soldiers been like him, there would have been no need of gallows, racks, hangmen, torturers, or surgeons, nor yet of sutlers or drummers to beat the tattoo, for nothing was further from his thoughts than guzzling, debauchery, gambling, or duelling. Whenever he was ordered on a convoy, patrol, or any kind of raid he would stagger along like an old woman on crutches. I am certain that if this good dragoon had been a less staid and virtuous soldier I would never have become his prize, for he would doubtless have ignored the lousy boy that I was and gone chasing after my lieutenant-colonel. No new suit could I expect from him, for he himself went about in rags and tatters, almost like my hermit. His saddle and harness, too, were barely worth three bits, and his horse so weak from hunger that neither Swedes nor Hessians had need to fear his hot pursuit.

All this prompted his captain to send him on picket duty to a convent by the name of Paradise. Not that he would be of much use there, but to let him mend his fortunes and give him a chance to re-equip himself—and also because the nuns had asked for just such a pious, quiet, and conscientious fellow. So he rode off to the convent, and I followed on foot, since he had only the one horse. 'By Jove, Simpkins,' he said as we went along (for he could never remember the name Simplicius), 'what feasts we shall have when we get to Paradise!' 'The name,' I replied, 'is of good omen. God grant that the place does it honour!' 'Indeed,' he said (not altogether understanding my meaning), 'if we could drink six gallons of the best beer every day they would not grudge it. Be a good lad and patient, and I'll soon have me a new coat made. Then you can have the old one, which will still serve you nicely as a jacket.' Well might he call it old, for I do believe it still remembered the Battle of Pavia, so weatherbeaten and threadbare did it look, and the promise of it gave me little joy.

Paradise fulfilled our highest hopes, and pretty maids instead of angels so plied us with food and drink that I was soon as sleek as ever I had been. Rich beer we had, best Westphalian hams and sausages, and tasty and very tender beef cooked in salt water and commonly eaten cold. There I learned to spread the black bread an inch thick with butter and a layer of cheese on top to make it slide down my gullet more smoothly. With a leg of mutton in front of me spiced with garlic, and a tankard of good beer, I was at peace with the world and forgot all my past sufferings. In short, this Paradise suited me as well as if it had been the true one; the only cares I had were knowing that it could not last for ever and that I was still going about dressed in rags.

Yet just as misfortunes had once threatened to overwhelm me with their multiplicity, so now, it seemed, luck intended to square the account. My master sent me to Soest to collect the remainder of his baggage, and on the way I found a parcel containing several ells of scarlet for a coat, as well as red lining to go with it. I took it to a mercer in Soest, and in exchange got enough common green woollen cloth for a suit with trimmings, the tailoring of it, and a hat into the bargain. Now all I lacked was a pair of new shoes and a shirt. I gave the shopkeeper the buttons and braid that were with the coat, and for these he provided me with what I still needed. So I returned in style to Paradise, where my master scolded furiously that I had not brought him my find. He threatened me with a beating and was sorely tempted to strip me and wear the suit himself—except that he felt ashamed, and the suit, moreover, would not have fitted him. I, on the other hand, thought I had done very well.

The old miser, however, felt embarrassed that his lad went better dressed than he, so he rode to Soest, borrowed money from his captain, and fitted himself out to his taste, promising to repay the captain from his weekly picket money, which he did. He might perhaps have raised the sum out of his own savings, but he was far too shrewd for that. If he had, he might well have had to surrender his comfortable billet in Paradise, where he meant to spend the winter, to another starveling. As it was, the captain must let him stay where he was if he wanted to have his money back. From that time on we led the laziest life in the world, our greatest exertions being at bowls. As soon as I had fed, watered, and groomed the dragoon's nag in the morning I spent the rest of the day loafing like a squire.

The convent also had a musketeer as picket from the Hessians, our enemies. He was a furrier by trade, and therefore not only a master-singer but an excellent fencer. So as not to lose his skill, and to relieve his boredom, he practised daily with me with every weapon, and I soon became so adept at it that I was not afraid to have at him whenever he liked. My dragoon, on the other hand, played him at bowls, and they never wagered for anything other than who should drink most beer at table. In this way all losses went to the convent's account.

The convent had its own game preserve and employed a huntsman for it. He, too, was dressed all in green, so I kept him company and learned from him that autumn and winter all the tricks of his trade, especially about small game. For this reason—and because the name Simplicius was somewhat unusual, difficult to pronounce, and hard to remember for simple folk—I was commonly called 'the little huntsman'. On our expeditions I came to know the country like the back of my hand, something which I later put to excellent use. I also read all manner of books which the convent's steward lent me whenever bad weather prevented me from roaming about the countryside. As for the noble nuns, when they discovered that I had a good singing voice and could play the lute and even a little the clavichord, they began to take a closer interest in my behaviour. A well-made body and a handsome face helped to persuade them that my bearing, manner, and, indeed, all that I said and did was full of nobility and grace. So, all unawares, I became a most popular young squire who, to everyone's surprise, put up with such a slovenly dragoon.

After I had spent the winter in this happy state my master was relieved, which so affected him after his comfortable life that he began to sicken. The effect of a violent fever on a constitution already undermined by long years of soldiering was swift, and three weeks later I had to bury him. This is the epitaph I wrote for him:

Old Niggard lieth here, a soldier brave and good,
Who never in his life did shed a drop of blood.

By right and custom the captain should have inherited his
horse and musket and the army commander the rest of his
estate. But as I was at that time an alert and well-grown lad
who promised to make a good soldier when his time came,
I was offered it all on condition that I signed on in the dead
dragoon's place. I accepted the more readily as I knew that
my master had a fair number of ducats sewn away in his old
trousers—his life's savings. When I came to give my name—
—Simplicius Simplicissimus—for entering in the roll the
clerk (whose name was Cyriack) could not spell it and said:
'There is no devil in Hell by that name!' I quickly retorted:
'And is there one by the name of Cyriack?' To this he could
find no answer, though he thought himself a wit. My captain,
however, was delighted. It gave him a good opinion of me
from the start, and great hopes of my future prowess as a
warrior.

CHAPTER XXVII

Simplex becomes the huntsman of Soest,
His enemies know him to their cost.

THE Commandant of Soest thought me a likely lad for his
stables, and so it did not please him that I had become a
soldier. He had hopes of getting me yet, instancing my youth,
and that I was not of an age to do a man's work. He remon-
strated over this with my master, and also summoned me to
him and said: 'Listen, little Huntsman, I want you to be
my servant.' I asked what my duties would be. He replied:
'You are to help tend my horses.' 'Sir,' I said, 'we do not see
eye to eye. I would rather have a master whose horses tended
me. But since I am not likely to find one, I prefer to remain
a soldier.' He said: 'Your beard needs to grow a little yet.'
'Oh, no,' I answered, 'I am a match for any eighty-year-old.
It is not the beard that conquers a man, or billy-goats would
stand in high esteem!' 'If your courage is as forward as your

tongue,' he said, 'perhaps you will pass muster.' 'Of that you shall have proof as soon as opportunity offers,' I retorted, and thereby gave him to understand that I would not take employment as a stable-lad. So he let me be as I was and said the proof of the pudding would be in the eating.

Then I went after my dragoon's old trousers, and when I had dissected them there was enough in their entrails for a good charger and the best musket I could lay hands on; and all, I insisted, must shine like a new pin. I had another green suit made for me, because I greatly fancied the name of 'Huntsman', and my old one, which I had outgrown, I gave to my lad. So I rode through the streets with him like a young lord and thought myself a fine fellow indeed. I even adorned my hat with a magnificent plume like an officer, which quickly made me enemies and rivals with whom I exchanged bitter words and in the end even blows. But as soon as I had shown one or two of them what I had learned from the furrier in Paradise, and that I was accustomed to give as good as I got, they left me in peace and even sought my friendship. I volunteered for patrols on horseback and on foot, for I was well mounted and a better runner than most; and whenever we encountered the enemy I made sure that I was in the thick of the fighting. This soon made me a name among friends and foes alike, and I was highly regarded on both sides. I was given the most dangerous raids to carry out and even entrusted with the command of entire patrols. Then I began to loot like a Bohemian, and whenever I picked up anything of consequence I gave my officers so large a share that I could carry on my business even where it was forbidden, because I had protectors in high places.

General Count Götz had left three enemy garrisons in Westphalia—at Dorsten, Lippstadt, and Coesfeld—to which I was a constant nuisance. With small patrols I lay in wait at their gates, now here now there, and caught many a fat prize. As I always escaped unharmed, people began to think that I could make myself invisible and was proof against shot and sword. So I became feared like the plague, and thirty of the opposition were not ashamed to take to their heels if they knew me in the neighbourhood with half that number. In the end I reached the point where I was called upon whenever a contribution had to be levied anywhere. This made my purse as big as my name; my officers and comrades loved their Huntsman, the foremost enemy partisans were terrified, and the country-folk kept on my side by a mixture of fear and love: I knew how to punish the obstinate and to reward lavishly those who had given me even the smallest assistance. Indeed, I spent almost half my booty on rewards and on payments to spies. In this way no party, convoy or patrol left the enemy's gates without my being informed of its departure. I then tried to guess its purpose and laid my plans accordingly. With luck on my side I frequently succeeded, and everybody marvelled at it because of my youth. Even brave enemy officers and soldiers would have given much only to get a glimpse of me. I also treated my prisoners with great courtesy, so that they often cost me more than my share of the prize was worth, and if I could, without being false to my duty and allegiance, be of service to an enemy—especially an officer— I never failed to do so.

Such conduct would quickly have earned me a commission had it not been for my extreme youth. For whoever wanted to command a troop at my age must be of noble birth as well as a good soldier. Moreover, my captain could not promote me because he had no vacancy in his company, nor would he let me go to another, because he would have lost more in me than a milch cow. But I was at least made a corporal. This honour of being promoted over the heads of older soldiers (although no great matter) and the praise I received daily were spurs that urged me on to even bolder ventures. I schemed all day long what I might do to make myself yet greater and more renowned and admired; such foolish thoughts even kept me awake at night. I fretted that I could not have daily encounters with the enemy, because I feared I was missing opportunities to prove my courage. I often wished that I was fighting in a second Trojan war and did not consider, fool that I was, that the pitcher goes to the water until one day it breaks. But that is the way with a young and heedless soldier who has money, luck, and courage: arrogance and pride soon beset him, and it was arrogance which made me hire two servants in place of my stable-lad, fitting them out splendidly and mounting them on good horses. It earned me the envy of all the officers, who grudged me that which they themselves lacked the spirit to achieve.

CHAPTER XXVIII

How Simplex, as a devil, stole the priest's food,
But later made the damage good.

A ND here I must tell of an adventure or two which happened to me while I was with the dragoons. Though of no great importance, they make a diverting tale, for my concern was not only with great enterprises and I was by no means above lighter ones if they promised to increase my fame.

My captain had orders to occupy the fortress of Recklinghusen with fifty men on foot, to carry out an ambush. Foreseeing the need to spend a few days hiding in the forest before we could accomplish our task, every man took with him a week's provisions. But when the rich convoy for which we were waiting did not arrive as expected, we began to run out of bread, nor could we go a-plundering unless we wanted to betray our presence and thereby ruin our plan. Presently we began to feel the pangs of hunger, and as I had no clients in that part of the world (as I had elsewhere) who would secretly bring us provisions, we must think of some other means of replenishing our supplies if we did not want to return home empty-handed. My companion, a student from the South who had but recently run away from school and enlisted, sighed for the flesh-pots which his parents had heretofore provided for him and which he had foolishly rejected and abandoned. As he recalled those ample meals he also remembered the schoolmaster in whose house he used to eat them.

'Ah, brother,' he said to me, 'is it not a disgrace that I have studied so long and yet learned nothing which would now help me to a good supper? Brother, I know for certain that if only I could go to the priest in yonder village I should have the feast of my life.' I pondered on his words awhile, bearing in mind that those of us who knew the countryside dared not go abroad for fear of being recognized, while those who were strangers did not know where they might steal or secretly purchase what we needed. In the end I decided to make use of the student and told the captain of my plan. Though it was not without danger, he had such trust in me and our affairs were in so sorry a state that he agreed to it.

I exchanged clothes with another soldier and with my student wandered off to the aforementioned village, choosing a long detour, though it lay only about half an hour's walk away from us. We soon recognized the house nearest the church as the vicarage, for it was built like a town house and adjoined a wall which surrounded the entire close. I had already told my companion (who was still wearing his thread-bare student's cloak) what he should say. As for me, I intended to give myself out for a journeyman painter, reckoning that the peasants were not likely to want their houses painted, and I would therefore not be called upon to practise my trade. The reverend gentleman was most polite. When my companion told him a pack of lies about how he had been ambushed on his journey by soldiers and robbed of all his provisions, he invited him in for a slice of bread and butter and a drink of beer. I, for my part, pretended that I was on my own, saying that I would have something to eat at the inn and then return to fetch him so that we might continue on our way. Then I set out towards the inn—not so much to appease my hunger as to spy out the land and see what I might carry away that night. As good fortune would have it, I saw a peasant plugging a baking oven in which he had put large loaves of Pumpernickel to bake through for a day and a night. 'Plug on,' I thought to myself, 'it will not take us long to find our way to such welcome provender!' As I already knew where I could come by what I wanted, I spent little time at the inn, buying only some white loaves which they call Stutts in those parts to take to my captain, and then went back to the vicarage. There I found my companion already well-fed and the priest apprised that I was a painter travelling to Holland to perfect my art. He made me very welcome and invited me to accompany him to the church,

111

where he wanted to show me some paintings in need of repair. Unless I wanted to give the game away I must needs do as I was bid. He led us through the kitchen, and when he opened the night-lock on the heavy oak door I thought I saw a Jacob's ladder rising into a black sky. But instead of angels it was full of hams, sausages, and sides of bacon hanging in the chimney. I looked at them full of confidence, for they seemed to smile at me, and made a quick wish that they might all suddenly be spirited to my companions in the forest. But in vain; they stayed where they were and obstinately refused to move. Then I thought of ways and means by which I might make them join the loaves in the baking oven, but could not readily conceive of any, for the vicarage, as I have told, was surrounded by a wall, all the windows were heavily barred, and in the yard there lay two enormous dogs which would assuredly not sleep at night if someone came to steal what was theirs to gnaw as a reward for their faithful services.

We entered the church and talked knowingly about painting. But when the priest tried to commission me to carry out repairs on a few of the pictures and I made excuses and pleaded pressing business elsewhere, the verger said. 'You, fellow, look to me more like a run-away soldier's boy than a journeyman painter.' I was no longer used to being addressed so rudely, but had perforce to take it in good part. So I just shook my head a little and replied: 'And you, fellow, give me a brush and a pot of paint, and in a trice I will paint you a fool such as you are.' The priest made a joke of it and reproached us both for telling each other the truth so bluntly in so sacred a place—giving us to understand that he believed us both. Then, with another drink for the road, he sent us on our way. But as for me, I had left my heart behind with the hams and the sausages.

We returned before nightfall to our companions, where I donned my own suit and weapons again and reported to the captain what we had discovered. Then I selected six good men who would help us carry home the bread and returned about midnight to the village. We succeeded in lifting the bread from the oven without making a sound, for we had with us one who had a way with dogs. But as we went by the vicarage I could not bring myself to pass by without the sides of bacon. I stood still and searched earnestly for a way of entering the kitchen, but found none except the chimney, which must for this once serve me as a door. We carried the loaves and our weapons to the churchyard and hid them in the mortuary. From a barn near by we took a ladder and a rope, and as I had learned in my youth in the forest to climb inside hollow trees and was as expert as a sweep at scaling chimneys, I climbed on to the roof myself. It was tiled in double rows and most convenient for my purpose. I tied my long hair in a top-knot above my head and descended with one end of the rope down the chimney to my beloved hams. Losing no time, I tied one ham, side of bacon, and sausage after the other to the rope, which those on top hauled up with equal expedition and passed on to those beneath to carry to the mortuary. But, alas, when I had finished and tried to climb up again, a staunchion broke under my weight, poor Simplicius fell to the ground, and the luckless huntsman found himself caught as in a mousetrap. My companions on the roof lowered the rope to pull me up, but it broke before they had got me off the ground. 'Huntsman,' I thought to myself, 'now you will have to suffer a chase in which you are like to lose as much fur as Actaeon did of old!' For the priest had been awakened by the noise of my fall and had ordered the cook to bring a light. She came to me in the kitchen in her night-shift and stood so close that its folds touched me. She seized an ember, held the candle to it, and began to blow. I, however, blew much harder than she, which so frightened the good woman that she dropped both ember and candle and beat a hasty retreat to her master. This gave me a breathing space in which to collect my wits and try to think of a way out, but none would occur to me. My companions called down the chimney that they intended to break into the house and rescue me by force; but I forbade them, ordering them instead to return to their weapons in the mortuary, to leave only Happy-Go-Lucky on the roof, and to wait and see whether I might not, after all, get free without an uproar which would hazard our whole enterprise. If I could not, they were then to do the best they could. Meanwhile the clergyman himself had struck a light while his cook told him that there was a fearsome ghost in the kitchen with two heads (perhaps she had seen my top-knot and taken it for a second head). All this I heard, and therefore rubbed my face and hands with soot, ashes, and coal until I looked anything but the angel the pious ladies in Paradise had thought me, and the verger, had he seen me, would have been obliged to admit that I was at any rate a quick painter. Then I began to make a great noise in the kitchen, throwing utensils this way and that. My hands encountered the kettle-ring, which I hung around my neck, and the poker I kept in my hand to have a weapon in case of need. All this, however, did not deter the pious priest, who advanced in procession with his cook carrying a candle in each hand and a pitcher of holy water over her arm. He himself was arrayed in cassock and stole, holding the sprinkler in one hand and a book in the other, from which he began to read exorcisms, asking me who I was and what business I had there. Seeing that he believed me to be the Devil, I thought it only right that I should behave like Satan and seek my way out with lies. So I replied: 'I am the Devil and have come to wring your and your cook's necks!' He continued with his exorcisms and pointed out to me that I had no business either with him or his cook, adjuring me with powerful incantations to return whence I had come. To this I replied, in a voice like thunder, that I would like nothing better, but that unfortunately I could not.

Meanwhile Happy-Go-Lucky, who was a died-in-the-wool rascal and ever wide-awake, had started a most hideous din on the roof. Hearing what transpired in the kitchen, that I was pretending to be the Devil and that the priest believed me, he hooted like an owl, barked like a dog, spat and squealed down the chimney like a whole sackful of fighting cats, or clucked like a hen about to lay an egg. For the fellow could imitate the voices of animals to perfection, so that peasants would keep indoors when he howled like a pack of wolves. All this terrified the priest and the cook, but I felt sorry to have him exorcise me as the Devil, for whom he took me because he had read or heard somewhere that the Devil likes to appear in a green suit.

114

Amidst all this confusion I observed that the night-lock on the door to the churchyard was open and the door only bolted. Quickly I pulled back the bolt, slipped out of the door into the churchyard (where I found my companions waiting for me with their muskets cocked), and left the priest to exorcise the Devil at his leisure. After Happy-Go-Lucky had clambered down from the roof, bringing my hat with him, we gathered up our provisions and left the village to return to our companions, having no further business there except, perhaps, to return the rope and ladder.

Our entire party feasted on what we had stolen, and so blessed was our loot that no one felt any the worse for it. Moreover, we all laughed fit to split our sides over my adventure, except the student, who regretted that we had robbed the priest who had treated him so hospitably. He swore by all the saints that he would gladly pay him for his bacon, if only he knew how; all of which did not prevent him from eating his share as heartily as if he had already done so. We remained two more days in our hide-out and waited for the long-expected convoy. When it came we lost not a single man in the engagement, while taking more than thirty prisoners and as splendid booty as ever I had part in. For my exploits I received a double share, consisting of three fine Friesian stallions with as much merchandise as they could carry at a fair pace. Had we had time properly to sort and salvage our prize, every man of us would have come away rich. But we had to leave more behind than we took, for we were in haste to get away, retiring for greater safety to the town of Rehnen, where some of our troops were stationed.

There I began to think again about the priest whose bacon I had stolen. The gentle reader will perhaps consider me bold, reckless, and overweening, but not satisfied with having robbed and terrified the pious cleric, I now proceeded to vaunt myself with the adventure. I took a sapphire set in a gold ring which I had won on the expedition and sent it by messenger to the priest with the following letter:

'Most Reverend Sir, etcetera! Had I of late had food enough to live by in the forest I would have had no cause

115

to steal your Honour's bacon—giving you, I fear, a great fright into the bargain. I swear by Almighty God that the latter was no part of my design and therefore hope you will the more readily forgive me. As for the bacon, it is only fitting that it should be paid for, and I enclose this ring which comes from those on whose account the theft was committed, asking your Honour to be good enough to accept it. For the rest, I assure the Reverend Gentleman of the most willing and devoted services of him whom your verger does not consider a painter and who is commonly known as

'The Huntsman.'

To the peasant whose baking oven we had emptied, the patrol sent, from the common pool of prizes, sixteen rix-dollars for his loaves. I had taught our men that it is useful to oblige country folk in this manner, for they can often help a patrol in difficulties or, if they feel so inclined, betray or sell them and cost them their necks. From Rehnen we went to Münster and thence to Hamm and back to our quarters in Soest, where a few days later I had a reply from the priest.

'Honoured Huntsman, etcetera! If he whose bacon you stole had known that you would appear to him in the guise of the Devil he would not have been so eager to meet the famous Huntsman face to face. You have paid the borrowed bread and meat so dear that it would be churlish of me to complain of the fright—the more so since it was caused, and that against his will, by so notable a personage, to whom I herewith extend full pardon, coupled with an invitation to call another time without fear on him who does not hesitate to exorcise the Devil. Vale.'

This was my way of handling these matters on many occasions, and I achieved a great reputation thereby. The more I spent on bounties of this kind, the more prizes came my way, and I was well content that this ring, though worth about a hundred rixdollars, had served its purpose well.

And with that I end the Second Book.

BOOK III

CHAPTER I

*The Huntsman tells of many a ruse
And how he began God's gifts to abuse.*

THE kindly reader will have gathered from the preceding book how ambitious I had become in Soest and how I sought and found honour, glory, and favour by exploits which in another might well have been considered cause for punishment. Now I will tell how my folly led me on and plunged me into ever greater hazards and dangers. I was, as I have already mentioned, so eager for honour and glory that it often kept me awake at night, and in the long watches I thought of many strange ruses and projects. I invented a shoe which could be put on back to front, with the heel where the toe should be. I had thirty pairs made in various sizes at my own expense, and when I distributed these among my lads and we went out on patrol with them, no one could follow our tracks. We would wear now these shoes and now our proper ones, putting the false ones in our packs; and if someone came to a spot where we had changed our footwear it looked for all the world as if two patrols had come together there and then jointly vanished. If, on the other hand, we kept our false shoes on, it appeared as if we were going to a place where we had already been or coming from one we were about to visit. So my comings and goings, whenever I left tracks, were more confusing than any maze, and no one could have caught me by following them. Sometimes I was almost within reach of the enemy when they set out on a long march to find me, at others miles away from a thicket they had surrounded in the certainty of finding me inside. As with our patrols on foot, so also with those on horseback. It was nothing uncommon for me to dismount at a fork or cross-roads and have the horses shod back to front. As for the ordinary ruses of leaving a strong trail when a patrol is weak, or a weak one when it is strong but wants to hide its strength, all these were such common fare for me that I do not even trouble to tell them. I also invented an instrument with which I could hear, on a calm night, a trumpet being blown nine miles away, a horse neighing or a dog barking at six miles, and men talking at three. This art I kept very secret and acquired great credit by it, for no one thought it possible. But in the daytime this instrument (which I used to carry in my knapsack with my telescope) was of less use, except in very lonely, quiet places. For it picked up every sound indifferently, and listening to it then was like standing in a market, where a man cannot understand his neighbour's word for all the other noises.

I am well aware that to this day there are many who do not believe this tale of mine, but whether they do or not, it is no more than the truth. I will undertake, with this instrument, to recognize a man by his voice as far away as you might, in the daytime, distinguish him by his clothes through a telescope. But I cannot blame any who refuse to believe what I am now writing, for even those who saw it with their own eyes would not credit it when I listened through my instrument and told them: I hear troopers coming—their horses are shod; I hear peasants, for the horses' hooves are bare; I hear carters, but I can tell by their speech that they are only peasants; there are musketeers coming, about such-and-such a number, I can tell by the clanking of their bandoliers; there is a village over there, for I hear cocks crowing, dogs barking, and so on; a herd of animals is passing by yonder, there are cows lowing, sheep bleating, pigs grunting, and so forth. My own companions took such talk at first for jesting, fooling, and bragging, and when experience taught them that I was never wrong they firmly believed that it was magic and that I got my knowledge from the Devil and his Dam. And so, I fancy, would my readers. Nevertheless, I often escaped the enemy by means of this instrument when they had wind of me and came to seize me; and I believe that if I had passed on the knowledge of my invention it would by now be in common use, for it would be of great value in war, and particularly in a siege. But I must return to my story.

If I could not go on patrol I went out thieving on my own, and for miles around neither horse, cows, pigs, nor sheep were safe in their stables when I was about. For horses and cattle I had special shoes with which I fitted them until we reached a hard road, so that their tracks did not show. Even with large sows, which are lazy and dislike travelling at night, I had my way if they grunted and showed reluctance. I made them a well-salted pap from flour and water in which I soaked a sponge tied to a stout piece of string. Then I let the pig I was after eat the sponge with its mush, keeping the string in my hand, when it would follow me willingly and without further ado, repaying me for my pains with fine hams and sausages. Whenever I brought home such booty I shared it faithfully with my companions and officers, which got me permission to go out again on the next occasion and helped me out of trouble if my thefts were ever discovered.

For the rest, I thought myself far too great a personage to rob the poor, steal chickens, or pilfer anything else of little account; and by-and-by began to lead a life of luxury, with guzzling and swilling, forgetful of my hermit's teaching and with no one in authority over me to guide my youth. My officers were as bad as I, for they shared the spoils at my table, and those who should have warned and punished me only encouraged my vices. I became so godless that there was no roguery which I would not do, and in the end was secretly disliked and envied by all: by my companions for my luck at stealing and by the officers because I was so bold and successful on patrol and made a greater name for myself than they could. Had I not been so lavish with my bounty, I am sure that one side or the other would quickly have betrayed me.

CHAPTER II

The Huntsman of Soest deals with one who tries
To pass himself off in the same disguise.

As a further aid to my exploits I designed a number of devil's masks complete with clothes and even cloven hooves, with which to frighten my enemies or disguise myself from our own side if my thieving took me in that direction. While I was thus engaged I heard that there was a fellow in the town of Werle, a very skilful partisan, who wore a green suit and committed all manner of outrages in my name, plundering and raping here, there, and everywhere, but especially among our own supporters. This led to such angry complaints against me that I would have been in sore trouble had I not been able to prove that I was elsewhere when such-and-such a crime was chalked up to my account. I was resolved not to let this pass unpunished, still less to allow him to continue using my name and person for his looting and to my disgrace. With full knowledge of the Commandant of Soest I challenged him to meet me, either with swords or pistols, and when he failed to appear let it be known that I would have my revenge at all costs—if need be in the house of the Commandant of Werle himself, who did not punish his insolence. Moreover, I announced that if I met him on patrol I would treat him as an enemy.

So angry was I that I threw away my masks—with which I had intended to do great things—and tore up my green livery and publicly burned it outside my quarters in Soest, though the dress—not counting the plumes and harness—was worth more than a hundred ducats. In my rage I swore that anyone who henceforth called me Huntsman would pay for it with his life, even if I hanged for it afterwards. I also refused to lead any more patrols (which, not being an officer, was in any case no part of my duties) until I had taken revenge on my double in Werle. I kept to myself, doing no more soldiering than to mount my guard and carry out any other orders, and these lazily, like any old sweat. The news soon spread and made the enemy's patrols so bold and insolent that they showed themselves almost daily outside our very gates, which riled me much. But what I found insufferable was that the Huntsman of Werle continued to impersonate me and took much booty in my name.

Yet while it was generally assumed that I had decided to rest on my laurels and rise no more, I was gathering intelligence about my impostor's habits and soon discovered that he aped not only my name and dress but also my habit of stealing whatever I could lay my hands on at night. I laid my plans to catch him accordingly. Over several months I had trained my two servants like gun-dogs, and they would have gone through fire for me if need be, for they were excellently provided in my service and had more than their share of loot. I now sent one of them to Werle to my impersonator, to say that I, his former master, had apparently decided to live a life of ease and sworn never again to go on patrol. He had therefore decided to leave me and offer his services to a Huntsman who seemed, with my clothes, also to have taken on my qualities of courage and enterprise. He was also to tell the impostor that he knew the countryside like the back of his hand and could help him to much valuable loot, and so forth.

The fool believed him and took him on. Then, one night, with his companion, he let himself be guided to a sheep-fold where he hoped to capture some fat rams. There, with my other servant and Happy-Go-Lucky, I was waiting for them. I had bribed the shepherd to chain up his dogs and let his visitors burrow into the fold undisturbed, for we would spice their mutton for them as they deserved. When they had made a hole in the wall the Huntsman of Werle wanted my servant to go through first. 'No,' said he, 'I might get knocked on the head by someone waiting for me inside. I can see that you are a raw hand at thieving. First we must inspect.' With that he drew his sword, put his hat on the tip, and pushed it several times through the hole, saying: 'That's the way to see whether our host is in.' When he had done, the Huntsman of Werle was the first to go through. Happy-Go-Lucky at once seized him by the sword-arm and asked him if he surrendered. His companion, alerted, tried to escape, and I, not knowing which

121

of the two was the Huntsman, ran after him and quickly caught him. 'Who goes there?' I asked. 'Imperial army,' said he. 'So am I. What regiment?' 'We're from the dragoons in Soest, come to collect a few rams. If you're one of ours, comrade, I hope you will let us pass.' I answered: 'And who, if one may ask, are you from Soest?' 'My fellow in there is the huntsman.' 'Rogues, that's what you are!' I said, 'or why do you rob your own supporters? The Huntsman of Soest is not such a fool as to let himself be caught in a sheep-pen.' 'I meant of Werle,' he said, and as we were arguing my servant and Happy-Go-Lucky came up with my double. 'Well now,' I said, 'is this how we meet, you jail-bird you! If I did not so much respect the Imperial arms you bear to fight the enemy, I would put a bullet through your head here and now. I am the Huntsman of Soest, and as for you, I shall call you a knave until you have taken up one of these swords and crossed it with me.'

As we spoke my servant (dressed, like Happy-Go-Lucky, in a frightful devil's mask with goats' horns) laid at our feet a pair of swords which I had brought with me from Soest, and I let him choose his weapon. This so frightened the poor Huntsman that he soiled his breeches, and such was the stench of it that we nearly left him in possession of the field. He and his companions shivered like wet dogs, fell on their knees, and begged for mercy. But Happy-Go-Lucky, in a hollow and terrible voice, as if from the pit, said to the Huntsman: 'Fight, or I'll break your neck!' 'Oh, please, worshipful Master Devil, I did not come to fight. If you will only let me off the fighting I'll do whatever else you want.' While he was jabbering, my servant thrust one sword in his hand and gave me the other. But the Huntsman was trembling so much that he could not hold his. The moon shone brightly, and the shepherd and his herdsmen could see clearly from their hut what was going on. I called them closer so as to have witnesses of this affair. The shepherd pretended not to see the two dressed up as devils and asked what we were doing, arguing around his sheep-pen. If we had a quarrel we should settle it elsewhere; he had no part in it, paid his contributions regularly, and wished to be left in peace. Then he turned to the two from Werle and asked them why they let me torment them so instead of knocking me over the head. 'You oaf,' I said, 'they wanted to steal your sheep.' 'Well,' he replied, 'if that is so they know what they can do with my sheep!'

Then I started once more insisting on my duel, but the poor Huntsman could hardly stand on his feet for fear, till in the end I almost pitied him; and when he and his companion again begged most movingly for mercy I forgave them everything. Not so Happy-Go-Lucky, who remembered the shepherd's parting remark and made them kiss the back-sides of three of the sheep, that being the number they had intended to steal. Then, being a devil, he scratched and mauled their faces so that they looked as if they had been fighting with cats, and with this poor revenge I was content. The Huntsman, however, soon disappeared from Werle, so ashamed was he; and his companion spread the story, which he affirmed with terrible oaths, that I had two real and palpable devils at my beck and call—all of which made me even more feared but also less loved.

CHAPTER III

Another convoy brings more loot,
With glory, honour, and praise to boot.

OF this I soon became aware and therefore mended my godless ways, devoting myself for a time to virtue and piety. I went on patrols again as before, but showed myself so affable and discreet towards friend and foe alike that all who fell into my hands found me very different from my reputation. Moreover, I put an end to my reckless extravagance and saved many fine ducats and jewels which I hid here and there in hollow trees in the countryside around Soest. This I did on the advice of a famous sooth-sayer of Soest who swore that I had more enemies in the town and in my regiment who hankered after my money than ever I had among the enemy. But if, from time to time, the rumour spread that the Huntsman had vanished, those who rejoiced at it found me suddenly at their elbow, and no sooner did a place have news that I was plaguing its neighbour than it discovered me on its own doorstep. For like a whirlwind I was everywhere at once, so that my fame spread even wider than when there were two of us roaming under my name.

One day I was sitting with some twenty-five musketeers in ambush not far from Dorsten, waiting for a convoy which was to come that way. When our look-out in a tree reported its approach I climbed up to him and saw through my telescope that they had no men on foot with them but only an escort of some thirty horse. From this I quickly concluded that they would not come up through the forest where we were waiting for them but skirt it, keeping to the open fields in the plain, where we were no match for them. Determined not to return empty-handed after our long watch, I quickly changed my plan.

Just in front of us a small stream ran down a gulley to the plain, presenting no obstacle to a man on horseback. I posted myself with twenty men at the lower end and gave strict orders how each was to pick his victim and who was to shoot and who to hold his fire. Happy-Go-Lucky and the rest I left in our ambush at the top of the gulley, having told them what to do. Some of the older men thought me mad. Did I think the convoy would come this way, where they had no business and where no peasant had come in a hundred years? Others, who believed I could work magic (for which at that time I had a great reputation), thought I would put a spell on the enemy which would guide them into our hands. But I needed no Devil's art for this—only Happy-Go-Lucky. For when the convoy, keeping well together, was about to pass in front of our position the student, at my command, began to low like a cow and neigh like a horse till the whole wood echoed with it, and anyone would have sworn it was full of horses and cattle. As soon as the escort heard it their thoughts turned to booty, hoping to snap up something in a countryside much ravaged by war and generally bare of loot. At full tilt and in great disorder they came galloping into our ambush as if each wanted to be the first to meet his fate. And meet it they did; our first salvo emptying thirteen saddles and several others falling in the ensuing confusion.

124

Then Happy-Go-Lucky came charging down the gulley towards them, shouting: 'This way, Huntsman!' which threw them into such a panic that they did not know which way to turn, and abandoned their horses to escape on foot. But I captured them all, their commander, a lieutenant, included, and then turned to the carts, unharnessing twenty-four horses and otherwise taking only some bales of silk and Holland cloth. I dared not stay to strip the dead, far less to search the carts thoroughly, for some of the drivers had taken to their horses as soon as the skirmish began, and might have alerted the garrison of Dorsten, who would have cut off our retreat.

When all was over and we making off with our prisoners as if the Devil were at our heels the lieutenant was overcome at the thought of his error, having carelessly delivered a good troop of cavalry into the enemy's hands and caused the death of thirteen brave men. He became desperate and refused the quarter I had given him, trying, as it were, to force me to have him shot. For he realized that his misjudgement not only burdened him with shame and heavy responsibility but also spelt death to his further promotion—if not to himself. I humoured and consoled him, saying that good soldiers had before now been forsaken by a fickle fortune without giving way to despair. His behaviour, I said, revealed a faint heart; a brave soldier should be thinking how he could redeem his error. Whatever happened, he would not make me violate my word and do something so shameful and contrary to the customs of war. Seeing me remain firm, he began to abuse me, hoping to rouse my anger. He said I had not fought him fairly and openly, but had acted like a rogue and an assassin, taking his men's lives like a robber and arch-scoundrel. This greatly frightened his own men and so infuriated mine that they would have riddled him with bullets like a sieve had I let them; and, indeed, I had much trouble to prevent it. As for me, I did not permit myself to be moved by his talk, but called friend and foe to witness what had happened and ordered the lieutenant to be bound and guarded as a madman. I promised him that when we got back to our quarters— and if my officers allowed—I would let him take his pick of my horses and weapons and show him in open combat that ruses are an honourable device of war. Why—I asked—had he not stayed with his carts as in duty bound or why, if he wanted to know what the wood contained, did he not send a detachment to reconnoitre in the proper way? That would have been more fitting than now to make all manner of accusations which deceived no one.

Both friend and foe agreed with me in this and said that among a hundred partisans there was not one who would not have replied to such insults by shooting the lieutenant and all the other prisoners as well. Next morning I brought booty and prisoners safely to Soest and got more honour and glory from this patrol than from any before. But as for a duel or fight with the lieutenant, the Commandant would not allow it, saying I had already vanquished him twice. Meanwhile, the greater the praise heaped upon me, the greater also became the envy of those who already grudged me my luck.

CHAPTER IV

Simplex finds a devil in a chest,
Happy-Go-Lucky gives horses best.

A T that time Count Wahl, who commanded the Imperial forces in Westphalia, was mustering troops from all the garrisons for a mounted sweep through the bishopric of Münster and the surrounding country. He wanted most particularly to settle accounts with two companies of Hessian cavalry in the bishopric of Paderborn who were causing our forces much trouble. I was detailed for the sweep with our dragoons, and when a fair force had been assembled at Hamm we quickly moved off, without waiting for the remainder of the expedition, to assault these companies in their stronghold, a poorly fortified small town. They tried to break out, but we drove them back behind their stockade and offered them free passage with their personal baggage, leaving their horses and weapons behind. This they refused, preferring to fight it out on foot inside their walls. So it came about that I could try my luck in an assault that very night, for the dragoons were ordered to lead the way. So well did I succeed that I and Happy-Go-Lucky were among the very first into the town, and that without a scratch. The streets were quickly cleared, for all who bore arms were put to the sword and the citizens had no stomach for fighting. So we entered the houses. Happy-Go-Lucky said we must choose one with a big dung-heap in front of it, for this betokened the owner's wealth and usually meant an officer's billet. We selected a suitable one, Happy-Go-Lucky making for the stables and I for the house itself, it being understood that we shared with each other whatever we found. We each lit a candle and I called for the master of the house but got no answer, for they were all in hiding. I entered a room which was empty except for a bed and a locked chest. This I chopped open, hoping to find something of value, but when I lifted the lid a thing as black as coal jumped up, which looked to me like the very Devil himself. I swear that never in my life was I so frightened as when I saw this black thing so unexpectedly. 'Back with you to hell, Satan!' I exclaimed, and despite my fright raised the hatchet with which I had opened the chest. But I had not the heart to bring it down on the creature's head, for it knelt down, raised its hands, and said: 'Oh, massa, I beg by de good God, gib me my life!'

I concluded that he could not be the Devil, having talked of God and begged for his life. I told him to get out of the chest (which he did, stark naked) and cut him a piece of my candle so that he could show me the way. Obediently he led me to a small room where I found the master of the house and his household, who begged for mercy with every appearance of fear and trembling, though the blackamoor and I must have presented a diverting enough spectacle. I granted their request the more readily, as we were not in any case allowed to harm civilians and as they surrendered to me the baggage of the captain who had lived with them, which contained, among other things, a locked and tightly packed wallet. The master of the house also told me that the captain and his men, except for the moor and one servant, had gone out to their posts to defend the town.

Meanwhile Happy-Go-Lucky had caught this servant and

127

six fine and well-appointed horses in the stables. These we brought into the house, locked it, told the moor to dress, and ordered the master to serve us whatever he had prepared for the captain. But when the gates of the town were opened, guards posted, and our Commander, Count Wahl, let in, he chose this very house for his quarters. So in pitch darkness we had to look for another billet, finding it with our companions who had also entered the town by assault. There we settled in comfort and spent the rest of the night eating and drinking, after Happy-Go-Lucky and I had divided our spoils. I got for my share the moor and the two best horses, one of them an Arab with which I later made a great show. From the wallet I had several valuable rings and a golden snuff-box set with rubies and a miniature of the Prince of Orange. All the rest I left to Happy-Go-Lucky, yet my own share, horses and all, came at the very least to two-hundred ducats' worth. But for the moor, who had given me so great a fright, I got no more than two dozen rixdollars from our Commander, to whom I presented him.

CHAPTER V

Deals with trifling things and small,
But merry to relate withall.

WHEN I returned to Soest I found that the Hessians from Lippstadt had captured the servant I had left behind with my baggage, as well as one of my horses from the pasture. From my servant the enemy learned something of my ways and methods, which made them admire me the more, since they had until then believed the common gossip that I was nothing but a sorcerer. He also told them that he had been one of the devils who gave the Huntsman of Werle such a fright at the sheep-fold. When the latter heard it he was so ashamed that he could not bear to stay in Lippstadt any longer but went off to join the Dutch. For me, however, it turned out the greatest blessing that they had caught my servant, as will be seen hereafter.

I now began to behave with greater gravity than before, having good hopes of early promotion to command a troop. I began to keep company with officers, as well as with young noblemen who were my rivals for advancement and consequently my deadliest enemies, though they professed the greatest friendship. Nor was I in great favour with the lieutenant-colonel, who had orders to promote me over the heads of his kinsmen. My captain also disliked me because I went better dressed, mounted, and armed than he, and no longer squandered money on the old miser as before. He would have wished me death rather than promotion, for in that case he would have inherited my beautiful horses. As for my lieutenant, he hated me for a single thoughtless word that had escaped me a little while ago. It happened like this: During our recent sweep we had been posted together as look-outs in a position so exposed that we must lie flat on our bellies even at dead of night. While I was taking my turn on guard the lieutenant came creeping up to me on his stomach like a snake, whispering: 'Sentry, sentry, do you notice anything?' 'Yes, sir,' I replied. 'What, what!' he asked. 'I notice that the lieutenant is frightened.'

From that day on he was my enemy; he sent me wherever the danger was greatest and tried constantly to find occasion to fault me before I became an ensign and could answer him back. The sergeants, too, detested me because I was to be promoted over their heads. Even the common soldiers began to waver in their friendship and affection, for it seemed to them that I despised them, no longer seeking their company but sticking to the big fish, who loved me none the better for it. The worst was that no man told me how they all felt about me and I myself did not notice, since many professed their friendship who would sooner have seen me dead.

So I lived securely, like a blind man, becoming ever more proud; and though I knew that some disliked my display, which exceeded that of noblemen and high-ranking officers, I did not mend my ways. I did not scruple, when I became an ensign, to wear a ruffled collar, scarlet trousers, and white lawn sleeves braided with gold and silver, which was then the dress of the highest officers and therefore an offence to all who saw me in it. But I was a terrible young fool and cared for no one's opinion. Had I borne myself differently and used the money with which I so needlessly bedizened myself for bribes in the right places, I would soon have had my troop and fewer enemies into the bargain. Nor did I stop at my own person. I caparizoned my best horse so lavishly with saddle, bridle, and armour that when I rode out one might have taken me for a second Saint George. Nothing vexed me more than not to be of noble birth and therefore unable to dress my servant and stable-lad in my own livery. There's a beginning to everything, I thought to myself: if you have a coat-of-arms the livery goes with it, and if you are made an officer you are entitled to your own signet even if you are not a squire.

No sooner said than done. I had a coat-of-arms devised for me by a herald, displaying three red masks in a white field, and for a crest the head and shoulders of a young jester, in a calf-skin suit with hare's ears and little bells. I thought this would go well with my name—Simplicius—and also hoped that in the high rank I was soon to occupy the jester would remind me of what I had been in Hanau and guard me from overweening pride. So I actually became the first of my name, race, and escutcheon, and if anyone had tried to mock me with it I would doubtless have offered him the choice of swords or pistols.

Although I was not yet interested in women, at that time I went with the noblemen whenever they visited one of the many young ladies of the town—mainly to preen myself in my handsome clothes and plumes. I can truthfully say that my good figure earned me much attention, but behind my back I overheard the spoilt minxes likening me to a beautiful wooden statue, which had beauty but neither strength nor sap. For as I still knew nothing of love I had nothing to commend me to them, nor could I give them any pleasure except by playing the lute. When more accomplished friends, to show their wit and win the ladies' favours, chaffed me for my awkwardness and lack of graces, I would say that I was content to find my pleasure in a sharp word or a well-polished musket. Often the women took my part in this, which made the men so angry that they would gladly have killed me, but not one of them had the stomach to challenge me or provoke me to a challenge. Yet a blow, or even a few sharp words, would have been enough, for I was more than a little touchy. From this the women concluded that I must be a redoubtable young man and said candidly that my figure and proud bearing recommended me more than all the compliments Cupid ever invented. And that, of course, embittered the men even more.

CHAPTER VI

Simplex, on horseback, encounters a spook;
He tells of the splendid treasure he took.

I HAD two fine horses which were all the joy I had in the world at that time. Every day, if I had no other duties, I would take them for an outing or to the riding school; not because they needed further training, but in order to let people see that these beautiful animals were mine. Then, as I rode through the streets—or rather, as the horse pranced along under me—the common people would say: 'Look, there is the Huntsman! What a fine horse and what magnificent plumes!' or 'By God, what a splendid fellow he is.' All this sounded sweetly in my ears and pleased me as much as if the Queen of Sheba had compared me with Solomon in all his glory. But in my folly I did not hear what wiser people thought and my enemies said of me. The latter, since they could not rival me, doubtless hoped I would break my neck. Others probably reflected that if each had his due in this world a lad like me would not be able to cut so extravagant a figure. In short, sensible men must surely have thought me a young fool whose high and mighty airs could not last long; built, as they were, on sand and nourished by nothing more substantial than haphazard plunder. If I am to admit the truth I must confess that such men judged rightly, though I did not realize it at the time. My only real merit was that of being a match for any opponent; that is to say I was a good soldier though no more than a boy in years. But the reason for my prowess was this: that nowadays the lowliest stable-lad can shoot and kill the bravest hero. Had gunpowder not been invented, I would no doubt have had to sing a very different tune.

It was my habit, on my rides, to explore every road and path, every ditch, bog, thicket, hill, and stream, so that I should know and remember them and put the knowledge to good use in any encounter with the enemy. One day, with this in mind, I was riding—not far from the town—past an old ruin which had once been a mansion. It struck me at once that this would be a good place for a look-out or a refuge, especially for us dragoons if we were overwhelmed and pursued by enemy cavalry. I rode into the courtyard, whose walls were almost in ruins, to see if one could retire there, if need be, on horseback and defend it dismounted. As I was closely inspecting all this and passing by the cellar, the walls of which were in fair condition, I could not, do what I would, make my horse go where I wanted, although as a rule it was not in the least nervous. I spurred it till it grieved me but to no purpose. I dismounted and tried to lead it by the bridle down the crumbling steps, which evidently caused its fear, so that next time I would know how to manage it. But every time it started back, trembling. With blows and good words I got it down at last, but as I stroked and patted it I found that it was sweating with fear and that its eyes seemed fixed on one corner of the cellar where it absolutely would not go, yet where I could see nothing to trouble even the most timid of horses. As I was regarding the trembling animal with amazement, I myself was seized by such terror that it was as if someone had lifted me up by my hair and poured a bucket of cold water down my back. I still could not see anything, but the horse's trembling redoubled and I began to think that we must both be bewitched and would meet our end in this cellar. I tried to go back, but the horse would not move, which so increased my fear and confusion that I hardly knew what I was doing. At last I took my pistol from the saddle-holster and tied my horse to an elder-tree growing there, intending to make my way out on foot and ask people working near by to help me bring out the horse. As I was handling the pistol it occurred to me that a treasure might be hidden in the old ruin and this the reason for its being haunted. I looked about me more closely, and especially into the corner where my horse would not go at any price, and noticed a stretch of wall, about the size of the entrance to an alcove, unlike the rest in texture and workmanship. But as I tried to approach it my former terror returned and my hair stood on end, which confirmed my opinion that a treasure must be hidden there. I would ten times rather have fought a duel than have had to endure such fear. I was in torment but knew not from what —seeing and hearing nothing. I took the other pistol from its holster as well, with the intention of making my escape on foot and leaving my horse to its fate, but found I could not climb the steps. A hurricane seemed to be forcing me back, and my terror turned to panic.

At last it occurred to me to fire my pistols, which the peasants in the fields near by might hear and come to my help. This I did, seeing no other remedy or hope of escaping from that accursed place. So angry was I, or so desperate (I cannot now remember exactly which) that in firing I pointed my pistol straight at the spot which seemed to be the cause of my strange adventure, hitting the distinctive piece of wall so hard with both bullets that it made a hole through which a man could stick his two fists. As the pistols went off my horse neighed and pricked up its ears, at which I felt deep relief. But whether the monster or ghost vanished at that moment, or whether the poor horse was pleased by my shooting I do not know.

At all events my courage also returned and I went without fear or further hindrance to the hole which my shots had opened up. I broke down what remained of the wall and found there such a treasure of silver, gold, and jewels as I could have lived on to this day if only I had known how to secure and invest it. There were six dozen old French silver goblets, a large gold cup, some tankards, four silver and one gold salt-cellars, one old French gold chain, various diamonds, rubies, sapphires, and emeralds set in rings and other ornaments; also a whole casket full of large pearls—but all spoilt and discoloured from lack of use—and finally, in a rotting leather bag, eighty of the oldest Joachim dollars of finest silver, and 893 gold pieces with the French coat-of-arms and an eagle—coins which no one would accept because, they said, one could not read the inscription. These coins, the rings, and the jewels I put into my pockets, boots, and pistol holsters. I had no bag with me, for I had been riding merely for my pleasure, so I took down my saddle-cloth (which was lined and made a passable sack) and stowed in it all the rest, hanging the gold chain round my neck. Then I mounted my horse in high glee and rode off for home.

As I emerged from the courtyard I noticed two peasants who took to their heels when they saw me. Having six legs and being in an open field, I quickly overtook them and asked them why they had tried to run away in such terror. They said they had taken me for the ghost who haunted the old ruined manor and who was reputed to deal severely with any who approached too close. They also told me that for fear of it hardly anyone ever went near the place, unless it were a stranger who had lost his way and chanced upon it. The story went that an iron chest full of gold lay in the ruin, guarded by a black dog and a maiden under a curse. The legend, which they had from their grandfathers, said that one day a strange nobleman would come that way who knew neither his father nor his mother, who would free the maiden from her curse, open the chest with a key of fire, and take away the treasure. They told me several other foolish tales of the same kind which I will not repeat because they were so preposterous.

I asked them what they were doing there, seeing that they dared not enter the ruin. They replied that they had heard a shot and a loud cry, and had come running to see what was afoot. I told them that it was I who had fired the shot, having taken fright in the place and hoping someone would come to my aid, but that I knew nothing of the cry. To this they answered that a man might fire many a shot in the old ruin without anyone in the neighbourhood going to his aid, for fear of the ghost. Indeed, had they not seen the young gentleman emerge, they said, they would not have believed him when he said he had been inside.

Then they wanted to know all manner of things, but especially what the place was like inside and whether I had seen the maiden and the black dog sitting on the iron chest. I could, had I wished, have spun them a fine yarn, but I said nothing—not even that I had raised the treasure—but made my way home, where I examined my hoard with the utmost delight and satisfaction.

CHAPTER VII

Simplex tries to make a choice,
And listens to a good friend's voice.

IT is my belief that those who know the power of money and treat it as their God have much reason on their side; for if there is anyone alive who has witnessed its mighty and well-nigh divine virtues it is I. I know not only the sentiments of a man with a good supply of it but have also experienced more than once the afflictions of those who have not a farthing to their names. With this experience both of riches and poverty I venture to maintain that money has all and more of those powers and virtues commonly ascribed to precious stones. Like the diamond, it dispels melancholy; like the emerald, it induces a desire and inclination to study (which is the reason why commonly more students come from rich homes than from poor); like the ruby, it overcomes timidity and makes a man merry and content. It often causes sleeplessness, like the garnet, yet like the jacinth, may also have the effect of bringing peace of mind and a good night's rest. Like the sapphire and the amethyst, it refreshes the heart and makes a man companionable, well-mannered, alert, and kindly; it dispels bad dreams, brightens and clears the mind, and wins lawsuits like the sardonyx (especially when used to grease the judge's palm); it also quenches lechery and lewd desires— mainly because it can be used to buy beautiful women. In short, the power of money is well-nigh infinite.

As far as mine was concerned, which I had acquired by plunder and by the discovery of this treasure, its effects were strange and varied. First, it made me even haughtier than before, so that I became quite vexed with having no better name than Simplicius. Like the garnet, it disturbed my sleep, for I spent many a long night wondering how to invest and increase it. It made me an expert mathematician, for I calculated what my unminted silver and gold might fetch, added to what I had hidden away here and there and what was in my purse, and arrived at a handsome total even without the precious stones. It also gave me a taste of its own perversity and malice, teaching me the truth of the saying that the appetite grows with what it feeds on and making me such a miser that it was enough to make the world my enemy. It inspired me with many mad ideas and plans, but did not help me to carry out any of them. At one moment it occurred to me to quit the war, settle down somewhere, and watch the world go by. But the next I thought better of it, in view of the unfettered life I led and the hopes I had of making my mark. Then I thought: Go to it, Simplici, have yourself knighted and use the money to raise a company of dragoons of your own for the Emperor! That will make you a fine gentleman who may yet go far. But when I reflected how a single unlucky encounter could lay my nobility low, or the conclusion of a peace put an end to it and the war at one blow, I did not like this idea either. Another time I wished I were a fully-grown man, for then, I thought, I would marry a beautiful and rich young girl, buy a nobleman's estate somewhere, and lead a peaceful and comfortable life. I would raise cattle and make an ample and honest living by it. But knowing that I was much too young for it, I had to abandon this idea, too.

Of such plans I had many, until at last I decided to take the greater part of my fortune to a wealthy man to keep in a safe city, and to wait and see what fortune still had in store for me. I made the Commandant a present of two silver-gilt tankards and my captain a pair of silver salt-cellars, which served no purpose but to make their mouths water for more, for the pieces were rare antiques. To my faithful comrade Happy-Go-Lucky I gave twelve rixdollars, and he, in return, advised me to separate myself from my treasure quickly or expect to suffer for it, for officers dislike common soldiers having more money than they. He also told me that he once saw a soldier murdered by his comrades for money. Until now, he said, I had been able to keep the extent of my plunder secret, for everyone believed I spent it all on clothes, horses, and weapons. But from now on I would not deceive anyone into thinking me poor, for rumour was already exaggerating the value of the treasure, and it was common knowledge that I was no longer as lavish as I used to be. Often had he heard the men muttering about it; if he were in my place he would let the war go hang, settle down somewhere, and leave God to look after His own. I replied: 'Listen, brother, how do you expect me to give up so easily the hope of getting a troop?' 'A troop!' said Happy-Go-Lucky, 'you will get your troop when I am Emperor of China. All the others who aspire to the same thing will see you dead a thousand times before they let you have one, even if a post falls vacant. Do not teach me to eat herrings, for my father was a fisherman! Take my advice, brother, for I have seen more of war than you have. Can you not see how many a sergeant's beard has turned grey in the ranks who long deserved to be a captain? Do you not think that they, too, have merit? Indeed, as you yourself admit, they have a better claim than you.' To this I had no answer, for Happy-Go-Lucky, true comrade that he was, had spoken from the heart and without flattery. But secretly I gritted my teeth, for I had a marvellously high opinion of myself.

However, I considered his words carefully, and it came to me that I had not a single natural-born friend who would help me in my hour of need or avenge my death. But clearly though I saw this, my ambition and greed would not let me quit the war and live in peace, and I reverted to my first resolve. When at that very time an opportunity occurred of going to Cologne (whither a hundred of us dragoons were to escort a convoy of merchants and their carts from Münster), I packed my treasure, took it with me, and gave it to one of the first merchants of that city to keep, against a receipt in writing. There were seventy-four marks in unminted fine silver, fifteen marks in gold, eighty Joachim dollars, and a sealed casket with various rings and jewels weighing eight and a half pounds. Of coin there were 893 pieces of antique gold, each the weight of one and a half gold florins.

CHAPTER VIII

Simplex is captured in the end,
But his enemies treat him like a friend.

On the journey back I reflected at length on how I should bear myself if I wanted to regain some of my former esteem. For Happy-Go-Lucky had put a troublesome flea in my ear and convinced me that I was disliked by all—which was true. These reflections greatly sharpened my understanding, and I perceived that a man who lives thoughtlessly is little better than an animal. I pondered why this or that person should hate me and how to deal with each, in order to regain his goodwill. What surprised me most was that all these people were so false; giving me kind words though they did not love me. So I resolved to behave like the rest of them, to say to each what would please him most and to show respect even to those whom I despised. Above all, it dawned on me that it was my vainglory that had earned me most enemies, and I decided that I would henceforth show myself humble though I did not feel it, consort again with common soldiers, doff my hat to my superiors, and moderate the splendour of my dress until my condition should have changed for the better.

I had borrowed a hundred rixdollars from the Cologne merchant, to be repaid with interest when he returned my treasure to me, of which I intended to spend half on the convoy during our return journey, having at last realized that a tight fist makes no friends. So eager was I to mend my ways that I was determined to make a start on this very journey. But I made my reckoning without my host, for as we were passing through the duchy of Berg, I leading the advanced guard with a corporal and five men, we fell into a well-prepared ambush of fifty horsemen and eighty musketeers. They let the advanced guard pass so as not to alert the main escort, merely sending a detachment of a cornet and eight troopers after us to keep us in sight till their people had attacked the convoy and we turned back to help protect the carts. When we did so they bore down on us and asked if we would surrender. For my part I was well mounted, having my best horse under me, but did not want to take to my heels. I wheeled on to a small hillock to see what honour was to be gained by fighting, but the noise of the volley our people received quickly showed me how matters stood, and I turned to escape. The cornet, however, was prepared for this, too, and had cut off our retreat. As I made ready to hack my way through, he again offered me quarter, taking me for an officer. I reflected that it was better to save one's life than to put it to so uncertain a hazard, and asked him if he would keep his promise of quarter like an honest soldier. 'Yes, upon my word!' he replied, so I handed him my sword and let myself be taken prisoner. At once he asked me for my rank and title, for he took me for a nobleman and therefore an officer. When I told him that I was commonly known as the Huntsman of Soest he said: 'Then you are in luck not to have fallen into our hands four weeks ago, when I would not have been allowed to offer you quarter or, if I had, to keep my promise; for at that time you were considered an avowed sorcerer.'

This cornet was a brave young cavalier and not more than two years older than I. He was delighted with the honour of having captured the famous Huntsman, and therefore kept the quarter he had promised me very faithfully and after the fashion of the Dutch, who do not take from their Spanish prisoners anything that is carried under the belt. He did not even have me searched, but I myself gave him the money from my purse when they came to divide the spoils. I also told him secretly to see to it that he got my horse and saddle, for in the latter he would find some thirty ducats and the former had hardly its equal anywhere. This so impressed the cornet that he took a liking to me and treated me like a brother. When he mounted my horse he gave me his to ride. As for the convoy, there remained only six dead and thirteen prisoners, eight of whom were wounded. The rest escaped, but lacked the spirit to try to recover what they had lost in open country, which, being all of them mounted, they might well have done.

When spoils and prisoners had been shared out, Swedes and Hessians (for the expedition was drawn from two different garrisons) separated that very evening. The cornet kept me, the corporal, and three other dragoons whom he had captured and took us to a fortress only a few miles from our own garrison. Since in my time I had caused them many a sleepless night, my name was well known there, and I myself more feared than loved. As we drew within sight of the place the cornet sent a trooper ahead to give the Commandant notice of his arrival and to tell him how he had fared and who the prisoners were. This caused great crowds to gather, for everyone wanted to see the Huntsman. One said this and the other that, and it was for all the world as if royalty had entered the place.

We prisoners were taken straightway to the Commandant, who was amazed at my youth. He asked me if I had ever served on the Swedish side and where I came from. When I told him the truth he asked me if I would not like to fight for the Swedes again. I replied that I did not really care one way or the other, but seeing that I had sworn allegiance to the Emperor it seemed to me that I ought to keep it. Then he had us taken to the prize-master, but allowed the cornet, at his request, to entertain me as his guest because I had previously given the same treatment to my prisoners, among whom had been his brother. In the evening a number of officers, some of them soldiers of fortune and others noblemen by birth, assembled at the cornet's quarters, and he invited me and the corporal to join them and treated us, to tell the truth, most civilly. I made as merry as if I had lost nothing and spoke openly and confidingly as if I had been among my best friends instead of a captive among my enemies. At the same time I was studiously modest in my demeanour, for I could easily imagine that the Commandant would be fully informed of my behaviour; which, as I learned later, was indeed the case.

The next day we prisoners were taken one by one before the adjutant, who examined us. The corporal was first and I

140

next. As soon as I entered the room the adjutant exclaimed at my youth and said, as if in reproach: 'Child, what have the Swedes done to you that you make war on them?' This vexed me the more since I had seen soldiers no older than I on the other side, so I answered: 'The Swedish soldiers took away my marbles and I wanted them back!'

This retort embarrassed the officers who were with him, and they spoke to him in Latin, saying that he should talk to me seriously, for he could see that I was not a child. From their remarks I gathered that he was called Eusebius. Then he asked me my name, and when I told him said: 'There is no devil in Hell of that name!' So I replied: 'And none, either, I presume, by the name of Eusebius,' paying him back as I had our old clerk Cyriack. But it did not please the officers, who told me to remember that I was a prisoner and had not been brought before them for fooling. This rebuke in no wise embarrassed me or persuaded me to apologize. I merely replied that since they had taken me prisoner as a soldier and presumably did not intend to let me run away like a child I, for my part, did not expect to be treated like one. As they had questioned me, so had I answered and hoped I had not done amiss. Then they asked me where I came from, about my family and birth, and whether I had ever served on the Swedish side. They also asked me about the fortifications of Soest, the strength of its garrison, and other similar questions. I answered everything briefly and to the point, and about Soest as much as I thought I could with honour. But about my having been a jester I said nothing, for I was ashamed of it.

CHAPTER IX

The Swedes soon set the Huntsman free,
But make him keep them company.

THE garrison of Soest, meanwhile, had learned the fate of the convoy and that I, the corporal, and the others had been captured. They also discovered where we had been taken and the very next day a drummer arrived for a parley to fetch us back. He was given the corporal and the three others, as well as a letter from the Commandant which he had first sent me to read and which ran as follows:

'Monsieur, etc.'

'The bearer of this letter—the drummer—brought me your Excellency's message and received in return the corporal and the three other prisoners, their ransom having been duly paid. As for Simplicius the Huntsman, I regret I cannot return him since he previously served on our side. If, however, I can be of service to your Excellency in anything else without prejudice to my duty to my Sovereign, I am always your Excellency's obliging servant.

'N(athaniel) de S(aint) A(ndré)'.

Little though I liked this letter, I had cause to be grateful that it had been shown to me. I asked for an interview with the Commandant, but was told to be patient; he would send for me as soon as he had dealt with the drummer, which would be the following morning.

When the time came it was around the hour for dinner that the Commandant had me summoned, and I had the honour of sitting at table with him for the first time. During the meal he drank my health very affably, but without a word about his intentions concerning me, nor would he let me broach the subject. When we had finished and I was somewhat fuddled he said: 'My dear Huntsman, you will have gathered from my letter on what grounds I am keeping you here. Nor is this in any way unjustified or contrary to reason or the customs of war, for you confessed both to me and to the adjutant that you served with the main army on our side. You will therefore have to resign yourself to accepting service in my regiment, where in due course—and subject to your good behaviour—I will accommodate you as you could never have hoped to be accommodated in the Imperial army. If you refuse, you will not take it ill, I hope, if I return you to the lieutenant-colonel from whom the dragoons captured you.'

'Sir,' I said, 'seeing that I am bound neither to the Swedish Crown nor to its Allies by any oath, far less to that lieutenant-colonel, but was no more than a stable-lad in his service, I do not feel obliged to engage myself with the Swedes and so break the oath I swore to the Emperor. I therefore most humbly beg of you, sir, not to expect this of me.' 'What!' said the Commandant, 'do you then despise service under the Crown of Sweden? I would have you remember that you are my prisoner and that rather than let you return to Soest to serve with the other side I will have you tried or let you rot in prison. You may make up your mind accordingly!' His words frightened me, but I refused to give in, saying I prayed God would protect me both from such a fate and from perjury. For the rest I entertained the humble hope that the Commandant would treat me as a soldier, and in accordance with his reputation for justice. 'Justice indeed!' he said, 'I know only too well how I ought to treat you in strict justice. Think it over and do not give me cause to do so!' And with that I was taken back to prison.

The following day he summoned me again and asked me sternly if I had changed my mind. I replied: 'This, Sir, is my resolve: that I would die rather than be forsworn. But if your Excellency will be pleased to set me free and not force me into military service, I will gladly give you my word of honour that for six months I will bear no arms against Swedes or Hessians.' To this the Commandant readily agreed, we shook hands on it and he waived my ransom into the bargain. Then he ordered his clerk to draw up an agreement in duplicate which we both signed, and in which he promised me my freedom under his protection for as long as I remained in the fortress under his command. I, in return, pledged myself while there to do nothing to injure its garrison or Commandant, nor to conceal anything that might harm them, but on the contrary to do all in my power for their aid and comfort and to help them defend the place if attacked.

Afterwards he entertained me again at table and did me more honour than ever I could have hoped for in the Imperial army. In this way he won me over by degrees, so that I would not have returned to Soest even if he had released me from my promise and let me go; whereby, without bloodshed, he did his enemy much damage, for the partisans of Soest were never again of any account.

CHAPTER X

The Huntsman's mind is turned to love,
And easy game the ladies prove.

BEING now at a loose end for six months I decided to perfect myself in the arts of musketry and fencing. The idea was sound and the execution to match, but it was not enough wholly to protect me from idleness, which is the root of much evil; the more so as I was my own master and owed obedience to nobody. True, I spent much time reading books from which I derived great profit, but others that I chanced upon did me as much good as a bone does to a cow. The incomparable 'Arcadia', which I read to acquire eloquence, was the first to turn my mind from good stories to tales of love and from serious history to romances of chivalry. Thereafter I picked up books of this kind wherever I could, and if I laid my hands on one I would not put it down until I had read it from cover to cover, even if it took me days and nights on end. They taught me love-sickness instead of eloquence, but the evil did not at that time grow so strong in me that one could describe it, with Seneca, as a divine frenzy or, as it is called in Thomas à Kempis' *Garden of Roses*, a burdensome disease. For wherever my fancy alighted I obtained my desire quickly and without much trouble, so that I had no cause for complaint like some lovers, who are full of fanciful thoughts, cares, desires, secret sorrows, anger, jealousy, passion, rage, tears, boasts, threats, and a thousand other follies, and out of sheer impatience long for death. I had money and was generous with it; a good voice which I constantly exercised with all manner of instruments; and instead of dancing, which I never grew to like, I displayed my bodily skill on the fencing-floor. I also had a smooth and pretty face and acquired agreeable manners, so that women—even those I did not much

144

desire—pursued me of their own accord more than I cared for.

This was about the time of Martinmas, the season of the year when we Germans eat and drink too much, which in some places is carried on until Shrovetide. I was invited to many houses, both by officers and burghers, to help them eat the Martinmas goose, and made numerous acquaintances with their ladies. My playing of the lute and singing drew their attention, and my habit of accompanying the love-songs (which I composed myself) with graceful gestures and amorous glances so beguiled them that many a pretty maid fell in love with me before she was well aware of it. To show that I, too, was not without means I gave two banquets myself— one for the officers and the other for the most prominent burghers. My hospitality was lavish, earning me a good name and entry into many houses. But it was the women I was after, and though with a few I did not find what I sought (for even in those days there were some who could resist temptation), I still frequented their company so that no suspicion might fall on those who showed me more favour than a modest maiden should, and in order that the chaste ones might believe that I visited their more compliant sisters also for no other purpose than polite conversation. Moreover, I succeeded in persuading each that she was the only one to enjoy my favours.

I had exactly half a dozen who loved me and whom I loved, but none had my heart—much less my person—to herself. In some I liked the eyes, in others the hair, in a third her particular charms; in each, in short, something that the others lacked. So if I visited one rather than another it was only for such reasons or for the sake of novelty, and because in any case I would not scorn an offer and had no intention of settling in one place. My lad, who was an arch-rogue, had his hands full with pandering and the conveyance of love letters to and fro, which he did so discreetly that there was never the least talk about it. In this way he gained many favours from the ladies, but yet it was I who paid most, for I was generous with him and found much truth in the saying that what you gain on the swings you lose on the roundabouts. But as I say, all was done so discreetly that not one in a hundred suspected me of philandering, except perhaps the parson, from whom I borrowed fewer books of devotion than I had done before.

CHAPTER XI

The Huntsman is caught with his prey in bed,
And cannot escape until he is wed.

OPPOSITE my lodgings lived a lieutenant-colonel on half pay who had a most beautiful daughter of noble bearing. I had long sought to make her acquaintance, although at first sight she did not seem to me the woman with whom I would want to spend the rest of my life. Nevertheless, I took many a walk for her sake and cast frequent amorous glances in her direction; but she was so carefully guarded that never once could I carry out my intention of talking to her. Nor did I dare to accost her too impertinently, for I was not acquainted with her parents and the family seemed much too superior for a fellow of my humble origins. The closest I came to her was on the way to and from church, when I would seize my chance to approach her and heave a passionate sigh or two, which I did most convincingly albeit from a false heart. But her manner of receiving them was so aloof that I could only presume she would not be easily seduced like a common burgher's daughter, and the despair of ever possessing her greatly inflamed my desires.

The lucky star which at last brought us together was one which schoolboys carry in procession at this season, in memory of that which guided the Three Wise Men to Bethlehem. I took it for a good omen that it was this that lighted me to her house and made her own father send for me. 'Sir,' he said, 'the neutral position you hold between citizens and soldiers is the reason for my approach to you. I have a matter to arrange in which both sides are concerned and for which I need an impartial witness.' I thought he had goodness knows what weighty affairs in mind, for ink, paper, and quills were ready on the table, so I offered my most willing services with all manner of compliments, saying it would be a great pleasure and I would be most happy to oblige him in any honourable undertaking.

It turned out to be no more than the preparations for a so-called Kingdom (as is the custom in many places) to celebrate the festival of the Three Kings from the East. I was to see that all the 'offices' were properly drawn by lot without regard to person. For this task, which I was to undertake jointly with the colonel's secretary, my host treated us to wine and confectionery, for he was fond of the bottle himself, and it was already past supper-time. The secretary wrote, I read the names, and the maiden drew the lots, while her parents sat by and watched. I do not rightly remember how it happened that we became better acquainted, but they complained of the tedium of long winter evenings and gave me to understand that I would be welcome to help make them pass more quickly—the more so since they did little entertaining otherwise. This, of course, was the very opportunity I had been looking for.

From that evening on, though I behaved decorously enough towards the girl, I showed all the symptoms of love-sickness, so that she and her parents had every reason to believe that I had swallowed the bait. Yet my intentions were anything but serious and my only concern how to enjoy married bliss without a wedding. Like a witch, I donned my finery only at night, when I went to see her. The days I spent poring over romances from which I composed love letters to my mistress, for all the world as if I lived a hundred miles away or had not seen her for years. In the end I became almost a member of the household, for her parents—far from placing obstacles in the way of our spooning—asked me to instruct her in the art of playing the lute. So now I had as free access to her in the daytime as in the evenings, and my theme-song

The bat and I
By night do fly,

lost its point. Instead, I composed a song praising my good fortune which allowed me glad days as well as happy even-

147

ings in which to feast my eyes on the charms of my beloved and solace my heart with her presence. But the song also lamented the hard fate which embittered my nights, instead of granting me the felicity of spending them, like the days, in sweet dalliance. Though this was somewhat forward, I sang it to her with many a deep sigh to a beguiling melody, the very accompaniment on the lute being designed to tempt the wench to make my nights as happy as my days. But her response was cool, for she was quick-witted and neatly parried even my best-turned compliments.

I took good care not to mention matrimony, and to handle the subject cautiously whenever it arose. My maiden's married sister soon became aware of this, and from then on put every possible obstacle in our way and took care that we saw less of each other privately than before; for she could see that her sister loved me dearly and that the affair was likely to come to a bad end.

There is no need to describe at length all the follies of my courtship, for the romances are full of such stuff. Enough for the reader to know that at last I prevailed upon my mistress to grant me a kiss and then some other liberties. I pressed my advantage by arousing her desires with all manner of caresses, until one night my sweetheart let me in and I lay down beside her in her bed as if it were the most natural thing in the world. As the outcome of such situations is generally known, the gentle reader might well imagine that some impropriety now took place. Far from it! All my efforts were in vain. I encountered such resistance as I would never have expected to meet in a woman, for her mind was set only on honourable matrimony. And though I promised it her with the most solemn oaths, she would not let me have her out of wedlock, allowing me only to lie beside her on the bed, where at last, worn out by my fruitless struggle, I fell asleep.

I had a rude awakening at four o'clock in the morning when I found the lieutenant-colonel standing beside the bed with a pistol in one hand and a candle in the other. 'Croat,' he yelled, 'quick, Croat, fetch the parson!' I was now wide awake and perceived the full extent of my peril. 'Alas,' I thought, 'I am to be shriven before he dispatches me!' I saw

148

green and yellow specks before my eyes and did not know whether to open them or keep them shut.

'You fly-by-night,' he said to me. 'Do I find you dishonouring my house! Who would blame me if I broke your neck and that of this baggage here who has become your whore! Ah, you beast! My hands are itching to tear out your heart, hack it into small pieces, and feed it to the dogs!' He gnashed his teeth and rolled his eyes like a wild animal, while I was at a loss what to do and my bed-fellow merely wept. At last, when I had somewhat recovered from my shock, I tried to say something about our innocence, but he told me to hold my tongue and began to harangue me again, proclaiming that he had trusted me and I had requited his trust with the greatest perfidy in the world. Meanwhile his wife had joined him and now began a brand-new sermon of her own, until I felt I would be better off lying in a hedge of brambles. I do believe they would have carried on like this for another two hours or more had not the Croat arrived with the parson.

Before that I had tried several times to rise to my feet, but the colonel forced me with threatening gestures to stay where I was. This taught me how little courage a man has who is caught red-handed, and how a thief must feel when he is found in a house even though he has not yet stolen anything. I thought of happier days when I would have sent this lieutenant-colonel and two such Croats packing had I met them, but now I lay there like a poltroon lacking the heart even to use my tongue to any purpose, let alone my fists.

'Behold, parson,' he said, 'the fine spectacle to which I am obliged to call you as a witness of my dishonour!' And with that he began again to rant and rave so that I could distinguish no more than a few phrases about breaking necks and washing hands in blood. He foamed at the mouth like a wild boar and seemed completely demented, so that I thought at any moment he would put a bullet through me.

But the good parson begged him with great eloquence to do nothing irrevocable, for which he might later be sorry. 'My dear colonel,' he said, 'do, I beg of you, listen to reason and remember the saying that it is no good crying over spilt milk! This handsome young couple, the like of which you

149

will not easily find however far you seek, is not the first to succumb to the temptations of the flesh. The fault they have jointly committed—if we must call it a fault—they can as easily remedy together. Far be it from me to condone their manner of entering into the married state, but neither is it deserving of the gallows or the rack. Nor need you, Sir, fear any dishonour from this trespass (which is as yet known to no one but those assembled in this room) if you will only keep it secret and pardon it, giving your consent to their union and letting it be solemnized according to the rites of the Church.'

'What?' said he, 'am I to let them off their deserved punishment, and honour and compliment them instead? I would rather have them tied together in the morning and drowned in the River Lippe! Either you marry them this very instant, which is the purpose for which I had you fetched, or I will wring their necks like a pair of chickens.'

'What am I to do?' I thought. 'Take my medicine or die! At least she is a girl of whom you need not be ashamed; indeed, considering your origin, you are not fit to touch the ground she treads on.' Nevertheless, I insisted and swore with many oaths that we had done nothing improper together. But to this they retorted that then we should have comported ourselves in such a way as not to arouse suspicion. After what had happened such suspicions could never be allayed.

Then the parson married us sitting up in bed, and when it was done we were ordered to get up and leave the house together. At the door the lieutenant-colonel told me and his daughter that he never wanted to set eyes on us again. But I, having recovered my composure and now with my sword at my side again, answered him with a quip: 'I cannot understand, dear father-in-law, why you arrange these matters with so little propriety. When other couples marry their nearest and dearest conduct them to the bed-chamber. You, on the other hand, drive us not only out of bed but out of your house, and far from wishing us good fortune in matrimony you deprive me of the happiness of beholding my father-in-law's face and serving him. Truly, if this were to become the custom, marriage would breed little friendship in the world.'

CHAPTER XII

Simplex is by his bride beguiled,
And with her parents reconciled.

THE people at my lodgings were much surprised when I
brought this wench with me, and their surprise turned
to amazement when they saw how unconcernedly she went to
bed with me. For though the trick that had been played on
me gave me furiously to think, I was not such a fool as to
disdain my bride. But even as I embraced her I was busy
thinking how best to deal with this affair. First I felt I had
suffered the most terrible insult, which could be effaced only
by a suitable revenge. But when I reflected that this must strike
at my father-in-law and therefore also at my devoted and
innocent wife, my resolution turned to water. Then I was
overwhelmed by shame and resolved to keep to my room
and never show my face abroad again, but on consideration
I realized that this would be the very height of folly. In the
end I decided that the first thing I must do was to try to regain my father-in-law's friendship, and thereafter pretend to
the world that nothing untoward had happened and that my
marriage had been of my own choosing. 'Since all this has
come about in so odd and unusual a fashion,' I thought, 'you
must behave accordingly. If people were to discover that the
marriage was against your will and forced upon you, you
would have insult added to injury.'

With such thoughts in my mind I arose early, though I
would gladly have tarried longer in bed with my charming
bride. First I sent for my brother-in-law—the husband of my
wife's sister—and briefly told him how closely we were related, asking him to send his wife to help prepare the marriage feast and also to try to placate our father-in-law on my
behalf, while I went to invite the guests who were to seal
the peace between us. To this he readily agreed.

Next I went to the Commandant and related to him with
much ribaldry the events of the previous night, which made
him shake with laughter. Indeed, the tale put him in such

151

good humour that I prevailed upon him to attend our feast, which he promised to do and also to bring my father-in-law with him. Moreover, he promptly dispatched a cask of wine and the carcass of a stag to my lodgings, and so I had a banquet prepared fit for a king. I succeeded in assembling a numerous company, who not only made very merry among themselves but, above all, brought about so complete a reconciliation between my father-in-law and me and my wife that he now wished us luck with even greater warmth than that with which he had previously cursed us. As for our marriage, I had it put about that we had arranged it so strangely on purpose, in order to forestall any unseemly pranks by people who might wish us ill. For me, indeed, this quick marriage was not without its benefits, for had the banns been read in church in accordance with custom I might well have had trouble with half a dozen burghers' daughters who knew me better than they should and who were now in a fine pickle.

CHAPTER XIII

Simplex goes to fetch his hoard,
But finds its guardian fled abroad.

THE ways of fate are strange indeed. One man's misfortunes come upon him slowly, one by one; another's overwhelm him like an avalanche. My own had so sweet and delightful a beginning that I did not even recognize them for what they were, but took them for the greatest happiness. I had hardly spent a week in blissful wedlock with my dear wife when I donned my Huntsman's suit, slung my musket over my shoulder, and bade her and her friends farewell, in order to fetch back from Cologne the treasure I had deposited there. I made my way safely through the enemy's lines, knowing the countryside as if I had been born there, and did not meet a soul until I reached Deutz, which lies on the opposite side of the Rhine from Cologne.

But when I crossed over to Cologne and inquired after the

merchant with whom I had left my treasure I was told that I would have little joy of him, for he had gone bankrupt and fled. Though my property was held under seal by the Council and he himself had been ordered to return, there was little hope that he would comply, for he had taken with him all his property that could be moved, and much water would flow under the Rhine bridges before the affair was settled.

You may imagine, gentle reader, how this news enraged me. I swore like a trooper, but to what purpose? It did not bring me back my treasure, and I had little hope of ever seeing it again. I had taken only ten rixdollars with me for the journey, so that I could not stay as long as the affair demanded. Delay, moreover, was fraught with danger for me, for I had reason to fear that I might be denounced as a member of an enemy garrison and might lose not only my possessions but my life as well. Yet it seemed equally senseless to return with nothing attempted and cravenly to abandon my claim with nothing more to show for it than a wasted journey. In the end I decided to stay in Cologne until the case came up for trial, and meanwhile to inform my wife of the reasons for my delay. I therefore went to an advocate who was also a notary, told him of my intentions, asked him to assist me and promised him that if he could hasten the matter he should have a handsome present on top of his fees.

Thinking me a good catch, he readily agreed, and also undertook to board and lodge me. The next day we went to the officials in charge of the bankruptcy proceedings, handed them a certified copy of the merchant's receipt, and also showed them the original, but were told that we must wait until the affair was settled in its entirety, because some of the items listed in the receipt could not be found.

So I prepared myself for another spell of idleness, which I would while away in acquainting myself with life in a big city. My host was, as I have said, an advocate and notary, in addition to which he entertained half a dozen lodgers and also kept eight horses in his stables to hire out to travellers. For these he had two grooms—an Italian and a German—who served either as drivers or riders in addition to tending the horses. With this three- or four-fold trade he made a good living, and doubtless put a goodly sum aside as well; for as no Jews were allowed in the city, he had the greater scope for usury.

CHAPTER XIV

Short rations fall to Simplex' share,
His host keeps floors and tables bare.

THE fellow had, in fact, all manner of means by which he amassed money: he fed on his guests—not his guests on him. With what they paid him he and his household could have had a well-furnished table, if only the old niggard had used it for that purpose. But he kept us on short rations and hoarded his takings. At first I did not eat with his guests, being short of funds, but with his children and servants. Their diet was Spartan indeed and gave my stomach, used as it was to good Westphalian fare, much cause to grumble. The only meat we ever saw was what the students had left the week before, well picked over and grey with age like Methuselah. His wife, who did all the cooking (for he would afford her no maid), poured a black and sour kind of sauce over this and peppered it well, after which we gnawed the bones so clean that you could have carved chessmen out of them there and then. Yet still they were not done with but put in a special basin, and when our skinflint had enough of them together he hacked them small and boiled them to extract the last dram of fat. Whether this was used for lacing the soup or greasing the boots I never could discover.

On fast-days, of which there were more than enough and all faithfully observed (our host being most scrupulous in this respect), we had to whet our teeth on stinking herrings, salt cod, rotten stock-fish, and other stale sea-food, for he bought whatever was cheap and did not shun the trouble of going to the fish market himself, seizing what the fishmongers were about to throw away. Our bread was black and usually stale, and our drink a thin, sour ale which seared my guts, but which he insisted was fine March beer.

154

I heard from the German groom, moreover, that things were even worse in summer, when the bread turned mouldy, the meat was full of maggots, and their best food a few radishes for dinner and a handful of lettuce for supper. I asked him why he stayed with the miser. He replied that he spent most of his time on journeys, and was therefore more concerned with the travellers' tips than with the mouldy old Jew, who, he said, would not allow even his wife and children into the cellar because he grudged them the very drippings from the wine barrels. What I had experienced so far, he said, was nothing; if I stayed a little longer I would see that he would not hesitate to skin a flea for its fat.

One day he brought home six pounds of tripe which he put in the larder. His two children, as luck would have it, found the skylight open, so they tied a fork to a length of string and fished out the tripe, which they cooked in great haste and gulped down equally quickly, saying afterwards that the cat had taken it. But the old garbage-picker did not believe them; he weighed the cat and found that skin, hairs, and all weighed less than the tripe had done. Seeing that he was so shamelessly mean, I insisted that I would no longer eat at his private table, but with his guests, never mind the cost. Matters were a little better there, but not much, for all the food was only half-cooked, achieving a twofold profit for our host: once in the fuel he saved, and then because we could not digest so much of it. I also noticed that he counted every mouthful we ate and grimaced mournfully if we showed too hearty an appetite. His wine was well-watered and of a kind which did not assist the digestion. The cheese which was served at the end of every meal was hard as stone, and the Dutch butter so salt that nobody could eat more than half an ounce at one sitting. The fruit was brought to the table days before it was ripe enough to eat, and if one of us grumbled about it he would scold his wife furiously in our hearing, but secretly tell her to carry on as before.

For the rest, his house was as tidy and clean as a new pin, for he would suffer nothing under foot—not the smallest blade of straw or scrap of paper or anything else that would burn.

Rather would he pick it up himself and carry it to the kitchen, saying that many drops of water made a stream and thinking, no doubt, that many tooth-picks heat a furnace. The ashes he gathered more carefully than others do threads of saffron, for he knew where he could sell them.

BOOK IV

CHAPTER I

Simplex is sent off to France,
And straightway led a merry dance.

ALL this, you may imagine, tried my patience sorely, and I played many pranks on my host to punish him for his insatiable greed. I taught his boarders how to extract the salt from the butter by boiling it and how to grate the hard cheese like the citizens of Parma do and moisten it with wine—all these lessons being so many stabs at the skin-flint's heart. By one of my conjuring tricks I separated the water from the wine at table, and I composed a song in which I compared the pinch-penny to an old sow which is good for nothing until the butcher has it dead upon his trestles. But as a bow too far bent will break and an over-sharpened blade become notched, so I, by my pranks, provoked him to swift revenge, for he did not keep me there to set his household by the ears.

Two young noblemen who were boarded with him received a letter of credit from their parents one day, with orders to travel to France and learn the language there. As it happened, our host's German groom was away at the time. The Italian, he said, he could not trust to take the horses to France, for he did not know him well and feared he might forget to return, and so lose him his horses. He therefore asked me if I would do him a favour by escorting the youths and the horses on their journey. My own affairs would not mature for another month or more, and if I gave him the necessary powers he himself would meanwhile promote them as energetically as if I myself were there to do it. The noblemen added their pleas to his, and my own desire to see France also prompted me to it; for in this way I would be able to do it without special expense, whereas if I stayed where I was I would only idle away four more weeks and spend my own money into the bargain. So I took to the road as the young noblemen's postillion, and nothing worth mentioning happened to us on our way.

But when we arrived in Paris and put up at our host's correspondent, where the noblemen encashed their letter of credit, I was arrested almost immediately, and the horses seized, on behalf of a man who claimed that my host owed him a sum of money. Moreover, the man sold the horses with the full approval of the local magistrate, and I could do nothing about it. So there I sat like a fly in a spider's web, not knowing what to do, and certainly not how to arrange my long and at that time very dangerous return journey.

The two young noblemen showed me the greatest sympathy and gave me a correspondingly handsome gratification. They also insisted that I stay with them until I had found either a good master or a good opportunity to return to Germany. They took lodgings, and I spent some days there tending one of them who was indisposed after the long and unaccustomed journey. I served him so well that he gave me his suit, which he had discarded for a new one cut according to the latest fashion. They advised me to spend a few years in Paris and learn the language. What I had in Cologne, they said, would not run away, since our capable host was looking after it. While I was still considering this suggestion a doctor, who called daily on my sick nobleman, heard me play the lute and sing a German song, which so pleased him that he offered me board and lodging, and a good wage as well, if I would go to him and teach his two sons. He knew I would not refuse a good master, for he realized better even than I how my affairs stood. So we quickly came to an agreement, to which the two noblemen gave their whole-hearted approval, recommending me warmly to my new master. I would not, however, engage myself for more than three months at a time.

CHAPTER II

The doctor is a man of worth,
But loath to rise above his birth.

I soon recovered my good spirits in my new home and proved the better a teacher for my master's sons. They were being brought up like a pair of princes, for the doctor, Monsieur Canard by name, was as haughty as he was rich, and determined to show off his wealth. It was a disease he had caught from the great noblemen whose houses he visited daily and whom he aped in everything. His establishment resembled that of a duke, with nothing missing but the title, and his conceit was such that he treated even a marquess, if one chanced to visit him, as no more than his equal. He was generous and charitable, and would not take even modest fees from the needy, preferring to treat them for nothing and so make the better a name for himself.

Being of an inquiring disposition and knowing that my master, when he visited the sick, boasted of having me in his retinue, I helped him to prepare his medicines in his laboratory and became quite familiar with him—the more so since he enjoyed speaking with me in German. One day I asked him why he did not take the style and title of a manor he had recently bought near Paris for 20,000 crowns, and why he wanted to make doctors of his two sons and made them study so hard. Since he already had the right to a title, would it not be better if he bought them some office, as other cavaliers did, and established them at Court? 'No,' he replied, 'if I visit a prince he says, "Pray be seated, doctor", but a nobleman is told to wait his turn in the ante-chamber.' 'But are you not aware, Sir,' I said, 'that a doctor has three faces? First, of an angel when he arrives; then, of a god if he cures; and finally, of a devil when the patient is restored and wants to be rid of him? So a doctor's standing lasts no longer than the wind in his patient's bowels; when it is gone and the rumbling over the doctor's standing, too, has an end and he is shown the door. So a nobleman has more honour from his

159

waiting than a doctor from his sitting, for the nobleman waits
on his prince at all times and is always at his side. The doctor,
I recall, recently had to take some of his prince's stool in his
mouth to test the taste. I would rather stand and wait ten
years than try another man's dung, even if they seated me
on a couch of roses.'

He answered: 'I did not *have* to do it, but did it willingly,
so that the prince, seeing to what lengths I went to ascertain
his condition, would pay me the better. And why should I not
try the dung of a man who may pay me a hundred crowns
to do it, whereas I pay him nothing for whatever filth he may
have to eat at my prescription? You talk of these things like a
German; if you were of a different nationality I would say
you talk of them like a fool!' And at that I left it, for I could
see that he was about to grow angry. Rather, to humour him,
I asked him to forgive my simplicity and changed the subject.

CHAPTER III

Simplex learns the actor's art,
And conquers many a lady's heart.

MONSIEUR CANARD, who had more venison to waste than
many another man—even with a game preserve of his
own—has to eat, and received more presents of meat than he
and his household could consume, also had many parasites who
daily sat at his table, so that it appeared as if he kept open
house. One day the King's Master of Ceremonies and other
courtiers of rank visited him, and he entertained them
lavishly, for he knew well the value of friends who were close
to the King and stood high in his favour. In their honour
and as a climax to the meal he asked me to play a German
song on my lute. I gladly consented, for I was in the right
mood, and, like most musicians when the mood is upon them,
gave of my very best. This so delighted the company that the
Master of Ceremonies said it was a thousand pities that I
knew no French, for otherwise he would have commended me
warmly to the King and Queen. He said that never in his

life had he encountered such a combination of handsome looks, beauty of voice, and skilful playing in one person. A comedy was soon to be performed before the King at the Louvre, and if he could produce me at it he thought I might do him great credit.

Monsieur Canard translated this for me, and I replied that if I was told what part to play and what songs to sing and accompany on my lute I could easily learn melody and words by heart and perform them even though they were in French. Why should my wit be less than that of schoolboys, who were also used for this purpose and must be taught the gestures as well as the words? The Master of Ceremonies, seeing me so willing, made me promise to come to the Louvre next day to see if I would serve.

So I presented myself at the appointed time. The tunes of the various songs I had to sing presented no difficulty, for I had the music in front of me. Then I was given the French words to learn by heart and to study the pronunciation. I was also given a German translation so that I might fit my gestures to the words. I found it no great trouble and learned more quickly than anyone had expected, and so well, moreover—according to Monsieur Canard—that not one in a thousand would have thought me other than a natural-born Frenchman. When finally we came together for the first rehearsal I sang, played, and acted my part as Orpheus lamenting his Eurydice with such a sincere show of grief that they all swore I must have played it many times before.

In all my life I have never had a more pleasant day than that on which we performed the play. Monsieur Canard gave me some potion to improve my voice, but when he attempted to improve my looks with paint and my curly, jet-black hair with powder he found that he merely spoilt it. I was crowned with a wreath of laurels and dressed in an antique, sea-green shirt which left my neck and most of my breast, my arms, and my legs to half-way up my thighs naked. A flesh-coloured taffeta cloak which resembled a flag rather than a garment was draped over it.

In this attire I languished for my Eurydice, sang a prayer to Venus for help, and finally led off my bride—a scene in which I excelled, with sighs and longing looks at my Beloved. Later, when I had lost my Eurydice, I donned a garment of similar cut but all in black, from which my white skin shone forth like driven snow. In this I lamented my lost spouse and became so engrossed in my part that real tears welled up into my eyes and sobs bade fair to strangle my voice. But I recovered myself perfectly before I reached the nether regions and the presence of Pluto and Proserpine, to whom, in a most moving song, I recalled their mutual love and asked them to judge from it of my and Eurydice's sorrow at being separated. I entreated them, with the most piteous gestures—accompanying myself on my harp the while—to let her return to me. But when I had obtained their consent I thanked them in a merry song and so transformed my face, voice, and manner from grief to joy that all the audience marvelled at it. Then, when all unawares I lost my Eurydice once more, I imagined to myself the most terrible danger into which a man might fall and turned as pale as if I were about to faint. Being at that moment alone on the stage and every spectator's eyes on me, I played as I had never played before and had the reward of being acclaimed the best actor. Later in the play I seated myself on a rock and began to lament the loss of my Beloved in sorrowful words and heart-rending melodies, calling on all creatures to weep with me; and there gathered around me all manner of tame and wild animals, trees, mountains, and suchlike, so cunningly made that it truly appeared as if all were done by magic and enchantment.

Nor did I put a foot wrong until the very end, when, having foresworn all women, I was strangled by the Bacchantes and cast into the water (which was done in such a way that only my head was visible, the rest of me being in perfect safety below the level of the stage), and the dragon was to devour me. But the fellow who was working the dragon from inside could not see my head, and so let the dragon's head snuffle about beside me. This struck me as so ridiculous that I could not suppress a grimace, which the ladies, who were devouring me with their eyes, did not fail to notice.

From this comedy I earned much praise, as well as a generous purse and a new name, for from then on the French called me only 'Beau Alman'. It being carnival time, there were several other plays and ballets of this kind in which I performed. But in the end I found that I was drawing upon myself the envy of my fellow-actors as surely as I was the eyes of most of the spectators—especially the women. So I decided to put an end to my exploits, especially after I had received some hard knocks when, as Hercules and almost naked, I had to fight with Achelous for Dejanira, and was handled more roughly than illusion required.

CHAPTER IV

Abducted by a lady's ruse,
Simplex does not dare refuse.

MY acting brought me to the notice of highly placed persons, and fortune seemed to smile on me once more when I was offered a place at court—something which many a fine nobleman seeks in vain all his life. One day, while I was in Monsieur Canard's laboratory, a lackey came and asked for him, having a letter to deliver. 'Monsieur Beau Alman,' Monsieur Canard said to me, 'this letter concerns you. It is from a great nobleman who asks you to call on him at once, for he wants you to instruct his son on the lute. He asks me to plead his cause with you, graciously promising that your efforts will be well rewarded.' I replied that if I could oblige him by being of service to another I would most gladly do it. So he told me to change my dress while he went to prepare a meal for me; for I had a fair way to go, he said, and would hardly arrive at my destination before nightfall.

I dressed carefully, and hurriedly ate some of the food Monsieur Canard set before me, notably a pair of delicate little sausages which seemed to me quite strongly medicated. Then I accompanied the lackey who for an hour led me along devious streets until, towards evening, we arrived at a garden gate which stood ajar. He opened it wide to let me pass and shut it again behind me, leading me on to a pavilion in a corner of the garden. We followed a long passage until we came to a door at which he knocked. It was opened almost immediately by an old lady who welcomed me most civilly in German and asked me to come in. The lackey, who knew no German, bowed low and took his leave. The old lady seized my hand and led me into a richly furnished room, the walls of which were covered with the most costly tapestries. She bade me take a seat so that, while I rested, she might acquaint me with the purpose for which I had been brought to this place.

I readily complied and sat down in a chair which she had placed near the fire, for it was a chilly night. She herself sat down near me and said: 'Monsieur, if you know anything of the power of love and how it masters even the bravest, strongest and wisest of men it will not surprise you that a weak woman has also succumbed to it. You have not been called here—as you and Monsieur Canard were made to believe— by a gentleman for the sake of your lute, but for the sake of your beauty by one of the greatest ladies of Paris, who fears she will die unless she can soon gaze on your graceful figure and have her delight in it. She has therefore commanded me—as a compatriot of yours—to inform you of her desire and beg you, more passionately than ever Venus begged Adonis, to come to her this evening and let her feast her eyes on your beauty—a wish which I trust you will not deny a lady of her quality.'

I replied: 'Madam, I do not know what to think, far less what to say! I cannot believe that a lady of such great quality would be interested in my poor person. Moreover, it seems to me that if the lady is truly as exalted as you say, she would have sent for me by daylight instead of having me brought to this secluded place late at night. Why did she not command me to come to her directly? What business have I in this garden? Forgive me, most gracious lady, if I, a lonely stranger in this country, fear some trap, and this the more since I have evidently already been deceived concerning the gentleman who was supposed to have summoned me. However, if I found that some treacherous plot was being hatched against my life, I can assure you that I would know how to make use of my sword before I died.'

164

'Gently, gently, my dear fellow-countryman,' she replied, 'these are mere idle fancies. Women are strange and devious in their plans, and it is not always easy to follow them. If she who loves you more than anything else in the world had wanted you to know her person all at once she would, indeed, have had you brought straightway to her house instead of here. There lies a hood,' she said, pointing to the table, 'which you will have to wear when you are led from here to see her, for it is her intention that you should know nothing of the place—far less the person—where you have been. I therefore beg and entreat you as earnestly as I can to behave towards the lady in accordance with her high dignity and the great love she bears you. If not, be warned that she has the power to punish your arrogance and contempt this very minute. If, however, you treat her as she wishes, be assured that the least step you have taken on her behalf will not go unrewarded.'

It had grown dark as we spoke, and I was worried and full of apprehension, so that I sat there like a statue. I had been left in no doubt that I would find it hard indeed to escape from this place unless I agreed to what was asked of me. So I said to the old lady: 'Very well, then, madam, if things are as you say I will entrust my person to a compatriot, hoping that your native German probity will forbid you to suffer any harm to come to an innocent stranger. Do, therefore, what you are commanded. The lady of whom you speak will not, I trust, prove to have a basilisk's eyes with which to turn me to stone.' 'God forbid!' she said, 'it would be a thousand pities if a body such as yours, fit to be the glory of an entire nation, were to die so long before its time. I assure you that you shall find greater delights than ever you imagined in your life.'

When she had my consent she called out, 'Jean and Pierre!' Two men at once stepped out from behind a tapestry, armed from head to foot, with halberds and pistols at the ready, which gave me such a fright that the colour drained from my cheeks. The old lady observed it and smiled: 'There is no need of such fear when one is about to see a woman.' Then she ordered the soldiers to take off their cuirasses, pick up some lanterns, and carry with them only their pistols. She slipped the black velvet hood over my head, took my hat under

165

her arm, and led me by the hand along many twisting passages. I noticed that we passed through many doors and also across a paved courtyard. After a quarter of an hour we climbed a narrow staircase, a door opened, we went along yet another passage and up a spiral staircase, then a few steps down, and at last into a room where the old lady took the hood from my head. I found myself in a most elegantly decorated room, its walls covered with beautiful paintings, a night table set with silver jugs and basins, and a bed hung with draperies of gold thread. In the centre stood a lavishly appointed table, and by the fire a bath-tub which, though pretty enough in itself, seemed to me to spoil the entire appearance of the room. The old lady said to me: 'Welcome, my fellow-countryman! How say you now? Do you still think you are being treacherously done by? Be at ease and carry yourself as you did of late in the theatre when you retrieved your Eurydice from Pluto; I assure you that here you shall find a more beautiful mistress than ever you lost there.'

CHAPTER V

Eight days is Simplex made to stay,
And then, with thanks, sent on his way.

FROM this I gathered that I had not been brought here merely to be admired, but for a more active role. So I said to my guide that it profited a thirsty man little to sit beside a forbidden well. To this she replied that the French were not so small-minded as to forbid anyone a drink—especially when the supply was so plentiful. 'Indeed, madam,' I said, 'your words would delight me more were I not already married.' 'Nonsense,' retorted the godless old witch, 'they will not believe you when you tell them that tonight, for married cavaliers are not greatly prized in France. Yet even if it were true I cannot think that you would be so foolish as to go thirsty rather than drink from a strange well, especially if perhaps it sparkles more and has better water than your own.'

This was our conversation while a young gentlewoman who had been tending the fire took off my shoes and socks, which were soiled all over from my blindfold journey—the streets of Paris being at best well-nigh paved with filth. Then came orders that I was to be bathed before dinner and the young gentlewoman went to fetch what was required. All smelt of perfume and fine soap, the towels were of pure linen edged with precious lace. I felt bashful and reluctant to strip naked in front of the hag, but I had no choice. I was made to sit in the tub and let her scrub me while her young companion withdrew. After the bath I was clothed in a fine shirt, a magnificent dressing-gown of violet-blue taffeta, and silk stockings to match. Night-cap and slippers were embroidered with gold thread and pearls, and there I sat in state like the king of hearts.

Then the old woman, who tended me like a prince or a small child, dried and combed my hair while the young one, who had returned, set the table for dinner. When she had finished there entered three handsome young ladies whose low-cut dresses revealed as much of their snow-white bosoms as the masks they wore hid of their faces. All three seemed to me fair indeed, yet one far more beautiful than the others. I made them a profound and silent reverence, and they returned the compliment, so that we appeared like an assembly of mutes mimicking people with speech. All three ladies sat down at the same time, so that I could not tell which of them was highest in rank—far less which I was to serve. They all threw me glances full of admiration, love, and tenderness, and I could have sworn that they heaved many a sigh. But because of the masks I could not see the passion smouldering in their eyes.

My old crone, being the only one able to converse with me, asked me which of the three I thought most beautiful. I replied that I could not tell, at which she laughed so heartily that she showed every one of the four teeth she had left and asked me why. I said because I could not properly see them, but as far as I could tell none of them seemed ill-made. The ladies then wished to know what the old woman had asked me and my reply. She interpreted and added a lie of her own: that I had said that the mouth of each of them was fit for a hundred thousand kisses, for the mouths I was well able to see—particularly that of the one sitting opposite me. So from this piece of flattery I gathered that she was the highest in rank, and I studied her more closely than before. This was all the conversation we had at table, for I pretended that I knew not a word of French. The meal being so silent, we were the sooner finished, whereupon the ladies bade me goodnight and went their ways, nor was I permitted to escort them farther than the door, which the old woman immediately bolted behind them. So then I asked her where I was to sleep. She answered that I must content myself with the bed that was in the room, and with her company in it. The bed, I said, would do, if only I could have one of the three inside it. 'Indeed,' she said, 'not one of them will you have as a bed-fellow tonight.'

As we were speaking, the drapery round the bed was pulled back a little and a beautiful lady inside told the witch to stop her chatter and take herself off to bed. I seized a candle to look at the occupant of the bed more closely, but the hag extinguished it and said: 'Sir, if you value your head, go no farther! Lie down in the bed, but be assured that if you try, against her will, to see the lady's face you will never leave this place alive.' With that she left, locking the door behind her. The young gentlewoman who had been tending the fire doused it and also left by a concealed door behind one of the tapestries.

Then the lady in the bed said: 'Allez, Monsieur Beau Alman, gome to slip, sweet'eart. Gome 'ug me glose!' That much of my language the old crone had taught her. I got into bed to see how matters stood, and no sooner had I joined her than she clasped me to her, smothered me with kisses, and well-nigh bit my lower lip off in her passion. So hot was her lust that she fairly tore the buttons off my dressing-gown and ripped my night-shirt to pieces. She knew no other words than her ''ug me glose, sweet'eart!' For the rest, her gestures were enough, and though I thought of my dear wife at home, I was but human. The creature I found was so perfectly propor-tioned and charming that I would have had to be a log of wood to come chaste out of the adventure. Moreover, the little sausages the doctor had given me to eat were doing their work, so that I myself was more like a goat than a man.

In this way I spent eight days and as many nights in that place, and I believe the other three also lay with me, for they did not all speak like the first, nor were they all equally passionate. As I was also served the little sausages there, I must assume that Monsieur Canard had prepared them and knew well enough what business I was at. But though I spent eight whole days with these four ladies, I never once saw any of their faces unmasked except in the dark.

When the eight days were up I was blindfolded once more, led to the courtyard, and put in a closed carriage beside the old woman, who untied the bandage over my eyes during the journey and returned me to my master's house, the coach driving off quickly afterwards. My gratification amounted to two hundred pistols, and when I asked the old crone whether I should not give somebody a douceur out of that she replied: 'By no means! If you did you would offend the ladies, for they would think you imagined yourself to have been in a brothel, where everything has to be paid for.'

From then on I had a whole string of such clients who pressed me so hard that at last I wearied of the game from sheer exhaustion, and even Monsieur Canard's little sausages were of no avail.

CHAPTER VI

Simplex in secret from Paris takes flight,
But the smallpox reduce him to a pitiful plight.

MY employment earned me such fees in money and kind that they quite took my breath away, and I wondered no more that women go into brothels and make a trade of this sordid pastime, seeing it is so profitable. I, on the other hand, began to think seriously about the matter—not, indeed, for love of God or conscience' sake, but for fear that I might be caught red-handed one day and paid as I deserved. I therefore thought of returning to Germany, and this the more earnestly since the Commandant of Lippstadt had written to me that he had captured several Cologne merchants whom he proposed to hold as hostages for my property, and that he still kept an ensign's brevet for me, expecting me back before the spring. If I did not return by then he would have to give it to someone else. My wife, too, enclosed a letter full of expressions of affectionate longing for my return. Had she but known the kind of life I led, she would assuredly have sent me greetings of a different kind.

It was clear to me that I would not easily obtain Monsieur Canard's consent to my departure, so I planned to escape in secret as soon as an opportunity offered, for which (to my great misfortune) I had not long to wait. I happened to meet some officers of the Duke of Weimar's army, to whom I introduced myself as an ensign in Colonel de Saint André's regiment who had spent some time in Paris on private business. Now, however, I wished to return to my regiment and would be grateful if they would allow me to join them for the journey. They readily agreed and informed me of the day of their departure. I bought myself a nag, fitted myself out for the journey in great secrecy, gathered together my money (which amounted to some 500 dubloons, all got from depraved women by my shameless labours), and left without asking Monsieur Canard's permission. I did, however, write to him on the way, giving as the reason for my sudden departure the medicated sausages, which had disagreed with me and forced me to cut short my stay.

Two days' journey out of Paris I began to feel as if I had been stricken with St Anthony's fire, and my head ached so terribly that I could not rise from my bed. We were in a poor village without a doctor, and there I lay all unattended, for the officers continued on their way early in the morning, leaving me there, sick unto death, as being no concern of theirs. They did, however, commend me and my horse to the host when they departed, and left word with the mayor of the place that he was to treat me as an officer who served the King.

For several days I remained there, unconscious and in a delirium. They brought me a priest who could make nothing of my ravings, but seeing that he could not heal my soul, tried

170

at least to cure my body. He got them to bleed me, give me a hot drink, and wrap me up warm in bed to make me sweat. This did me so much good that I recovered my senses that very night, and with them a knowledge of where I was and how I had got there and fallen sick. The priest, when he returned the following morning, found me quite desperate. Not only had all my money been stolen, but I was covered with spots all over like a leopard, and quite certain that I had (saving your presence) the French disease which I deserved so much more than my many dubloons. I could not walk, stand, sit, or lie, and my impatience knew no bounds. For though I had no reason to think that my lost money had come from God, I was now so indignant that I swore the Devil had taken it from me. Indeed, I behaved like one demented, and the good priest's efforts to console me were not helped by the fact that I was uncertain in my mind which of my two worries was the greater.

'My friend,' he said, 'do, at least, behave like a reasonable human being, even if you will not bear your cross like a good Christian. Come to your senses! Having lost your money, do you also want to lose your life and your very hope of eternal salvation?' I answered: 'I would not care a fig about the money if only I did not have this disgusting, accursed disease, or if I were somewhere where I could be cured of it!' 'Be patient,' said the priest, 'even as the little children, of whom more than fifty are lying sick with the disease in this very village.'

When I heard that children, too, were suffering as I was my spirits rose, for I surmised that they could hardly be afflicted by the disease I suspected. So I took out my saddle-bag to see what was left in it. Apart from my fine linen, I found nothing but a snuff-box with a miniature of a lady set with rubies which I had been given in Paris. I removed the portrait and gave the priest the box, asking him to sell it in the nearest town so that I might have some ready money. In the event it fetched little more than a third of its value, and as this did not last me long, my nag had to go as well. All of which barely tided me over until the pock-holes began to dry up and I to mend.

CHAPTER VII

Simplex roams the countryside,
And plucks the peasants far and wide.

WHEREWITH a man sins, therewith is he commonly punished! These smallpox so disfigured me that from then on I was never again bothered by women. My face was marked like the floor of a barn where peas have been threshed, and so ugly did I become that my very curls, in which so many women had become entangled, grew ashamed of me and left their abode. In their place grew others which resembled hog's bristles more than human hair, so that I was obliged to wear a wig. Even as I retained none of my outward beauty, so also my voice was gone, for my throat had been full of sores. My eyes, which heretofore had kindled many a passion, were now as red and watery as those of an eighty-year-old crone who has the cataract; and to crown it all I was in a strange country where I did not know a living soul, did not understand the language, and had not a penny to my name.

I still had the fine suit I had bought for the journey and a saddle-bag full of good linen, but nobody wanted to buy it from me for fear of the infection which might go with it. So I shouldered my bag, took my sword in my hand and the road under my feet, and finally came to a small town which even boasted an apothecary's shop. There I had an ointment prepared to remove the pock-marks from my face, and having no money, gave the apothecary a fine, soft shirt for it, nor was he as finicky as the other fools who would not take my clothes. I thought that if only I could be rid of these hideous marks my other cares would also lighten. The apothecary also raised my spirits by assuring me that in a week or so I would have little left to show for my disease but the deep scars which the sores had burnt into my skin. It was market day in the town, and I saw a quack who made good money by selling trash to the crowds. 'Fool that you are,' I said to myself, 'why do you not ply the same trade? You must be a poor fish indeed if after all this time with Monsieur Canard you have not learned enough to earn your bread and butter by cheating these yokels.'

I ate ravenously at this time, and nothing seemed to assuage my hunger, though I had nothing to fall back on but a single gold ring set with a diamond worth about twenty crowns. I sold it for twelve, and realizing that this would not last me long with no money coming in, I resolved to become a leech. I bought materials for a mithridate which I made up into pills, for sale in small towns. For the peasants I chose a purgative made of juniper and mixed it with oak- and willow-leaves and other astringents. Of herbs, roots, butter, and sundry oils I concocted a green ointment for wounds of all kinds—it might have served to cure a galled horse—and of calamine, gravel, crabs' eyes, emery, and pumice a powder for cleaning teeth. I also had a blue lotion, made of lye, copper, salt of ammonia, and camphor, to cure scurvy, bad breath, tooth-ache, and eye-sores. I then collected a large number of small boxes, bottles, and phials in which I packed my wares and, to give them a more respectable appearance, had labels printed in French with the use for which each was intended. In three days I had finished my work and had barely spent three crowns on the ingredients and containers by the time I left the town. I packed up my drugs and set out towards Alsace, intending to stop at every village on the way to dispose of my wares. My plan was to reach Strasbourg, which was then a neutral city, take my chance of a ship down the Rhine to Cologne, and thence back to my wife. The intention was laudable, but nothing came of it.

The first time I tried my hand as a quack was outside a church, and I had little success. I was too shy, and neither the salesman's patter nor his bragging manner came to me easily. I saw that I must proceed differently if I wanted to make money and dispose of my trash. I went to an inn, and over dinner the landlord told me that there would be a gathering of all manner of people that afternoon under the lime-tree outside his house. There, he said, I might do a good trade if my wares were good, but there were so many quacks abroad that people were mighty close with their money unless they had solid proof that the medicine was outstanding.

Thus forewarned, I bought half a tumblerful of good Strasbourg gin and caught myself some toads of the sort called Reling or Möhmlein in those parts, which you find in spring and summer sitting and croaking in dirty puddles. They are yellowish or pinkish in colour, with dappled black bellies—not very pretty to behold. One of these I put in a tumbler half-full of water which I placed beside my wares on a table under the lime-tree. When the people began to crowd around me some thought that I was going to pull their teeth with a pair of pincers I had borrowed from the landlord's kitchen. But I addressed them thus: 'Good people and friends; I am no breaker of jaws, but have an excellent lotion for the eyes which cures redness and watering.'

'So I see,' said one, 'from your own eyes, which look like a pair of will-o'-the-wisps!' I retorted: 'True enough, but had I not had my lotion I would assuredly now be blind. Nor do I want to sell the lotion. What I am selling is this mithridate, the tooth-powder, and the ointment for wounds. The lotion I give away free with any of these. I am no loud-mouthed quack, good friends, and if I cannot prove my mithridate's potency to your satisfaction I do not expect you to buy it.'

With that I asked one of the bystanders to select a box of pills, took one from it and crumbled it into the tumbler with gin, which the people took to be pure water. Then, with the pincers, I took the toad from the other tumbler and said: 'Look closely now, friends! If this poisonous creature can drink of my mithridate and live, the pill is worthless and you can call me a quack.' Then I put the poor toad, which was born and bred in water and could abide no other element or liquid, into my gin and covered the glass with a piece of paper so that it could not escape. The creature, unaccustomed to the potency of the liquor, began to struggle and kick and generally behaved as if I had thrown it on to glowing coals, and after a little while it went limp and died. The yokels, seeing this striking proof of my skill, opened their purses as wide as their eyes. Never had they seen a more potent mithridate in all their lives, and I was kept busy from then on wrapping the rubbish in paper and pocketing their money. Some of

174

them bought three, four, five, or even six times the prescribed dose in order to have a store of so precious an antidote; they even bought for their relatives and friends who lived elsewhere, so that with this foolery, and on a day when there was not even a market, I had netted ten crowns before nightfall and still was left with more than half my stock.

That same night I left for another village, fearing that some peasant might try the experiment with the toad for himself and, finding that it failed, have me whipped out of town. But in order to have another means of demonstrating the excellence of my pill I made a yellow arsenic from flour, saffron and gall, and a sublimate of mercury from flour and vitriol. Now when I wanted to cause a stir I put on the table two glasses full of water, of which one had a fairly strong admixture of aqua-fortis or nitric acid. Into this I dissolved my pill and then scraped a certain quantity of my two poisons into each glass. The water which contained no pill (and also no aqua-fortis) turned black as ink, but the other, because of the acid, stayed as clear as before. 'Ho!' said the peasants, 'a truly marvellous mithridate, and so cheap, too!' Then, when I poured the two together, the whole mixture became clear as water again and the good yokels flourished their purses and bought the pill in such quantities that not only had I enough to eat but was soon able to buy a horse again and even put some money by before I reached the German frontier.

Wherefore, good peasants, do not put your faith in quacks on market day, for they are concerned only with your money, not your health.

CHAPTER VIII

In which Simplex once more a musket bears,
And gains some renown by catching hares.

WHILE passing through Lorraine my stock ran out, and as I wanted to avoid garrison towns, I had no chance of replenishing it. So I was forced to think of something new until I could make my mithridate again. I bought two pints of spirits, coloured the liquid with saffron and filled it in half-ounce bottles which I sold as gold-water of the highest quality, good against fever, and with my two pints earned thirty crowns. I was running out of bottles when I heard of a glass-blower in the neighbourhood of Fleckenstein and made for the district to re-equip myself. But seeking for by-paths, I was picked up by a patrol from Philippsburg which was quartered in Wagelnburg castle, and so lost all I had filched and cheated from the people I had encountered on my travels. The yokel who had been my guide told my captors that I was a leech, and so it was as a doctor that I was brought to Philippsburg.

There they questioned me and I told them the truth without beating about the bush. But they would not believe me, wanting to make more of me than I was, and insisted that I should and must be a doctor. In the end I had to swear that I was an Imperial dragoon from Soest and tell them on oath everything that had happened since, and what I now proposed to do. But I carefully concealed from them that I had taken a wife from the opposite camp and had been about to become an ensign there, for I still hoped to talk myself free, slip down the Rhine, and get back to my Westphalian hams. In this hope I was deceived, for they told me that the Emperor needed soldiers at Philippsburg as badly as he did at Soest, so they would keep me there until an opportunity offered of returning me to my regiment. If this did not please me I was free to stay in prison and be treated as a doctor until my release, for as such they had taken me.

So I came down from a horse to a donkey and with great reluctance became a musketeer once again. The change was the bitterer as we lived frugally on our rations, which were dreadfully small. I say 'dreadfully' advisedly, for dread seized me every morning when I received my hunk of black bread, knowing that it must last me through the day, though I could have made short work of it at a single sitting. To tell the truth, a musketeer in a garrison having to make do with dry bread—and not enough of that—is a miserable creature indeed. He is no better off than a prisoner, eking out his pitiful existence with the bread and water of tribulation. Indeed, the prisoner's lot is the happier, for he at least is quit of sentry duties and parades, and can lie quietly with as much or as little hope of final release as the poor garrison soldier.

There were some, it is true, who bettered their condition by various means, but none of these were to my liking or of a kind I considered suitable for my support. Some, in their misery, took wives who might be no more than whores, for no other purpose than to be maintained by them with sewing, washing, spinning, huckstering, or even stealing. There was among them a woman-ensign who drew pay as a corporal; another was a midwife, and so earned many a good feast for herself and her husband; others could wash and starch, and these washed the officers' and soldiers' shirts, stockings, smalls, and heaven knows what else, and each had her special nickname from her trade. Some sold tobacco and pipes to those that wanted them; others dealt in spirits, which they were suspected of mixing with water. One was a sempstress, skilled in embroidery and making patterns; another knew how to live entirely off the land, digging for snails in winter, gathering herbs for salad in spring, and birds'-nesting in summer, while in the autumn she found fruit and berries in plenty for her table. Some carried wood to market like mules, and others traded in what came most naturally to them.

Seeing that I was already married, this means of support was not for me. Some fellows made a living by gambling, at which they were more expert than professional card-sharpers, robbing their simpler comrades by means of loaded dice or marked cards—a profession I detested. Others worked like slaves on the fortifications or elsewhere, but for this I was too lazy. Some knew or practised a trade or craft, but I, poor ninny, had learned none. True, if they had needed a musician I could have served their turn, but in this poverty-stricken land they made do with drums and fifes. Some there were who mounted guard for others and hardly left the sentry-box, day and night, but I would have starved rather than so torment my body. Some looted a living on expeditions, but me they would not trust even to walk outside the gates. Some thieved like magpies, but this was a trade I hated like the plague. In short, wherever I turned I could find nothing to

177

appease my hunger. But what vexed me most was that I had to endure the mockery of my companions into the bargain, for they said: 'What! call yourself a leech and know only how to starve?'

At last I was compelled by hunger to entice some fine carp from the moat on to the rampart beside me, but when the colonel heard of it he had me beaten and forbade me, on pain of hanging, to exercise my skill a second time. In the end the misfortunes of others proved my salvation, for after I had cured a few men, who must have had some special faith in me, of jaundice and fever I was permitted to go outside the fortress walls under the pretext of gathering roots and herbs for my medicines. But I set traps for hares instead, and the very first night was so lucky as to catch two. These I presented to the colonel, and got as a reward not only a rixdollar but also permission to go and catch hares when I was off duty. As the countryside was almost deserted and no one there to catch the animals, they had multiplied enormously, which brought grist to my mill, for soon it seemed fairly to be snowing hares, as if I could charm them into my snares by magic. Moreover, when the officers saw that they could trust me, they also let me out on patrols, so that I resumed much of my former life at Soest, though they did not let me lead any expeditions as I had done in Westphalia, for which a thorough knowledge of the countryside and the River Rhine was needed.

CHAPTER IX

Simplex leads a life most foul,
Nor lets the parson save his soul.

THE gentle reader has heard much of the misfortunes that befell my body. As for the state of my soul, I must confess that with my musket I was a truly desperate customer who cared neither for God nor His word. There was no malice of which I was not capable, and all the blessings and favours God had so lavishly bestowed on me were quite forgotten. I prayed for no charity, either in this world or the next, and lived heedlessly by the Emperor's bounty like a dumb beast. No one would have believed that I had been reared by a saintly hermit; I rarely entered a church, and never for confession; since I did not trouble about my soul's salvation, I had no scruples about harming my fellow-men. Wherever I could do a man an injury I never neglected to do so and, indeed, took such pride in it that few who met me went their ways unscathed. This often earned me hard blows and even punishment by my officers. More than once was I threatened with torture or the gallows, but all to no avail. I pursued my godless ways so persistently that I seemed quite bent on rushing straight to hell. Though I committed no crime for which they could have hanged me, I was so depraved that but for sorcerers and sodomites no greater scoundrel walked the earth.

Of this the regimental chaplain became aware, and as a faithful shepherd of his flock sent for me at Easter-time to ask me why I had not come to confession and Holy Communion. But I answered his friendly admonitions with irreverent argument, so that the good man could do nothing with me. Since it seemed that Christ and His blood were wasted on me, he said at last: 'Oh, you miserable sinner! I thought you transgressed out of ignorance, but now I see that you persist in your evil ways from sheer malice and with fell intent. Who, do you think, will have mercy on your poor soul and its damnation? As for me, I declare before God and the world that I am innocent of your fate, for I have done and will continue to do whatever may avail for your salvation. But I fear that I shall have no further business with you than to see to it that your body, when your poor soul departs from it in its unhallowed state, is not buried in consecrated ground near pious Christians, but flung into the carrion-pit with the beasts of the field.'

Even this desperate threat moved me no more than his previous exhortations, and for this reason: I was ashamed of confession. Fool that I was! How often did I boast of my exploits in public, and even embellish them with lies. Yet now, when I was asked to repent and confess my sins to a single man standing in God's stead and to receive absolution,

179

I clung to an obstinate silence. Obstinate indeed, for I replied: 'I serve the Emperor as a soldier, and if I die a soldier's death it will be nothing unusual if I, like other soldiers (who cannot always be buried in consecrated ground but must take their chance of some field, ditch or wolf's or raven's belly), must make do with somewhere outside a church-yard.'

On such terms did we part, and the priest's holy zeal gained him no better reward at my hands than that I once refused him a hare (which he most earnestly begged of me), saying that since the animal had hanged itself on the rope of the snare and thus put an end to its own life, it was not fit to be buried in consecrated ground.

CHAPTER X

Simplex meets his long-lost friend,
Who brings his penance to an end.

IN fact, far from improving, my behaviour went from bad to worse. Once the colonel threatened to discharge me as an incorrigible rogue, seeing that I was good for nothing, but I, knowing he did not mean it, said I would gladly go if he would dismiss the hangman as well, to keep me company. So he let it be, for he realized that I considered it a favour rather than a punishment to be dismissed; and much against my will I had to stay with my musket and my hunger till well into the summer.

But with the approach of Count Götz and his army my deliverance also drew near. For when the Count established his headquarters at Bruchsal my friend Heartsbrother, whom I had helped out with money before Magdeburg, was sent by the staff to Philippsburg on some business and received with great deference. I happened to be on sentry duty outside the colonel's quarters; though he was wearing a black velvet coat, I recognized him at once, but had not the courage to address him, fearing that according to the way of the world he would be ashamed to know me; for by his clothes he must be of high rank and I but a lousy musketeer. But as soon as I was relieved I asked his servant for his rank and name, to make sure I was not mistaken. Even then I lacked the heart to speak to him, writing him instead the following note, which I had conveyed to him next morning by his valet:

'Monsieur, etcetera,
'If it should please your honour by your high influence to deliver from the most miserable condition in the world into which fickle fortune's wheel has cast him one whom once already, at the Battle of Wittstock, you saved from chains and bondage by your great courage, it would not only cost you little but you would also for ever oblige him who is already your faithful servant, though now the most wretched and deserted
'S. Simplicissimus.'

As soon as he read it he called for me and asked: 'Fellow-countryman, where is the man who gave you this?' I replied: 'Sir, he is a prisoner in this fortress.' 'Very well, go to him and tell him that I will get him free even if the rope is already about his neck.' 'Sir,' I said, 'there is no need, though I am grateful for your quick and ready response. I myself am poor Simplicissimus, who wants to thank you for saving him in the Battle of Wittstock and to ask you to deliver him from this musket which he has been forced to bear against his will . . .' He did not let me finish, but clasped me in his arms, promising me every help and generally doing all that one good friend should do for another. Before even asking me how I came to be in this fortress and in bondage, he sent his servant to the Jew to buy me clothes and a horse. Meanwhile I told him how I had fared, since his father had died in the camp before Magdeburg. When he heard that I was the huntsman of Soest (of whose exploits he had heard much), he exclaimed what a pity it was that he had not known it at the time, for he could certainly have got me a commission.

When the Jew arrived with a cartload of uniforms and clothing, Heartsbrother selected the best, made me put it on, and took me to the colonel, to whom he said: 'Sir, I have met in your garrison this man, to whom I am so greatly

181

indebted that I could not leave him in his present lowly condition even if his qualities merited no better. You would therefore oblige me by either giving him a better post or letting me take him with me to assure his promotion in the army, for which, perhaps, you lack opportunity in this place.' The colonel crossed himself from sheer amazement at hearing me praised for once and replied: 'You will forgive me, most noble Sir, if I suspect you of putting me to the test, to see whether I am as ready to oblige you as your high quality deserves. If so, I beg you to ask anything else of me that is in my power and you shall have proof of my loyalty. As for this fellow, he does not really belong to me but—so he says—to a regiment of dragoons, and is so insufferable a guest that he has given my provosts more work since he came than a whole company. One might truly believe that there is no water that will drown him.' Then he smiled at me and wished me luck in battle. We then all ate at his table, and afterwards Heartsbrother and I rode out of the fortress in great happiness. Some of my companions shouted 'Good luck' after me, but others, being envious, called: 'The greater the rogue the better the luck!'

CHAPTER XI

Simplex relates how much to deplore,
Is the marauders' tribe in war.

ON the way, Heartsbrother and I agreed that I was to describe myself as his cousin, so as to increase my standing. He also decided that he would get me another horse and a servant and have me enrolled in the Neuneck regiment, where I could serve as a volunteer until a commission fell vacant elsewhere in the army which he could procure for me.

And so, in a twinkling, I became once more the image of a good soldier. But that summer I performed no great feats except to help steal a few cows every now and then in the Black Forest, and to get a fair knowledge of Alsace and the Breisgau. For the rest, my ill-luck dogged me still, for after my servant and one horse had been captured by the Weimar troops at Kenzingen I had to work the other the harder, and finally rode it to death, leaving me no choice but to join the fraternity of marauders. True, Heartsbrother would gladly have bought me another horse, but as I had run through the first two so quickly, he held back, intending to let me dangle awhile till I had learned better management. Nor did I wish it otherwise, for I found the fraternity such good company that I could wish for no better situation until we moved into winter quarters.

I must now tell something of the marauding fraternity, for no doubt there are some, especially among those inexperienced in war, who know nothing about it. Nor have I yet found a writer who mentions in his writings anything about their customs, usages, rights, and privileges, though it would be as useful to peasants as to commanders to know what kind of fraternity this is.

First, concerning their name: I hope it will not be held against the gallant cavalier (Maraude) from whom they got it, otherwise I would not mention it so openly. This gentleman once brought to the army a regiment of new levies which were so old, weak, and crippled that they could not bear the marching and other hardships to which a soldier in the field is subject. Soon so many of them were out of action that the regiment was barely stronger than a troop, and wherever one met the halt and the lame, in streets and houses or behind fences and hedges, and asked them 'Of what regiment?' the answer usually was 'Maraude's'.

So it came about that in the end all those, whether sick or healthy, wounded or sound, who straggled outside the ranks or were not with their regiments in the line of battle were called marauders. Before this they had been called 'hog-snatchers' or 'drones', for they are like those bees which have lost their sting and can neither work nor make honey, but only eat. If a rider loses his horse or a musketeer his health, or his wife and children fall ill and he falls behind, you have a pair and a half of marauders—a rabble which can best be compared with gipsies. Not only do they swarm at will around the army, in front, behind, and in between, but their habits and customs are also like those of gipsies. You can see them huddled together behind hedges like partridges in winter, seeking shade or sun according to the season, or lounging round the fire, smoking tobacco and loafing while decent soldiers are with their regiments suffering heat and frost, thirst and hunger, and all manner of other miseries.

There goes a pack of them, pilfering along the line of march while many a poor soldier can scarcely stagger on for weariness under the weight of his weapons. All around the army they loot what they can find, and what they cannot use they destroy, so that the army, when it enters camp or quarters, often cannot find so much as a drink of clear water. When a serious effort is made to keep them with the baggage the train is often larger than the army itself. When, on the other hand, they move in bands, they have no sergeant-major to command them, no sergeant to discipline them, no corporal to mount the guard, and no drummer to summon them for reveille, picket-duty, or retreat. In short, there is no one who parades them for battle or assigns them their quarters, and they live like gentlemen of leisure. But when something reaches the troops from the Commissariat they are the first to claim their share, though they have not earned it. Their worst enemies are the provost-marshal and his force, who, if they go too far, will put iron bracelets on their wrists and ankles or even adorn them with a hempen collar and hang them by their precious necks.

They keep no watch, they dig no trenches, they mount no charge, they figure in no order of battle, yet they are fed and clothed. But the damage they do to commanders, peasants, and the army itself, if it has too much of this rabble, is indescribable. The most rascally stable-lad who does nothing but forage is of more use to his commander than a thousand marauders who make a trade of it and loaf without need. They are captured by the enemy, or the peasants rap them over the knuckles if they get the chance. So the army is weakened and the enemy reinforced, and even if such a knave (and by this I do not mean the truly sick, but the unhorsed riders who have spoilt their mounts through neglect and become marauders to save their skins), comes safely through the summer the army has no profit from him, for he must be re-mounted at great expense in order to have something else to lose in the next campaign.

This was the worthy fraternity which I joined and with which I remained until the day before the Battle of Witten-weir, when our headquarters were in Schüttern. As I was going with some of my companions on one of our customary raids in search of cattle, we were captured by Weimar troops, who had a better way of dealing with us: giving each of us a musket and allotting us to various regiments—and me to that of Hattstein.

CHAPTER XII

Simplex meets a doughty foe,
And in a hard fight lays him low.

I HAD good proof then that I was born unlucky, for about a month before these events I had overheard some officers of Count Götz' army discussing the war and one of them saying: 'If we win, we will have to spend the winter besieging Freiburg and the Forest towns, but if we are beaten we will be able to go into winter quarters.' From this prophecy I drew the correct conclusion—that we would be beaten—and said to myself: 'Rejoice, Simplicius, for you will drink good Rhine and Neckar wine in the spring and will have the Weimar army to thank for it!' But I had sadly miscalculated, for here I was with the Weimar army and condemned to spend the winter besieging Breisach, a siege which began immediately after the Battle of Wittenweir. I was a musketeer once more, on sentry duty day and night, or else digging trenches, and had noth-ing to show for it but that I learned something of the art of siege entrenchment, to which I had paid little attention when I lay before Magdeburg. My situation in general was lousy, for we were cooped close together; my purse was empty; wine, beer, and meat a rarity; and apples and hard, mouldy bread —what little there was of it—my only venison.

I found all this the harder to bear when I recalled the flesh-pots of Egypt or, to be more precise, the Westphalian hams and sausages of Lippstadt. Never did I think more fervently of my wife than when I lay half-frozen in my tent, saying to myself: 'Ho, Simplicius! Would it not be only right and just if someone was now paying you back for what you did in Paris?' With such thoughts I tormented myself like a veritable cuckold, though I had no reason to think my wife anything but virtuous and honourable. In the end I became so impatient that I unburdened myself to my captain and also wrote to Lippstadt, getting in reply a letter from Colonel de Saint André and my father-in-law saying that they had prevailed upon the Duke of Weimar to make my captain give me a pass and let me go.

So, about a week before Christmas, I set out with a good musket down through the Breisgau towards Strasbourg, where at Christmas-time I hoped to find a remittance of twenty rixdollars from my brother-in-law, and to make my way down the Rhine in the company of traders, for I would have to pass many Imperial garrisons on the way. But when I was just out of Endingen and passing a lonely house by the wayside a shot rang out, a bullet grazed the brim of my hat, and a big, burly rogue came out at me with a rush, shouting to me to drop my musket. 'Not to do you a favour, by God!' I said, and cocked my piece. But he whipped a huge weapon from its scabbard that was more like an executioner's sword than a rapier and lunged at me. Seeing that he was in earnest, I pulled the trigger and the bullet struck him in the forehead so hard that he reeled and fell. I seized my chance, quickly wrenched the sword from his hand, and tried to run him through with it. But I could make no impression on him before he recovered, jumped nimbly to his feet, and grabbed me by the hair. I threw the sword away and returned the compliment, whereupon a struggle began so fierce that each marvelled at the other's great and stubborn strength. Neither of us could gain the upper hand; sometimes he was on top, and sometimes I; then suddenly we were both on our feet again. But as each was bent on killing the other, the struggle could not last long. Seeing that my enemy so much desired my blood, I spat what was flowing freely from my mouth and nose in his face, which served to unsight him. We must have grappled with each other in the snow for an hour and a half or thereabouts, becoming at last so exhausted that the weariness of one contestant seemed unable to overcome the other's weakness with fists alone, and that neither would be able to account for the other by sheer strength and without the aid of weapons.

The art of wrestling, which I had often practised at Lippstadt, now stood me in good stead, or I would undoubtedly have been overcome, for my enemy was much stronger than I and also proof against bullets and steel. At last, when we were both weary almost to the point of death and I felt I could not hold him down another minute, my adversary said: 'Stop, brother, I surrender!' 'You would have done better to let me pass in the first place!' I retorted. 'And what do you gain,' he said, 'if you kill me?' 'Or what would you have gained if you had shot me dead, seeing that I have not a penny in my pocket?' Then he begged my pardon and I relented and let him get up, having first made him swear by all he held sacred that he would not only keep the peace but also be my faithful friend and servant. But had I then known his record of villainy and double-dealing I would not have believed or trusted him.

When we were both on our feet again we shook hands and promised that all that had happened should be forgotten, and each wondered at having met his match in the other, for my adversary assumed that I was covered with the same kind of knave's skin as he. Nor did I disabuse him, lest he should start the quarrel anew when he recovered his musket. He had a big lump on his forehead from my bullet, and I had lost much blood. But our chief complaint was of our necks, which were so twisted that neither could hold his head upright, so long and hard had we tugged at each other's hair.

Dusk was falling, and my adversary told me that I would meet neither cat nor dog, never mind a human being, until I reached the River Kinzig, and that he had a good roast and a drink prepared in a lonely hut near by. So I let myself be persuaded to accompany him, and on the way he protested with many sighs how sorry he was to have offended me.

CHAPTER XIII

Simplex finds a foe of old,
Who has become a robber bold.

A RESOLUTE soldier, accustomed to hazarding his life and holding it cheap, has no more sense than an ox. Not one man in a thousand would have gone he knew not where as the guest of one who had just made a murderous assault on him. As we went along I asked him where he came from. He said he had no master at present, but waged war on his own account. And where did I come from? I replied that I had been with the Duke of Weimar's army, but was now discharged and on my way home. He asked me my name, and when I answered 'Simplicius,' he turned round (for, not trusting him, I made him go in front), stared at me fixedly, and asked: 'And your second name is Simplicissimus?' 'Yes,' I answered, 'a coxcomb he who denies his name! What is yours?' 'Ah, brother,' he said, 'I am Olivier, whom you will remember from before Magdeburg!'

With that he threw away his musket and fell on his knees to beg my forgiveness for having tried to harm me. He said he knew well enough that he could have no better friend in the world than me, for according to the elder Heartsbrother it was I who would one day avenge his death. I, for my part, exclaimed in surprise at this strange meeting, but he said: 'There is nothing so very odd in that; the only things that can never meet are mountains and valleys. But what is truly strange is that we are both so greatly changed: I, from a secretary into a footpad, and you, from a clown into so valiant a soldier! I promise you, brother, that if there were ten thousand like us we could relieve Breisach tomorrow and in the end make ourselves masters of the whole world.'

As we talked we came to a small and lonely cottage, and though his boasting displeased me, I took care not to contradict him, for I knew his false and villainous nature. Though I did not trust him an inch, I went into the cottage after him. Inside was a peasant kindling a fire, to whom he said: 'Have

188

you cooked anything?' 'No,' said the peasant, 'for I still have the roast leg of veal I brought back today from Waldkirch.' 'Very well, then, go and fetch whatever you have and bring the cask of wine as well.'

When the peasant had gone I said to Olivier: 'You have a willing host, brother!' (calling him by that name to be the safer with him). 'May the devil thank him for it! Do I not keep him and his wife and children, and let him loot freely for himself as well? Moreover, all the clothes I steal I give to him in lieu of wages.' I asked him where he had left his own wife and children, and he told me that they were safe in Freiburg, where he visited them twice a week and brought back victuals and powder and shot. He went on to say that he had been a freebooter now for a long time and fared better that way than if he served a master; he intended to carry on with it until he had properly filled his purse. 'Brother,' I said, 'you practise a dangerous trade. What, think you, would they do to you if they caught you?'

'Ho!' he replied, 'I can see that you are still the same old Simplicius. I know full well that he who would gamble must put up a stake, but do not forget that no one is ever hanged until he is caught.' I said: 'Even if you are not caught, brother (and your chances are not bright since a pitcher that goes to the well too often is likely to break), yet the life you lead is the most shameful in the world, and I cannot believe that you would wish to die in it.' 'What!' he said, 'the most shameful? My brave Simplicius, I assure you that robbery is the most noble trade you can practise these days. How many kingdoms and principalities do you know which have not been built by force and robbery? Or where in the wide world is a king or prince blamed because he enjoys the revenues of his lands which his ancestors most likely acquired by force? What could be considered more noble than the profession I practise? I can see you are about to tell me that many men have been hanged, beheaded, or broken on the wheel for murdering, robbing, and plundering. True enough, for that is the law. But you will see no thieves hanged except those that are poor and miserable, and rightly so, for this excellent trade should be practised only by men of parts and high courage. Where have

189

you ever seen a person of high quality punished for having oppressed his subjects? Nor is a usurer prosecuted who practises his noble art secretly, in the guise of Christian charity. So why should I be blamed who do it openly, in good German fashion, without subterfuge or hypocrisy? My good Simplicius, you have not read your Machiavell! I am an honest soul and follow this way of life freely, frankly, and without shame. I fight and risk my life at it like the heroes of old, which gives me the incontestable right to practise my trade.'

To this I replied: 'Whether or not you have the right to plunder and steal, I still know that it is an offence against the laws of nature which forbid you to do unto others what you would not have them do unto you. It is also an offence against the law of the land, which says that a thief should be hanged, a robber beheaded, and a murderer broken on the wheel. Lastly and most important of all, it is an offence against God, who leaves no sin unpunished.' 'As I said before,' replied Olivier, 'you are the same old Simplicius who has not studied his Machiavell. If I were but to establish a monarchy by these methods I would like to see the man who preached against them!' We would have continued our argument, but the peasant returned with food and drink, so we sat down together to refresh ourselves, of which I, at any rate, was much in need.

CHAPTER XIV

Because of Heartsbrother's prophecy,
Simplex is dear to Olivier.

OUR food consisted of white bread and cold roast veal, washed down with a drop of good wine, and all consumed in a warm room. Olivier said: 'Is this not better, my Simplicius, than the trenches before Breisach?' I replied: 'Indeed it is, if only this kind of life could be enjoyed with less hazard and greater honour.' At this he roared with laughter and said: 'And are the poor devils in their trenches any safer than we, when they have to fear a sortie by the enemy at any moment? My good Simplicius, I can see that though you have taken off your fool's cap it has not changed your foolish head, which cannot grasp the difference between right and wrong. If you were anyone other than Simplicius, who according to Heartsbrother's prophecy is to avenge my death, I would teach you to admit that I live a nobler life than any lord.'

At this I thought to myself: 'This will not do! You must find other words than these lest this monster should decide to finish with you, now that he has the peasant to help him.' So I said: 'Who ever heard of an apprentice knowing a trade better than his master? If you lead as noble and happy a life as you say, brother, then let me partake of your felicity, seeing how sadly in need I am of good fortune.' To this Olivier replied: 'Be assured, brother, that I love you as much as myself, and that the offence I gave you today hurts me far more than the bullet with which you struck my forehead when you defended yourself like the good and brave soldier you are. So how could I deny you anything? Stay with me if you like, and I will care for you as for myself; and to prove to you that my words came from the heart I will tell you the reason why I hold you so dear. You will remember how true were the elder Heartsbrother's prophecies. Well, then, when we were lying before Magdeburg he prophesied to me as follows, and I have never forgotten his words. "Olivier," he said, "you may think what you will of our fool, yet will he astound you by his valour and give you the biggest beating of your life, you having provoked him to it at a time when you did not recognize each other. Yet not only will he spare your life, which he held in his hands, but much later will come to the place where you are killed and avenge your death." For the sake of this prophecy, Simplicius, I am prepared to share my very heart with you, for just as one part of it has already come true, you having fought me like a brave soldier and wrested my sword from me (which no one has ever done before), and then spared my life when I was lying under you and choking in blood, so do I not doubt that the rest of his prophecy (concerning my death) will also come to pass.'

Afterwards he asked me to tell him how I had fared since the Battle of Wittstock, when we were separated, and why I had been wearing fool's clothing when I came to the camp before Magdeburg. But as my neck was very sore I excused myself and asked him to tell me the story of his life instead, which by all appearances should provide many a rare tale. To this he readily agreed and began to tell me of his wicked life as follows:

CHAPTER XV

Olivier tells how as a child,
He was already running wild.

MY father—he said—was born of humble parents not far from Aix-la-Chapelle and apprenticed to a rich merchant who traded in copper. He bore himself so well that his master had him taught reading, writing, and arithmetic, and in the end put him in charge of all his dealings, as Potiphar did Joseph over all his household. This turned out well for both, the merchant growing ever richer because of my father's industry and foresight, and my father prouder because of his success, so that at last he grew ashamed of his parents and despised them, of which they often complained in vain. When my father was twenty-five years of age the merchant died, leaving behind his widow and a daughter who had recently had a mishap and given birth to a child, which soon followed its grandfather to the grave. When my father saw that the girl was left without father and child, but not without money, he did not fret about the loss of her maidenhead but counted her wealth and courted her, which her mother gladly permitted. Not only would it make an honest woman of her daughter but also provide her with a son-in-law who knew the business and was a shrewd trader. So, by his marriage, my father at one stroke became a rich merchant, and I his eldest son and heir whom, because of his wealth, he brought up in great luxury. I was clothed like a nobleman, fed like a lord, and tended like a prince, for all of which I had copper and zinc to thank rather than silver and gold.

Before I had completed my seventh year I began to show my paces, for the nettle that is to be stings early. There was no roguery of which I was not capable, and if I could play a trick on someone I never missed the chance, for neither my father nor my mother punished me for it. With other evil urchins of my kind I roamed the streets and was already bold enough to fight with boys older and stronger than I. If I got a beating my parents would say: 'How dare the big bully hit a little child!' but if I won (for I scratched, bit, and threw stones) they said: 'What a fine, strong little fellow our Olivier is!' So I became still bolder. They thought me too young for prayers, but if I swore like a trooper they excused it by saying that I was too young to understand what I was saying. So I went from bad to worse until they sent me to school, where I put into practice whatever malice other rascals invented but dared not carry out for fear of a beating. If I spoilt or tore my books my mother bought me new ones, so that my miser of a father should not be angry. I treated my master as I pleased, who dared not handle me severely because of the many presents he received from my parents and the knowledge he had of their foolish indulgence towards me.

CHAPTER XVI

His studies give him greater scope;
He barely escapes the hangman's rope.

THE more my father's wealth increased, the greater was the number of parasites about him who said how clever I was and how good at my studies, but either kept silent about my many vices or at least knew how to excuse them, realizing that this was the way to my father's and mother's favours. So my parents had greater delight in their son than ever a hedge-sparrow in rearing a cuckoo. They hired me a tutor and sent me with him to Liège—to learn French rather than to study, for they wanted to make a merchant of me, not a theologian. My tutor had orders not to be too strict with me for fear of imbuing me with a timid and servile spirit. He had to let me consort freely with other students lest I became a recluse, and he must remember that he was not to make a monk of me but a man of the world who could tell the difference between black and white.

But my tutor had no need of these instructions, being himself inclined by nature to all manner of profligacy. How, then, should he have forbidden me or dealt severely with my trivial faults when those he himself committed were far graver? His taste was mainly for drinking and whoring, but mine rather for violence and brawling. So I prowled through the streets with him and his kind at night, and soon learned from him more lechery than Latin. As for my studies, I relied on my good memory and quick intelligence, and so became the more superficial. For the rest, I was steeped in all manner of vices, knaveries, and mischief, and already my conscience was so wide that one could have driven a hay-wain through it.

This glorious life lasted a year and a half before my father came to hear about it from his factor with whom we lodged. He was ordered to keep a closer eye on me, to dismiss my tutor, ride me on a tighter rein, and examine my expenses more carefully. This vexed us both greatly, and though the tutor had been dismissed, we continued to be as thick as thieves. Since we could no longer spend as freely as before, we joined a fellow who robbed people of their coats at nights or even drowned them in the Meuse. What we acquired in this way at our great peril we squandered with our whores, and let our studies go hang.

One night, when we were roaming the streets as usual, looking for victims to rob, we were overcome, my tutor was stabbed to death, and I and five others—all thorough-going rascals—caught and laid by the heels. When we were called before the magistrate next morning I named my father's factor, who was a respected citizen of the town. He was summoned and questioned about me, and I was freed on his surety; but on condition that I stayed confined to his house until further notice. Meanwhile, the tutor was buried, the other five punished as rogues, robbers, and murderers, and my father informed of my situation. He hurried in person to Liège, settled my affair by bribery, and preached me a stern sermon on the sorrow and heart-ache I was causing him, and that my mother was nearly out of her mind because of my behaviour. He also threatened to disinherit me and send me to the Devil if I did not mend my ways. I promised amends and rode home with him; and that was the end of my studies.

CHAPTER XVII

Simplex hears what Olivier did
To trip Heartsbrother and take his seat.

WHEN my father got me home he found that I was rotten to the very core. I had not become a man of honour, as he had hoped, but a quarrelsome braggart who thought he knew everything. I had barely got my feet properly under the table before he said to me: 'Listen, Olivier, the more I see of you, the less I like what I see. You are a useless burden to the world, a rascal who is good for nothing. You are too old to learn a trade, too ill-mannered to serve a master, and useless to study and practise my business. To what purpose, alas, have I spent so much money on you? I had hoped to take pride in you and make you a man, but here I am buying you out of the hangman's hands and seeing you loafing idly in my sight. For shame! The best would be to put you on a treadmill and let you eat the bread of affliction until you had expiated your evil ways and become worthy of better fortune.'

To such lectures I had to listen daily until at last I, too, grew impatient and told my father that I was by no means wholly to blame, for he and my tutor, who had led me astray, must also take their share. That he had no joy of me was his just reward for having given none to his parents, whom he had left in penury until they died. At this he seized a stick to pay me out for my plain speaking, swearing by all that was holy that he would have me sent to the house of correction in Amsterdam. So I ran away and spent the night at a farm he had just bought, where I seized my chance and stole the farmer's best stallion, on which I rode to Cologne. There I enlisted as a soldier in the regiment of that very colonel with whom we lay before Magdeburg and who happened to be recruiting there at the time.

It was not long before my colonel's clerk died and I took his place. I became preoccupied with thoughts of greater things, hoping to climb the ladder rung by rung until I became a general. I learned deportment from our secretary, and my intention to become a man of note forced me to behave decently and honourably and abandon my usual churlish tricks. But still I seemed to be making no progress until the secretary died, whom I was determined to succeed. I greased palms wherever I could, for my mother, hearing that my manners were improving, continued to send me money.

But as the younger Heartsbrother was so greatly in my colonel's favour and so plainly preferred to me, I thought how I might strike him from the lists, especially when I found how wholly determined my colonel was to give him the secretary's post. To see my promotion thus delayed made me so impatient that I got our provost to make me steel- and bullet-proof, intending to challenge Heartsbrother to a duel and put him out of the way. But I could never come at him in this way, and what is more: the provost dissuaded me from it, saying: 'Even if you do away with him it will do you more harm than good, for you will have murdered the colonel's favourite servant.' Instead, he advised me to steal something in Heartsbrother's presence and give it to him; he would soon see to it that Heartsbrother was disgraced in the colonel's eyes. I followed his advice, took the colonel's gilt cup at the christening of his son, and gave it to the provost, who used it to put an end to Heartsbrother's pretensions. You will remember the occasion in the big tent when he filled your breeches with puppies by his magic.

CHAPTER XVIII

Simplex hears Olivier tell
What Heartsbrother foretold so well.

I SAW red when I heard from Olivier's own lips how he had dealt with my dearest friend and could take no revenge. Indeed, I was compelled to dissemble, for I dared not let him notice my rage, so I asked him to tell me how he had fared after the Battle of Wittstock.

'In that encounter,' he said, 'I bore myself not like a pen-pusher who knows only his inkpot, but like an honest soldier, for I was well-mounted and bullet-proof. Moreover, I was attached to no squadron, so that I could display my valour like one who intends to rise or die by the sword. I roamed around the battle like a whirl-wind, which was good exercise for me and proof for my officers that I was handier with the sword than with the pen. But all to no purpose; the luck of the Swedes prevailed, and I had to share our side's misfortune. Indeed, I was forced to accept quarter which previously I had refused to my opponents.

'So, like any other prisoner, I was pushed into a regiment of foot which was soon afterwards transferred to Pomerania for a rest, and as it contained many recruits and I showed notable valour, I was made a corporal. But I had no intention of growing roots there, resolved as I was to return as soon as possible to the Imperial side, which I favoured, though I would doubtless have had quicker promotion with the Swedes. So I decided to escape, and managed it as follows: I was sent with seven musketeers to levy arrears of contribution from some outlying garrisons. When I had collected the 800 florins that were owing I showed the money to my men, making their mouths water, and we agreed to divide it among ourselves and desert with it. This done, I persuaded three of them to help me kill the other four, after which we divided their money, too, leaving each man with 200 florins, and so we set out for Westphalia. On the way I persuaded one of the remaining three to help me shoot the other two, and when it came to dividing the spoils I strangled this last one, too, and so came safely to Werle with the money, where I took up my quarters and used it to lead a gay life.

'When the money began to run out, but not my taste for good living, I heard of a young soldier in Soest who was making much booty and a great name for himself into the bargain, which encouraged me to follow his example. Because of his green dress this man was known as the Huntsman, so I also had a green suit made for myself, and in his

197

name stole and looted so outrageously from our own side as well as the enemy's that in the end we were both forbidden to forage more. But though he observed the order and stayed at home, I continued to thieve to my heart's content in his name, till the Huntsman at last sent me a challenge. But the Devil might fight him, for it was said that he was in league with him and would have made short work of my bullet-proof skin.

'Yet did I not escape his wiles, for with the help of his servant he enticed me and my henchmen into a sheep-pen, where he tried to force me to fight him by moonlight and in the presence of two real devils whom he had as seconds. When I refused they forced me to humble myself beyond all measure, the news of which my comrades spread abroad, putting me to such shame that I ran away to Lippstadt and took service with the Hessians. But because they distrusted me, I did not stay there long, and drifted into service with the Dutch, where the pay, it is true, was regular but the war too boring for my liking, for they kept us in like monks and made us live as chastely as nuns. So once again I absconded, this time to wage war on my own behalf as you see me doing now. And let me tell you, brother, that I have since accounted for many a staunch warrior and amassed a tidy sum of money, nor do I intend to desist until I see that there is nothing more to be got. And now it is your turn to tell me the story of your life.'

CHAPTER XIX

Simplex hears of Olivier's scars,
And how, to come by them, it needed no wars.

WHEN Olivier had finished I could not marvel enough at Divine Providence. How manifestly the merciful Lord had preserved me from this monster in Westphalia in days gone by, and even seen to it that the monster was frightened of me! Only then did I realize what was the trick I had played on Olivier which old Heartsbrother had foretold, but which— to my great good fortune—Olivier himself had interpreted differently. For if this brute had known that I was the Huntsman of Soest he would most certainly have avenged what I did to him in the sheep-pen. I also reflected how cunningly obscure Heartsbrother's prophecy had been, and although his predictions were generally infallible, how unlikely and strange it was that I should avenge the death of this villain who deserved breaking on the wheel and hanging. I also congratulated myself on my wisdom in not being the first to tell my life story, for then he would have heard from my own lips how I had led him by the nose. As these thoughts passed through my mind I noticed some scars on Olivier's face which had not been there before Magdeburg, and it occurred to me that these might be the indelible imprints of Happy-Go-Lucky's finger-nails when, disguised as a devil, he had scratched his face so unmercifully. So I asked Olivier where he got them, adding that I doubted whether he had really told me the whole story of his life and not withheld the best part, since he had not told me who had marked him.

'Ah, brother,' he replied, 'if I were to recount all my escapades and knaveries it would in the end weary us both. But to prove that I am concealing nothing from you I will tell you the truth about this one, too, though I fear it reflects no great credit on me.

'I do believe that from my birth I was predestined to be marked in the face, for even in my boyhood I was fiercely scratched by my companions when I fought with them. Then, later, one of the devils attending the Huntsman of Soest handled me so roughly that the marks of his claws showed in my face for six weeks or more. But these, too, vanished in time. The weals you now see have a different origin, and this is how I came by them: When I was still in quarters in Pomerania with the Swedes I had a beautiful mistress and made my host surrender his bed to us. But the man had a cat which also used to sleep there, and was less ready than its master and mistress to relinquish its accustomed couch. So it came every night and caused us much inconvenience. At last my mistress, who in any case detested cats, became so exasperated that she solemnly swore she would show me no more favours until I had got rid of the animal. I was still hot for her, and therefore quite ready to do her bidding, deciding to combine my revenge on the cat with some entertainment for myself. I therefore put it in a sack, and taking my host's two sturdy mongrels with me (who had no love for cats and knew me well) went out to a large, open meadow for my sport. There being no tree anywhere near in which the cat could take refuge, I thought the dogs would chase it to and fro on the ground a while like a hare, and so afford me some welcome diversion. But the devil they did! Dog's luck they brought me instead, as the saying goes—or rather cat's luck (which few people can have experienced, or it, too, would surely long since have become proverbial). When I opened the sack the cat, seeing nothing but an open field with two savage enemies in it and no eminence to which it could escape, refused to venture into the open to be torn to pieces, but retired to my head instead, as the highest point available. In my struggle to dislodge it I lost my hat, and the harder I tried to tear the cat away, the more firmly did it embed its claws to maintain its hold. The two dogs did not long stand idly by watching this struggle, but joined in the game. Jaws snapping, they leaped at the cat from every side. This made the cat even less disposed to relinquish its refuge, to which it clung with all its might, digging its claws into my face and anywhere else it could find a foot-hold. And whenever a blow from its glove of thorns missed the dogs it infallibly landed on me. Nevertheless, it succeeded now and then in landing a stroke on their noses, which made them the more determined to bring it down with their paws, dealing me many a shrewd scratch in the face in the attempt. Yet if I groped for the cat with both my hands to pull it off, the animal turned its undivided attention to me, scratching and biting for all it was worth. In fact, both cat and dogs attacked, mauled, and ripped me so terribly that I lost all resemblance to a human being. Moreover, I stood in constant fear that the dogs, while snapping at the cat, would bite me by mistake and tear off my nose or an ear. My collar and ruff were as bloody as a smith's trave on St Steven's day, when the horses are bled, and I could think of nothing to do to put an end to my plight. In the end I threw myself to the ground to let the dogs get at the cat and so preserve my head from continuing as their battlefield. This at last gave the dogs their chance, and they made short work of the cat, but I did not by any means have the pleasant sport of it that I had hoped for, but mockery rather and the face you see before you. This so enraged me that I shot both the dogs dead when they had finished with the cat and gave my mistress, who had been the cause of this fool's errand, such a thrashing that I fairly beat the oil out of her skin. She ran away soon afterwards—no doubt because she could no longer stand the sight of my raddled stew of a face.'

I could have laughed aloud at this tale, but thought it wiser to commiserate with Olivier, and with that we went to bed.

CHAPTER XX

Seeing Olivier's lust for blood,
Simplex would gladly escape if he could.

NEXT morning Olivier roused me and said: 'Up, Simplici, let us go out in God's name and see whom we can rob!' We set out and soon came to a village which was utterly deserted and where we climbed the church tower for a better view. I found the place well stocked with provisions, and Olivier told me that he used it regularly as a look-out and had several others in the neighbourhood equally well furnished. As I was about to begin telling him the story of my life we saw a coach with two riders coming up the valley. So we descended from our church tower and entered a house by the side of the road, conveniently placed for an attack on passers-by. My orders were to keep my loaded musket in reserve, while Olivier with his first shot bowled over one of the riders and his horse, taking the party completely by surprise. The other rider took to his heels and I, at the point of my cocked musket, made the driver of the coach rein in his horses and dismount. Olivier immediately pounced on him and with a single blow from his broadsword split his skull down to the teeth. Then he fell upon the women and children sitting in the coach, who already looked more dead than alive, intending to butcher them, too. But I roundly refused to allow it, saying that he would carry out his intention only over my dead body. 'Oh, you foolish Simplicius,' he sighed, 'you are even simpler than I thought you!' 'Brother,' I retorted, 'what harm have these innocent children done you? If they were grown men and could defend themselves it would be a different matter.' 'Cook your eggs and you will hatch no chicks, that is what I say! I know these young blood-suckers well. Their father, the major, is a veritable tartar who flays his soldiers alive.' With that he made as if to attack them again, but I restrained him, and in the end made him relent. The woman was the wife of a major, with her maid and three beautiful children, for whom I felt sincere pity. To prevent them from betraying us too soon we locked them in a cellar where there was nothing for them to eat except fruit and turnips until someone came to release them. Then we plundered the coach and rode off with seven fine horses into the thickest part of the forest.

When we had tethered the horses I looked about me and a little way off saw a fellow standing stock-still by a tree. I pointed him out to Olivier, saying we ought to be on our guard against him. 'Why you fool,' he replied, 'that is a Jew whom I tied up there. But the frost killed him off some time ago.' With that he went over to the fellow and chucked him under the chin, saying: 'And many a fine ducat did you bring me, you old rogue!' At his touch a number of dubloons rolled from the poor devil's lips which he had kept hidden even in death. So Olivier explored his mouth with his fingers and brought forth twelve more dubloons and a fine ruby. 'This prize,' he said to me, 'I owe to you,' and he gave me the ruby, pocketed the money, and went off to fetch his peasant, ordering me to stay with the horses meanwhile, and—with a dig at my soft-heartedness and supposed lack of resolution—to take care the dead Jew did not bite me.

While he was away looking for the peasant I considered with a heavy heart how dangerous was my new mode of life. I thought of mounting a horse and escaping, but was afraid Olivier might catch me in the act and shoot me dead, for I suspected that he was merely testing my good faith and standing somewhere near by, watching me. Then I thought of running away on foot, but feared that in this way, even if I escaped Olivier, I would surely not escape the Black Forest peasants, who had the reputation in those days of giving captured soldiers short shrift. 'And suppose,' I said to myself, 'you took all the horses with you so that Olivier could not pursue you; then if you were captured by Weimar troops you would be broken on the wheel as a murderer caught red-handed.' In short, I could think of no safe means of escape, especially in a wild forest where I did not know my way. Moreover, my conscience began to prick me for having held up the coach and been the cause of the coachman's miserable end and the imprisonment of two women and three innocent children in a cellar, where they, too, perhaps, like the Jew, would perish and die. I tried to take comfort from my innocence and that I was compelled to all this against my will, but my conscience told me that my many past misdeeds had amply earned me the fate of falling into the hands of justice in the company of an arch-murderer and receiving my just reward. Perhaps, indeed, God in His wisdom had decreed that this was the way I was to be punished.

Then again I took heart and prayed to God in His goodness to rescue me from my plight, and in this fervent mood said to myself: 'Fool that you are; you are neither confined nor bound, the whole wide world lies open before you, have you not horses enough to carry you on your flight or, if you do not want to ride, feet fleet enough to let you make your escape?' But while I was still tormenting myself and racking my brains, Olivier returned with our peasant. He led us with our horses to a farm where we ate and then slept for an hour or two, turn and turn about. After midnight we rode on, and at noon the next day reached the Swiss frontier, where Olivier was well known and we were very well looked after. While we feasted, our landlord fetched two Jews, who haggled with us over our horses and finally bought them for half of what they were worth. All this was done so smoothly and calmly that there was little need for talk. The main thing the Jews wanted to know was whether the horses came from the Imperial or the Swedish army. When told they came from Weimar troops they said: 'Then we must not take them to Basle but ride them into Swabia to the Bavarians.' Their expert knowledge and familiarity with the military situation came to me as a considerable surprise.

We wined and dined like princes, and I much appreciated the excellent river trout and succulent crayfish which we were served. When night fell we took to the road once more, loading the peasant with roasts and other victuals like a pack-mule. Next day we came to a lonely farm, where we were again most hospitably welcomed and entertained and where, because of the bad weather, we stayed for several days. Finally, travelling always through the forest and along by-ways, we returned to the hut where Olivier had taken me when we first met.

CHAPTER XXI

Simplex sees Olivier die,
And the truth of prophecy.

WHILE we were sitting there, easing our limbs and rest-ing, Olivier sent the peasant off to fetch more food, powder, and shot. When he had gone, Olivier took off his coat and said to me: 'Brother, I cannot bear to carry this devilish money about with me any longer.' With that he untied a pair of rolls or sausages he was wearing next his skin, threw them on the table, and added: 'You will have to burden yourself with these until we both have as much as we need and can retire. This confounded money has given me weals all over.' 'Brother,' I said, 'if you had as little as I it would not gall you!' But he cut me short, saying: 'Come now, whatever is mine is yours, and whatever we win in future we will share.'

I took the two rolls and found them a goodly weight, for all the coins in them were gold. I told him it was all most inconveniently packed. If he would let me, I would sew it into our clothing in such a way as to halve the burden. He agreed, and we went together to a hollow tree, where he produced scissors, needles, and thread, with the help of which I made, out of an old pair of trousers, a sort of harness or waistcoat for each of us into which I sewed many a fine red penny. When we had put these on under our shirts we were armoured, so to speak, in front and behind with gold. When, in some astonishment, I asked him why he had no silver, he said that he had more than a thousand rixdollars hidden in a tree, from which he let the peasant defray the household expenses without ever asking him for an account, for he was not interested in such small change.

When we had stowed away the money we returned to our hut, cooked our supper, and spent the night warming ourselves by the stove. Just after daybreak, when we were least expecting it, six musketeers and a corporal with weapons at the ready entered the hut, burst open the door to our room, and called on us to surrender. But Olivier (who, like me, always had his loaded musket handy and his broadsword by his side, and who was sitting at the table while I was standing behind the door) replied with a bullet from each barrel which felled two of our attackers, while I accounted for a third and winged a fourth with shots from my musket. Then Olivier whipped out his terrible sword, which could slice a hair and was well-nigh the equal of King Arthur's Excalibur, and split open a fifth from the shoulder to the belly so that his bowels tumbled to the ground and he sank down beside them. I, meanwhile, smashed the butt of my musket on to the head of the sixth, sending him sprawling stone-dead. But at that very moment the seventh struck Olivier a similar blow with such force that his brains spattered the wall. No sooner had he delivered it than I landed one on him that sent him to join his fellows in their dance of death. The wounded man, seeing what fierce buffets were being exchanged, and me advancing towards him brandishing my musket, threw his piece away and took flight as if the Devil himself were after him. The whole fight had lasted no longer than it takes to say the Lord's Prayer, in which short space of time these seven brave soldiers had bitten the dust.

Finding myself master of the field, I examined Olivier to see if perchance he was still breathing, but he was stone-dead and it seemed absurd to leave a corpse with so much money.

So I stripped him of the golden fleece which I had made for him less than a day before and hung it over my shoulders with my own. Having smashed my musket in the struggle, I took his, as well as his broadsword, with which I was well armed. Then I left the place by the path I knew the peasant would follow. I sat down a little way off to wait for him and thought what I should do next.

CHAPTER XXII

Simplex' new riches are timely indeed,
When he finds Heartsbrother in need.

I HAD been sitting with my thoughts no more than half an hour when the peasant appeared, panting like a stag and running as hard as he could. He did not notice me until I was at his elbow. 'Why so fast?' I asked, 'what news?' 'Quick,' he replied, 'be off! A corporal is coming with six musketeers; they have orders to seize you and Olivier and bring you back dead or alive to Lichteneck. They caught me and wanted me to take them to you, but I made my escape and have run all the way to warn you.' 'You rogue,' I thought, 'you betrayed us so as to lay your hands on Olivier's hoard in the tree!' But I kept my thoughts to myself, for I wanted to use him as a guide, and told him that Olivier and those who had come to take him were dead.

As he would not believe me, I took him there so that he could see the dreadful carnage for himself. 'I let the seventh of those who came to seize us get away,' I said, 'and would to God I could bring these others back to life as well!' The peasant stood aghast and said: 'What now?' 'This,' I answered: 'you have three choices: either you guide me safely to Villingen by secret paths through the forest, or you show me Olivier's hoard of silver in the tree, or you die and keep these corpses company. If you guide me to Villingen, Olivier's money is yours; if you show me the money I will share it with you; and if you will do neither I shall shoot you dead and go on my way notwithstanding.'

The peasant would gladly have escaped, but fearing my musket, he fell to his knees and offered to lead me through the forest. So we set out hurriedly, marching all that day and the following night (there being, fortunately, light enough) without food, drink, or rest, until at daybreak we saw the town of Villingen lying before us and I let him go. The peasant was driven to such efforts by fear and I by the desire to bring myself and my money to safety; from which it would appear that gold gives a man great strength, for though I carried a heavy enough load of it, I felt no particular fatigue.

I thought it a good omen that they were just opening the city gates when I reached Villingen. I went straight to the inn and hardly knew whether I should eat or sleep first, so badly was I in need of both. In the end I decided to have some food and a drink first, and while I was eating, I racked my brains how to get myself and my money safely to my wife in Lippstadt, for I had as little intention of returning to my regiment as I had of breaking my neck.

As I was turning these things over in my mind, a man came limping into the room on a stick. He had a bandage round his head, his arm was in a sling, and he was dressed in such wretched rags that I would not have given him a penny for them. No sooner did the server see him than he showed him the door, for he stank abominably and was so overrun with fleas that you could have peopled a fair-sized village with them. The fellow begged him in God's name to let him stay awhile and warm himself, but to no avail. Only when I took pity and interceded for him did he grudgingly allow him near the stove. The fellow looked at me, as I thought, with a ravenous appetite and close attention as I sat eating a hearty meal, and from time to time he heaved a sigh. When the server left to fetch me a cut off the roast he came towards my table with an earthenware penny-pot in his outstretched hand, his intention clear. So I took my jug and poured his pot full of wine before he even had time to ask for it. 'Alas, good friend,' he said, 'for Heartsbrother's sake give me something to eat as well!' and when he spoke it pierced my heart, for I knew that this was Heartsbrother himself. I nearly fainted to see him in

207

such misery, but recovered myself enough to embrace him and make him sit down beside me, whereupon we both fell to weeping—I with compassion, and he with joy.

CHAPTER XXIII

Simplex hears Heartsbrother relate
How he was brought to his present state.

OUR unexpected meeting quite robbed us of our appetite and thirst; we could think of nothing but to ask each other how we had fared since we were last together. But as the host and the server were constantly coming and going, we could not talk as freely as we wished. The host wondered that I should suffer so lousy a fellow at my side, but I told him that this was natural in wartime, when old comrades met after a long parting. When I found that Heartsbrother was living in the poor-house, where he subsisted on alms and his wounds were carelessly dressed, I rented a separate room from the host, put Heartsbrother to bed, and summoned the best surgeon I could find, as well as a tailor and a sempstress to fit him out with clothes and rid him of his lice. I had the dubloons which Olivier had taken from the dead Jew's mouth in my purse; these I banged on the table and said to Hearts-brother, but so that the host could hear it: 'Look, brother, this is my money. I will spend it on you, and we shall use it up together', which made the host assiduous in our service. To the surgeon I showed the ruby which also came from the Jew and was worth about twenty rixdollars, saying that I was spending the little money I possessed on our food and lodging and for my comrade's clothes, but would give him this ring if he cured my friend quickly and completely. He was well content with this, and did his best for his patient.

So I tended Heartsbrother like my second self and had a simple suit of grey cloth made for him. When we were alone together and I was sitting by his bed I begged him to tell me frankly how he had come to this terrible pass, for I thought he might have been cast from his former eminence, degraded, and brought so low for weighty reasons or by his own fault. But he replied: 'Brother, you know that I was Count Götz' right hand and closest friend and adviser; you also know the sorry outcome of the recent campaign under his command, and that we not only lost the Battle of Wittweiler but also failed to relieve Breisach. This led to much malicious talk, and the Count himself has been summoned to Vienna to give an account of his generalship. I, meanwhile, live in this low estate of my own free will and out of shame and fear. How often have I wished that I could either die in my misery or at least stay concealed until the Count has proved his innocence! For as far as I know he has always been faithful to the Emperor. The fact that he has been dogged by misfortune this past summer is, in my opinion, due to Divine Providence (which grants victory as it lists) rather than to any neglect on his part.

'While we were trying to raise the siege of Breisach I became aware how incompetently the campaign was being managed on our behalf, so I girded my loins and joined the assault across the boat-bridge as if to finish the business single-handed, though it was neither my profession nor my duty. But I did it as an example to others and because we had failed so utterly to achieve anything during the summer. As luck—or rather ill-luck—would have it, I found myself in the van, and therefore among the first to come to grips with the enemy on the bridge, where blows fell thick and fast. But as I had been leading the assault, so, when we had to give ground before the furious onslaught of the French, I was now in the rear, and therefore the first to fall into the enemy's hands. I was shot simultaneously in the right arm and the thigh, so that I could neither take to my heels nor draw my sword; the mêlée on the narrow bridge was no place for parleys about giving or receiving quarter, and I was felled by a blow on the head. Being richly dressed, I was stripped in the confusion and thrown into the Rhine for dead.

'In this extremity I cried out to God and commended myself to His holy will, and even as I was uttering certain vows, He came to my help. The Rhine threw me ashore, where I plugged my wounds with moss, and although I was well-nigh frozen to death, some last ounce of strength bore me on, until with God's help I reached a group of marauders and soldiers' wives who, though they did not know me, took pity on my miserable state. These people told me that they had already despaired of the relief of Breisach, which pained me more than my wounds; but they tended and clothed me by their fire, and before they had properly bandaged my injuries I could see how even our troops prepared for a shameful retreat and abandoned our cause for lost—all of which was a great grief to me. I therefore decided not to make myself known to anyone, in order to escape certain mockery, and joined a group of wounded from our army who had their own surgeon with them. I gave them a small golden cross which I still had around my neck, and in return he dressed my wounds to last me until now. In such misery, dear Simplicius, have I eked out my existence so far, nor do I intend to reveal myself to anyone until I have seen how matters stand with Count Götz. Your kindness and loyalty have given me much comfort and confirmed my confidence that God has not wholly forsaken me. Indeed, when I came from early Mass this morning and saw you pass by the Commandant's house I felt that God had sent you to me as an angel, to help me in my affliction.'

So I comforted Heartsbrother as best I could and told him in confidence that I had more money than the dubloons he had seen, all of which was at his service. I also told him how Olivier had perished and how I had been compelled to avenge his death. This so raised his spirits that his body also benefited and his wounds began to mend apace.

BOOK V

CHAPTER I

Simplex, his boredom to assuage,
Joins Heartsbrother on a pilgrimage.

WHEN Heartsbrother had recovered his strength and his
wounds were healed he confessed to me that at the
moment of his greatest peril he had vowed to make a pilgrimage to Einsiedlen. Since he was now so close to Switzerland, he intended to seize the opportunity and make the
journey, even if he had to beg his bread on the way. The
project pleased me well, so I offered him my money and my
company. I would, indeed, gladly have bought two nags to
help us along, though my eagerness stemmed from no sense
of devotion but rather from a desire to see the Confederation
—the only country where peace still flourished. I was glad,
moreover, of the chance to be of service to Heartsbrother on
this journey, for I loved him almost more than myself. But he
declined both my help and my company on the pretext that
his journey must be undertaken on foot and, indeed, with his
shoes full of peas. If I were to accompany him I would not
only disturb his devotions but also subject myself to much inconvenience because of his slow and painful progress. He said
this, however, in order to be rid of me, for it offended his
conscience to undertake so holy a journey with the aid of the
spoils of robbery and murder. Nor did he wish me to incur
any more expense on his behalf, saying firmly that I had
already done more for him than my duty demanded or he
could ever hope to repay. This led to an amicable quarrel between us as touching as any I ever heard, for each maintained
stoutly that he had not done as much by far as a friend's duty
demanded, and was still deep in the other's debt. I reminded
him how we had become blood-brothers before Magdeburg
and reproached him for seeming to cast me out and making

us both forsworn. But nothing would move him to accept my company on his pilgrimage until at last I perceived that he had a horror of Olivier's money and my godless way of life. So I had recourse to white lies, assuring him that it was true repentance that drove me to Einsiedeln. If he prevented me from so praiseworthy an enterprise and I died without having accomplished it, how would he answer for it on the day of judgement? By this means I persuaded him to let me accompany him on his visit to the shrine, and he assented the more readily as I made a great show of contrition for my wicked life (though all of it was lies). I even convinced him that I, too, had imposed on myself the penance of walking all the way to Einsiedeln with peas in my shoes.

At last we set out, crossed the Swiss frontier that same night, and next morning reached a village where we equipped ourselves with long, black cloaks, pilgrim's staffs, and rosaries.

I found the countryside as different from other German provinces as if it had been Brazil or China. I saw people going about their business peacefully; the stables were well stocked with cattle; chickens, ducks and geese strutted about the farmyards. Travellers used the roads in safety, and the inns were crowded with revellers. There was no fear of the enemy, no dread of robbery, and no terror of losing property, life and limb. Beneath his vine or his fig-tree each man lived, compared with the rest of Germany, in sheer delight and happiness, so that the country seemed to me an earthly paradise, inhospitable though its climate might be. I found myself, as a result, constantly staring about me open-mouthed, the while Heartsbrother said his rosary, which earned me many sharp rebukes, for he wanted me to spend my time in prayer, as he did. But I could not get into the habit of it.

It was when we reached Zurich that he found me out and told me most forthrightly what he thought of me. The previous night in Schaffhausen I had found my feet very sore from the peas, and dreading another such march, had them cooked before putting them back in my shoes, which gave me a comfortable walk to Zurich. He, on the other hand, was in a sorry state and said: 'Brother, you are in a rare state of grace that you can walk so well despite the peas in your shoes!' 'To tell

212

the truth, my dearest Heartsbrother,' I said, 'I had them cooked, otherwise I would not have got this far.' 'Merciful God!' he exclaimed. 'What have you done! Better to have removed them altogether than to make a mockery of them. I fear God will punish me as well as you; do not take it amiss, brother, if from brotherly love I speak plainly to you: I greatly fear for your soul's salvation unless you bear yourself very differently before God. Be assured that there is no one I love more dearly than you, but know also that I shall find it hard to abide by that love unless you mend your ways.' His words shocked me into silence, and I was at a loss how to make amends. In the end I confessed to him freely that I had put the peas in my shoes only to please him and to make sure that he would take me on his pilgrimage. 'Ah, brother,' he said, 'I see that you are very far from the way of salvation—peas or no peas. God grant you grace, for otherwise our friendship cannot continue.'

From then on I followed him sadly, like a man being led to the gallows. My conscience began to stir within me, and in this mood all the knaveries I had committed in my life passed before my mind's eye. Then did I lament the lost innocence which I had brought with me out of the forest, but since had trifled away over and over again. Nor was my sorrow lightened by the fact that Heartsbrother hardly spoke to me any more, only looking at me every now and again with a deep sigh, as though lamenting my certain damnation.

In this manner we reached Einsiedlen, where we stayed for two weeks. There I thanked God for my conversion and contemplated the miracles from which the town got its fame, all of which prompted me to devotion and a search for divine grace. But my conversion was half-hearted at best, arising as it did from fear of damnation rather than from love of God. So, little by little, I reverted to my former luke-warm and indolent state, forgetting the fright the Evil One had given me; and when we had seen our fill of saintly relics, precious vestments, and other interesting sights, we continued our journey to Baden, where we intended to spend the rest of the winter.

CHAPTER II

Heartsbrother has good news of the Count,
But Simplex of his wife not a sound.

IN Baden Heartsbrother learned from common report that
Count Götz' affairs stood well; in particular, that the
account he had rendered to his Imperial Majesty had been
well received, that he was being released from confinement,
and had, indeed, been given command of another army. So he
wrote to him in Vienna, telling him how things stood with
him; and also to the Bavarian army about his baggage, which
he had left there, and began to take hope that fortune might
smile on him once more. We decided that when spring came
we would each go our separate ways—he to the Count and I
to my wife in Lippstadt.

But whereas Heartsbrother received a favourable reply and
excellent promises from the Count, I did not hear a word
from Lippstadt, although I wrote repeatedly and sent copies
of my letters by different routes. This displeased me and
persuaded me, when spring came, not to set out for Westphalia but to prevail on Heartsbrother to take me with him
to Vienna, in the hope that I might share in the good fortune
he confidently expected. So, with the help of my money, we
fitted ourselves out with clothes, horses, servants and weapons
like a pair of cavaliers and departed by way of Constance for
Ulm, where we took a ship down the Danube and after eight
days' journey arrived safely in Vienna.

CHAPTER III

Simplex and Heartsbrother soldier once more,
But with no better fortune than before.

STRANGE things happen in this fickle world of ours. It is
often said that if a man could but know everything he
would soon be rich. Yet I would rather put it this way: if a

man can but seize his chances he will become great and powerful. Many a skin-flint and pinch-penny (or by whatever other
name you want to call a miser), has made his fortune by knowing and using this or that advantage; yet this does not make
him great; he is and remains as contemptible as he was in his
poverty. But he who knows how to make himself great and
powerful will have riches added unto him. The kind of fortune which leads to power and riches smiled brightly on me
when I had been no more than a week in Vienna, giving me
every opportunity to climb unhindered the rungs that lead to
eminence. Yet I missed the chance. And why? I think because
fate, helped by my own fatuity, decided otherwise.

That very same Count Wahl under whose command I had
heretofore made a name for myself in Westphalia happened
to be in Vienna at the time. He was at a banquet with Count
Götz and several Imperial councillors, where the conversation turned to the subject of strange characters the war had
thrown up, outstanding soldiers, and famous partisans. The
Huntsman of Soest was mentioned, and Count Wahl told a
number of such remarkable anecdotes about him that the rest
of the company was much impressed that so young a fellow
should have done these things.

Heartsbrother, who was in attendance at the table and eager
to further my cause, begged the company's pardon and asked
for permission to speak. Then he said that he knew the Huntsman of Soest better than any man alive, and that he was not
only an excellent and fearless soldier but also a passable horse-
man, an outstanding fencer, a skilled armourer and gunner,
and a military engineer second to none. Moreover, he was at
this very moment in Vienna, where he had accompanied him
with the intention of serving once more under the banner
of his Imperial Majesty; but only in a post suited to his
abilities, for he had no desire to serve again as a common
soldier.

By this time the august company was so animated by the
wine they had drunk that they insisted on having their curiosity
about the Huntsman satisfied there and then; and Heartsbrother was sent to fetch me in a coach. On the way he instructed me how to behave in the company of these important

215

gentlemen, for my future fortune might depend upon it. So when I was presented to them I answered their questions very briefly but pithily—to their great admiration, for everything I said appeared to be weighty and well considered. In fact, the impression I created was altogether favourable, and this the more since Count Wahl's report had already stamped me as a good soldier. Meanwhile I also became somewhat befuddled with the wine and can well believe that I showed plainly how little accustomed I was to such courtly company. The outcome of it all was that a colonel of foot promised me a company, which I readily accepted, for I thought it was a fine thing indeed to be a captain. But next day Heartsbrother upbraided me for my frivolity, saying that if I had but held out a little longer I might well have achieved much more.

So I was presented as its captain to a company which, although fully staffed with officers, had no more than seven privates fit for duty. It also caused me some concern to discover that most of my under-officers were gnarled and motheaten cripples, and it was not altogether surprising that in our first sharp engagement, which occurred soon afterwards, we were miserably routed. In this battle Count Götz lost his life and Heartsbrother his testicles, which were shot away. I got my share in the leg, but it was little more than a scratch. We returned to Vienna to nurse our wounds and to be near our money, which was in safe keeping there. The wounds did not take long to heal, but Heartsbrother developed a dangerous condition, which the doctors were at a loss to understand, becoming paralysed in all his extremities like a choleric suffering from gall, though in all other respects such a disease was quite alien to his temper. Nevertheless, he was prescribed the waters and advised to go to Griesbach in the Black Forest.

Thus did our fortunes change all unawares. Shortly before, Heartsbrother had decided to marry a young noblewoman, to which end he had planned to have himself created a baronet and me an esquire. These plans he now must change, for having lost the wherewithall to found a new dynasty and threatened, moreover, with a prolonged illness as a result of his paralysis, he was in need of good friends rather than a wife. So he made his will, appointing me his sole heir, for he saw that for his sake I was casting my good fortune to the winds and relinquishing my command in order to accompany him to Griesbach and tend him until his health was restored.

CHAPTER IV

Simplex goes to see his son,
And finds he has fathered more than one.

As soon as Heartsbrother was well enough to ride we transferred our money (which we now held in common) by banker's draft to Basle, provided ourselves with horses and servants, and made our way up the Danube to Ulm and thence to the waters, for it was the month of May and agreeable to travel. At Griesbach we took lodgings and I went on to Strasbourg to collect some of our money which had been sent there from Basle, and to look for experienced physicians who might prescribe a treatment and cure for Heartsbrother. I returned with them to Griesbach, and they declared that Heartsbrother had been poisoned, though the dose had not been large enough to kill him outright, striking his limbs instead. This poison would have to be removed by means of medicines, mithridates, and sweat-baths, and the cure might take as much as eight weeks. Heartsbrother had no doubt as to who could have done this to him: it must have been someone who wanted to step into his shoes in the army. When the doctors told him that there was no real need for him to have gone to a watering place he became even more certain that whoever it was had bribed his field surgeon to get him out of the way. But he decided to stay at Griesbach nevertheless, for the air was healthy and there was good company among those who came to take the waters.

I did not want to let time go to waste, for I had a great desire to see my wife again, and as Heartsbrother had no special need of me, I told him of my intentions. He entirely approved the plan, commending me for it and giving me some valuable jewels, which I was to present to my wife from him with his apologies for having been the cause of my delay. So

I rode off to Strasbourg, where I provided myself with money and inquired after the best and safest means of travel. I soon discovered that to do the journey alone and on horseback was out of the question, for frequent patrols from hostile garrisons of both armies made the countryside unsafe. I therefore got a pass for a post-rider from Strasbourg and wrote a number of letters—to my wife, her sister, and her parents—as if to dispatch him with them to Lippstadt. Then I pretended to have changed my mind, getting the rider to return the pass to me, sent my servant and horse back to Griesbach, disguised myself in a red-and-white livery, and set out by ship down the Rhine to the neutral city of Cologne, and thence by paths I knew well to Lippstadt. There, like a messenger from afar, I inquired after my father-in-law and heard that he and his wife had both passed away some six months previously. My wife, having given birth to a son who was now in her sister's care, had died soon after her lying-in. So I delivered to my brother-in-law the letters I had written to him, my wife, and her father, whereupon he immediately made me welcome in order to find out from me (the messenger) how I (Simplicius) fared and whether I had made my way in the world. I spoke about myself at length to my sister-in-law, singing my praises for all I was worth, for the pock-marks had so altered and disfigured me that no one recognized me.

When I had told in great detail how many fine horses and servants Monsieur Simplicissimus had, and how he wore a black velvet cap trimmed with gold, she said: 'Indeed, I always used to think that he was not so ill-born as he pretended. The Commandant of this town assured my parents most earnestly that they had made a good match with him for my sister, virtuous young woman that she was, but I never thought it would end well. Nevertheless, he made a good beginning and was about to enter the service of the Swedes—or is it the Hessians I mean? He even went to Cologne to collect his possessions and bring them back, but it was an ill-fated journey. By some knavery he was spirited off to France, leaving my poor sister, who had barely had him for a month, behind with child. So did he to half a dozen other respectable young women, all of whom in due course (and my sister last of all) gave birth to boys. My father and mother being dead and my husband and I without hope of a child of our own, we have taken in my sister's little boy and made him our sole heir. With the help of the Commandant we have also gained possession of his father's treasure in Cologne, which amounts to some three thousand florins in cash, so that this child, when he comes of age, will have no cause to count himself a beggar. Besides, my husband and I love him so much that we would not part with him even if his father came in person to claim him. Of all his stepbrothers he is the handsomest, and the very image of his father. I am sure Simplicius, did he but know what a lovely son he has here, would let nothing deter him from coming to see the little darling, however reluctant the thought of the bastards he has fathered might make him.'

So she prattled on, and from the way she spoke I could tell how much she loved my child, who was playing at our feet in his first breeches—a sight that warmed my heart. I took the jewels which Heartsbrother had given me to present to my wife on his behalf, saying that Monsieur Simplicissimus had given them to me as a gift and greeting for his dear wife. But since she was dead, I felt he would approve my leaving them for the child. My brother-in-law and his wife accepted them gladly, concluding from their value that Simplicius could not lack means and must be a very different sort of fellow from what they had imagined. Then I asked leave to depart, and before I did to kiss young Simplicius in the name of his father, so that I could tell him of it as a token. My sister-in-law readily consented, but when I kissed the child both our noses began to bleed, and I felt as if my heart would break. Hiding my emotion, I hurriedly departed before they had time to ponder on the significance of the event; and after fourteen days of much trouble and danger reached Griesbach in beggar's attire, having been cleaned out on the way.

CHAPTER V

Heartsbrother dies and Simplex ere long
Takes another wife, and chooses wrong.

O N my return I found Heartsbrother's condition worse
rather than better, though the surgeons and leeches had
plucked him cleaner than a fat goose. He seemed to have
turned quite childish and could barely walk. I tried to divert
him as best I could, but with little success. He himself was
aware how weak he had grown and that the end could not be
long delayed, and his greatest comfort was that I would be
with him when he breathed his last.

In the meantime I made merry and sought my pleasures
wherever I might hope to find them, yet without in any way
neglecting Heartsbrother's care. I relished Griesbach the
more, the longer I stayed there, for not only did the stream
of visitors taking the waters increase daily but the place itself
and its way of life were to my taste. I became acquainted
with some of the gay young blades who frequented it and
began to acquire courtly speech and manners, for which I
had had little use before. Because I was often addressed as
'captain', a position few soldiers of fortune achieved at my
age, I was taken for a nobleman. This earned me the acquaintance of the richer dandies, and before long we were sworn
friends and boon companions, whose sole labour and concern
was eating, drinking, and gambling. Many a precious ducat
did I lose in this way, but I took little heed, for my purse was
still well lined with Olivier's legacy.

With Heartsbrother, meanwhile, things went from bad to
worse, until at last the physicians and surgeons gave him up
for lost, though not before they had battened on him to their
hearts' content, and he must pay his debt to nature. Before he
died he confirmed his last will and testament, which made me
heir to whatever he had inherited from his father. I arranged
a splendid funeral for him and dismissed his servants, each
with a suit of mourning and a bounty.

His going filled me with grief, the hurt being the deeper

for the knowledge that he had been poisoned; and though I could not alter it, yet it altered me. I eschewed all entertainment and sought only solitude in which to commune with my sorrow. To this end I often made my way to the forest, where I brooded over the friend I had lost and how I would never find his like again. I also pondered on my own future, considering many schemes without coming to any firm conclusion. Sometimes I thought of returning to the war, but then it occurred to me that the humblest peasant hereabouts led a happier life than a colonel, for no partisans ever came into these mountains, nor could I conceive why any army should want to lay them waste. Here every farmyard was prosperous and the stables as full of cattle as in peacetime, whereas down in the plain you could not find so much as a cat or a dog in the deserted villages.

Sometimes at twilight I lay in the grass by the river's bank under the spreading branches of a tree, listening to the nightingale, whose song was my sorrow's greatest comforter. It pleased me to imagine that it was this bird's sweet music that compelled the others to silent attention—either from modesty or from a desire to learn and later emulate something of the tune. One evening as I was thus engaged I saw a maiden approaching the opposite bank, whose coarse peasant dress moved me more than the finery of a lady of fashion could have done. She lifted from her head a basket with a load of butter she was carrying to market in Griesbach. This she plunged into the water to cool, for it was very hot and the butter on the point of melting. Then she seated herself in the grass, threw off her veil and peasant hat, and wiped the sweat from her face, giving me every opportunity to observe and feast my indiscreet eyes on her. I thought I had never in all my life seen a more beautiful creature. Her body was perfectly proportioned and without blemish, her arms and hands white as snow, her face fresh and lovely, and her black eyes full of fire and languorous glances. When she retrieved her basket to be on her way I called across to her: 'Sweet maid, you have cooled the butter with your delicate white hands, but with your bright, flashing eyes you have set my heart on fire!' But when she saw and heard me she ran off without a word as if the Devil were after her, leaving me burdened with all the wayward fancies which afflict a foolish lover.

The desire to bask again in the rays of this charming sun made me forget my longing for solitude, and the nightingale's song meant no more to me now than the howling of wolves. So I, too, made my way back to Griesbach, sending my servant ahead to accost the fair butter-seller and bargain with her until I caught up with them. This he did and I, when I joined them, wooed her with all my might, but encountered a heart of stone and such coldness as I would never have credited in a peasant girl. This did but increase my passion, though my experience in such matters should have warned me that she would not easily yield to such an approach.

Then should I have had either a redoubtable foe or a good friend. The foe to oblige me to give thought to him and forget my infatuation, the friend to restrain and dissuade me from the folly on which I was bent. But alas, I had nothing but my own and Heartsbrother's money to lead me astray, my blind passion to dazzle me, and my gross recklessness to ruin me and bring disaster on my head. I spent much money on panders, but achieved nothing, which drove me to even greater distraction. Fool that I was! Our very clothes provided an augury that should have warned me how ill-starred was my love. For we were both in mourning when first we met—I for Heartsbrother and she for the death of her parents. How, then, could our courtship lead to joy? In a word, I was thoroughly enmeshed in folly's net, and therefore as blind and bereft of sense as Cupid himself; and since I could find no other way to satisfy my hot desires, I resolved to marry her. For are you not—I thought—but a peasant's son yourself, and will never boast a castle as long as you live! Here you have a delectable corner of the world which has, compared with other lands, prospered and flourished throughout this cruel war, and you still have money enough to buy the best farm in these parts. So marry this honest peasant maiden and settle in peace and comfort on the land among your own kind. Where, moreover, could you find a more agreeable home than close to Griesbach, where people come and go and you have, as it were, a new world about you every six weeks, and can gain an impression of how the earth changes from one century to another.

Such and a thousand like fancies passed through my mind until at last I sought my sweetheart's hand in marriage and obtained—though not without difficulty—her consent.

CHAPTER VI

Simplex finds marriage hard to bear,
And hears from his dad who his parents were.

I PREPARED a lavish wedding feast, for I fancied myself in the seventh heaven. I bought the entire farmstead where my bride had been born and had a handsome new mansion built on it, as if intending to keep court rather than house. Even before the wedding I had acquired more than thirty head of cattle—as much as the farm could support throughout the year. In short, I provided the best of everything, down to the pots and pans, and whatever else my folly prompted. But I soon had a rude awakening, for I discovered—too late—the good reason why my bride had been so reluctant to accept me. More vexing still, I did not even have a friend with whom I could speak of the way I had been fooled. Though I knew well that I had only myself to blame, the knowledge made me neither more patient nor better mannered. On the contrary, seeing myself thus betrayed, I resolved to do unto her as she had done unto me and began to take my pleasures wherever I found them. So it came about that I was more often in good company at Griesbach than I was at home. In fact, for a year I let my farming take care of itself, and my wife, for her part, was as remiss as I. An ox I had slaughtered for the household she salted away in baskets, and when I told her to serve a sucking-pig she tried to pluck it like a fowl. She would grill crayfish and roast trout on a spit. From these few examples the gentle reader may judge what kind of a bargain I had of her. Moreover, since she was fond of a drop of good wine and liked to share it with her gossips, everything pointed plainly to my impending ruin.

One day, accompanied by some dandies, I was strolling down the valley to visit friends at the lower end of the town when we met an old peasant with a goat on a rope which he wanted to sell. Feeling that I had seen the man before, I asked him where he and the goat came from. He doffed his cap and said: 'Your honour, I cannot tell you.' 'Why?' said I, 'surely you have not stolen it?' 'No, to be sure,' replied the peasant, 'but I am taking it from a village there in the valley which I must not mention in the goat's presence.'

This reply made the company laugh, and as I changed colour they suspected that I was put out and vexed at having received so tart an answer from the peasant. But my thoughts were of a very different kind, for the big wart this peasant had in the middle of his forehead like a Unicorn convinced me that he was my Dad from the Spessart forest. However, I decided to play the sooth-sayer a while before revealing myself to him and delighting him with so fine a son as my clothes proved me to be. So I said to him: 'Good father, is not your home in the Spessart?' 'Yes, your honour,' said he. 'And is it not true that some eighteen years ago horsemen plundered and burned your house and farm?' 'God-a-mercy yes,' said the peasant, 'though it was not as long ago as that.' 'And did you not have two children in those days, a grown daughter and a little boy who minded your sheep?' 'Sir,' said the peasant, 'the daughter was my own, but not the boy, though I was rearing him as if he had been.' From this I gathered that I was not this coarse yokel's son, which pleased me in a way but also made me sad, for I thought that I must then be some bastard or foundling. So I asked my Dad where he had found the boy or what reason he had to rear him as his own. 'Eh,' he replied, 'it is a strange story about that boy. The war gave him to me, and the war took him away again.'

Fearing that the tale might bring to light something shameful about my birth, I turned the subject back to the goat, asking him if he was selling it to one of the inns for the pot, which would have surprised me, for the guests at Griesbach were not in the habit of eating old goats. 'Ah, no, your honour,' said the peasant, 'the kitchens there have plenty of goats of their own, and besides, they do not pay enough. This one is

for a countess who is taking the waters and whose physician
has prescribed herbs which the goat must eat. Then he mixes
the goat's milk with some potion, which the countess must
drink to be cured. It is said that she lacks a bosom, and if the
goat helps her it will be more than the physician and all his
leeches have been able to do.' As he spoke I tried to devise
some way in which I could talk to him more at leisure, and
when he had finished I offered him a rixdollar more for his
goat than he was to get from the countess or her physician.
To this he readily agreed (for even a small profit will quickly
change a man's mind), but on condition that he might first
inform the countess of my offer. If she was ready to match it
the goat was to be hers as the first bidder; if not, he would
let me have it, and at all events let me know the outcome of
the bargain in the evening.

So my Dad went his way and I mine with my friends, but
my pleasure in their company had vanished, and I soon turned
away, following the same road as my Dad had gone. I found
him still with the goat, for the others had not been prepared
to give him as much for it as I, which surprised me in people
of such wealth, but did not teach me to be less spendthrift
myself. I brought him to my newly bought farm, paid him for
his goat, and when I had half befuddled him with wine asked
him how he had come by the boy of whom he had spoken.
'Well, your honour,' he said, 'the Mansfeld war gave him to
me, and the Battle of Nördlingen took him away again.' 'That
sounds a diverting tale,' I remarked, and encouraged him,
since we had nothing better to do, to pass the time in telling
it. So he began as follows:

'When Mansfeld lost the Battle of Höchst his beaten army
scattered far and wide, for they did not know where to with-
draw. Many sought refuge in the Spessart forest, but though
they escaped death in the plains, they encountered it no less
surely in our mountains. And as neither army scrupled to
plunder and kill the other on our land, we peasants, too, took
a hand. In those days a peasant rarely went into the forest
without a musket, for we could not stay at home to tend our
fields. It was at that troubled time, and in a forest not far
from my farm, that I came upon a beautiful young noble-

woman on a fine horse, having been drawn to the place by the sound of shots. At first I took her for a man, for she rode like one, but then I saw her lift up her eyes and hands to heaven and call upon God in a pitiful voice and a tongue I could not understand. So I lowered my musket, which I had aimed at her, reassured by her gestures and lamentations that she was a woman in distress. As we drew closer she saw me and cried out: "Good man, if you are an honest Christian I beg you for God's mercy's sake to lead me to some compassionate woman who, with God's help, may deliver me of my womb's burden!" These words, so gently uttered, and her troubled yet most graceful and fair appearance touched my heart, and I took her horse by the bridle and led it over sticks and stones to the densest part of the forest, where I had brought my own wife, child, servants, and cattle for safety. There, less than half an hour later, she was delivered of that very boy of whom we spoke.'

Here my Dad ended his tale and wetted his whistle, for I plied him liberally with drink. When he had emptied his tankard I asked: 'And what happened afterwards to the woman?' He said: 'When her labour was done she asked me to be the child's godfather and to take him to be baptized as soon as ever I could. She gave me for this purpose her name and her husband's, so that they could be inscribed in the register. As she spoke she opened her saddle-bag, in which she had many fine things, and gave to me, my wife, our child, the maid, and another woman who chanced to be with us enough to give us good reason for contentment. But while she was at it and telling us of her husband she died under our hands, commending the child to our care with her last breath. It was no easy matter in those wild times, when no one dared to stay in his own house, to find a parson who would perform the baptism and the burial, but in the end it was done, and the parson and the headman of our village commanded me to rear the child until it was grown, and to take for my trouble and expense all the lady's property except some rosaries, jewels, and trinkets that I was to save for the child. So my wife fed him on goat's milk, and we were glad to have the boy, intending to give him our daughter in marriage when he

226

grew up. But after the Battle of Nördlingen I lost both the girl and the boy and all that I possessed.'

'You have told a most excellent tale,' I said, 'but you have forgotten the best part. You have not said what the woman, her husband, or the child were called.' 'I did not think that it would interest your honour,' he replied. 'The lady's name was Susanna Ramsay, her husband's Captain Sternfels von Fuchsheim, and because my own name is Melchior, I had the boy christened Melchior Sternfels von Fuchsheim, in which name he was inscribed in the register.'

So then I knew that I was the true-born son of my hermit and of Governor Ramsay's sister, but, alas, too late; for both my parents were dead, and of my uncle Ramsay I could learn nothing but that the citizens of Hanau had finally rid themselves of him and his Swedish garrison, and that he had become demented with rage and frustration as a result.

I plied my foster-parent with more wine until he was quite drunk, and the next day I sent for his wife as well. Then I revealed myself to them, but they would not believe me until I had shown them a black, hairy mark that I had on my chest.

CHAPTER VII

Simplex, by children sorely pressed,
Finds that a widower's state is best.

SOON after, I took my godfather with me on a journey to the Spessart to obtain firm proof and witness of my legitimate birth and descent. I got it without difficulty from the baptismal register, to which my foster-father's testimony was added. I also called on the parson with whom I had lodged at Hanau, who gave me a written statement concerning the place and time of my father's death, that I had lived with him until he died and thereafter for a time with Master Ramsay, Governor of Hanau, under the name of Simplicius. In fact, I had a complete document about my past drawn up by a notary, based on the testimony of witnesses, for I thought: who knows whether you may not need it one day! Before I had finished this journey, it cost me more than 400 rixdollars, for on the way home I fell into the hands of partisans, who unhorsed and robbed me, so that I and my Dad, or god-father, escaped with little but our bare lives.

At home, too, matters were no better, for when my wife learned that her husband was a nobleman she gave herself great airs and let the household go to wrack and ruin. But as she was big with child, I bore it in silence. To crown it all, disaster had struck my stables and carried off most of my best cattle.

All this I might have borne with patience, but, alas, mis-fortunes never come singly. In the very same hour in which my wife was delivered of her child, the maid, too, was brought to bed with hers, which as closely resembled me as my wife's was the spit and image of the farm-hand; and to complete my discomfiture, that very night a lady from Griesbach de-livered another child on my doorstep with a note saying that I was the father. So at one stroke I had three children in the house and quite expected others to crawl out of odd corners at any moment, to my very great distraction. But so it goes if a man indulges every passing lust and leads as wicked and godless a life as I did.

There was no help for it: I must needs have them bap-tized and accept the law's just punishment into the bargain. This fell out the heavier, as the government of the day was Swedish and I had been a soldier in the Imperial army. All these calamities were an earnest of my renewed and utter ruin, but whereas I was greatly troubled by them, they sat lightly upon my wife, who even twitted me continually about the precious treasure that had been laid at my door and the heavy fine I had had to pay. Had she known how matters stood between me and the maid, she would have plagued me even more. But the good creature was complaisant and agreed, for a sum equal to the fine it would have cost me, to name a young spark from Griesbach as the father, who had some-times visited our house during the previous year and attended our wedding, though she had no closer acquaintance of him. Even so, she had to leave the house, for my wife suspected us of what I imputed to her and the farm-hand, though she

228

dared not hint at it lest I should remind her that I could not have lain with her and the maid at the same time. Meanwhile, I was sorely tormented by the thought that I must rear the farm-hand's bastard, whereas my own two children could not be my heirs; and that I must even hold my tongue about it all and be grateful that no one else knew of it.

With such thoughts I tortured myself daily, while my wife continued to regale herself with drink; for since our wedding-day she had grown so accustomed to the bottle that it rarely left her lips, and she was seldom sober when she went to bed. But with her drinking she brought her child to an untimely grave and on herself such an inflammation of the breasts that she soon followed it, leaving me once more a widower, which so affected me that I well-nigh laughed myself into a decline.

CHAPTER VIII

His dad and mum for Simplex fend,
And faithfully his homestead tend.

So I was restored to my erstwhile freedom, but with a purse sadly depleted, and saddled with a large household over-burdened with cattle and servants. I therefore summoned my godfather Melchior and appointed him to be my father, my foster-mother, his wife, to be my mother, and the bastard Simplicius, who had been laid at my door, I took for my heir. I turned over my house and farm to the old people, together with all that was left of my fortune, save for a few gold pieces and jewels which I kept in case of dire need. For I had conceived such a loathing of the intercourse and society of women that I was resolved—seeing how I had fared with them—never to marry again. This old couple, who in matters of husbandry hardly had their equal, quickly set my household in a different mould. They got rid of unwanted animals and servants and stocked the farm with whatever was profitable. They bade me be of good cheer and promised that if I left them the management of my affairs they would always have a good horse for me in the stable and enough money to afford me a bottle of wine with my friends whenever I wanted it. Nor did it take me long to recognize what manner of people they were who now tended my farm. My Dad tilled the fields with the labourers and haggled over cattle, wood, and resin more keenly than any Jew. My Mum looked after the beasts and contrived to make and save more milk money than ten such wives as mine had been. Thus my farm was soon amply stocked, and provided with so much cattle and poultry that it was reputed the best in the province. I, meanwhile, strolled about the countryside and gave myself up to contemplation, for seeing how my Mum made more profit in wax and honey from her bees than ever my wife had wrung from cattle, pigs, and all the rest put together, I could easily imagine that she would not be caught napping on other matters, either.

CHAPTER IX

Simplex would like Christians to lead
A life like the Anabaptists in Hungary did.

As for my mode of life, it was quiet and withdrawn. My greatest pleasures and recreation was reading, and I acquired many books on all manner of subjects, especially those requiring much thought and concentration. I soon tired of grammars and text-books, such as students use, nor did books on arithmetic hold my attention for long. As for music, I had long conceived a veritable hatred of it and had smashed my lute into a thousand pieces long ago. Treatises on mathematics and geometry occupied me for a while, but when they had led me on to astronomy I discarded them, too, and devoted myself entirely to this subject and to astrology, from both of which I derived great pleasure. In the end, however, these sciences also seemed to me false and uncertain, and I began to study the art of Raimon Lull,* in which I found more sound than sense. Suspecting that it was no more than a passing fashion, I abandoned it and investigated instead the

* A thirteenth-century Catalan mystic, so obscure in his writings that many of his contemporaries thought him mad.

writings of the Hebrews and tried to penetrate the riddle of Egyptian hieroglyphics. Yet from all my studies and the knowledge they vouchsafed me I discovered at last that there was no greater or better art than theology, the science which teaches us to love and serve God.

Under its guidance I invented a mode of life for mankind which, if practised aright, might achieve a very paradise on earth. I envisaged a community of men and women, married and single, under a prudent Governor, who, like the Anabaptists, would devote the work of their hands merely to providing for their bodily needs, and for the rest would labour in the praise and service of God and their souls' salvation. Such was the way of life I had seen on the Anabaptists' farms in Hungary, and it so impressed me that I would willingly have joined them—or at least considered their practices blessed above all others—had these good people not been otherwise involved in false and abominable heresies. For in their habits and practices they seemed to me very like the Jewish sect of the Essenes, of which Josephus and others tell. They possessed great riches and an abundance of food, but never wasted any. No curse, murmur or outcry was ever heard among them, and, indeed, they never spoke an unnecessary word. Craftsmen worked in their workshops as if for their own households, and tutors taught the children as though they were their own flesh and blood. Nowhere did I see men and women mingle, and each worked separately at his allotted task.

There were special rooms reserved for the lying-in of mothers. Here they were delivered of their children entirely without the aid of their husbands, but by women who tended them with all the care in the world; other rooms were furnished entirely with cradles, where women assigned to the task nursed and swaddled the infants, so that the mothers were relieved of their care except for going to suckle them three times a day at the appointed time. For these tasks of midwifery and nursing only widows were employed. Elsewhere I saw groups of women engaged solely in spinning, so that more than a hundred spindles or spinning-wheels might be found in a single room; some women laundered, others made beds, tended the beasts, washed dishes, minded the stills, sorted the linen, and all, in short, had their special and allotted tasks. As with the women, so with the men. If anyone fell sick a nurse was appointed to tend him, and physicians and leeches were available to all men equally. But because of their healthy diet and orderly way of life ill-health was rare among them, and I saw many a fine-looking man enjoying a sturdy and peaceful old age there such as is not often seen elsewhere. The people had their fixed hours for eating and sleeping, but not a minute for play or idle strolling, save for the children, who, for their health's sake, took an hour's walk with their tutors after every meal, during which they were encouraged to pray and sing hymns.

There was no anger among these people, no jealousy, vengefulness, envy or hatred. They knew no worldly cares, no pride, and no self-reproach. In short, their lives were filled with a blessed harmony directed solely towards the increase of mankind and the kingdom of God. No man saw his wife except when he met her at the appointed time in his bed-chamber. This was furnished only with a bed, a chamber-pot, and an ewer with water and a white towel, so that he could go to sleep with clean hands and arise in the morning to return to his work. Moreover, they all called each other brother and sister, nor did this sober familiarity lead to any impurity of thought or conduct.

So blessed a way of life as the heretical Anabaptists enjoyed I, too, would gladly have embraced, for it seemed to me to excel even that of a monastery. If only, I thought, I could set up so honourable and Christian a community under my protection I would, indeed, become another St Francis or St Dominic. How blessed a deed it would be to convert the Anabaptists, so that they might teach us true Christians their way of life; or what an achievement if I could persuade my fellow-Christians to embrace so honourable and (to all appearances) so Christian a code! True, I told myself I was a fool to think of meddling with other people's lives and would be better employed in becoming a Capucin monk and so be rid of women once and for all. But then I thought: you may not feel tomorrow as you do today, and who can tell what road your way to Christ will take in times to come? Today you are inclined to continence, but tomorrow, for aught you know, you may be hot with passion.

Such thoughts much occupied my mind, and gladly would I have given my farm and my fortune to such a community of Christians for the sake of belonging to it. But my Dad warned me bluntly that I had little prospect of getting others to join.

CHAPTER X

Simplex leaves the Black Forest once more
To soldier in Russia—but finds no war.

THAT same autumn French, Swedish and Hessian troops came to relax among us and to blockade the neighbouring Free City—built by an English king and named after him.* So every man gathered together his cattle and most valuable possessions and fled to the mountain forests. I followed my neighbours' example and left my home pretty well empty. A Swedish colonel on half pay got it as his billet and found some of my books in my study, for in my haste I could not remove everything. Among them were several treatises on mathematics and geometry, as well as some on fortifications, written for engineers. From this he readily guessed that the owner of the billet could be no common peasant. So he inquired about me and even approached me in person, persuading me, by a mixture of compliments and veiled threats, to visit him on my own farm. There he treated me most courteously and ordered his men not to damage or waste any of my property needlessly. With these civilities he prevailed upon me to give him a full account of myself, and particularly of my family and descent. He professed himself astonished that in the midst of war I could bear to sit so quietly and passively among peasants that other men might tie their horses to my fence, whereas I could more honourably have tied mine to other people's. I would do better, he said, to buckle on my sword again and not let the gifts with which God had endowed me go to

* Offenburg—after King Offa.

waste by the fireside and behind the plough. He was certain if I went into Swedish service my ability and knowledge of warfare would quickly raise me to high rank.

I received his suggestion coldly and said that promotion was never assured if a man had no friends to help him. To this he replied that my qualities would soon procure me both friends and promotion; moreover, I would doubtless find influential kinsmen in the main Swedish army, for many Scottish noblemen and men of rank served in it. He himself (so he said) had been promised a regiment by Torstensohn; if this promise were fulfilled—of which he had no doubt—he would immediately make me his lieutenant-colonel. With such and similar promises he made my mouth water; and as peace still seemed far away, and I could therefore expect nothing better than more billeting of troops and perhaps ultimate ruin, I decided to take up soldiering once more and promised the colonel I would go with him provided he kept his word and gave me the post of lieutenant-colonel in his promised regiment.

So the die was cast: I sent for my Dad, or foster-father, who was still in the mountains with the cattle, and assigned my farm to him and his wife, to be theirs for life and afterwards, since I had no legitimate heirs, to go, with all my other property, to my bastard son Simplicius. Then I collected my horse and whatever money and jewels I still possessed, settled all my affairs and left instructions for the education of the afore-mentioned bastard. The blockade of Offenburg was suddenly lifted, and we found ourselves unexpectedly out of our quarters and on our way to the main army. On the journey I acted as the colonel's steward and maintained him, his servants, horses, and entire household by theft and plunder, which in military language is called foraging.

Torstensohn's promises, of which the colonel had talked so loudly on the farm, were not by any means as firm as he had boasted; on the contrary, he seemed to me to be held in no great esteem. 'Ah, me,' he would say to me then, 'some malicious cur must have blackened my name at headquarters! If this is how matters stand I won't stay here for long!' As he guessed that I, too, would not stay long with him in these circumstances, he invented a letter ordering him to raise a new regiment in the Baltics, where his home was, and persuaded me to embark with him at Wismar and accompany him on his mission. But there, too, I had no better luck, for he had no orders to raise a regiment and was, moreover, nothing but an impoverished nobleman who lived on his wife's money.

Though I had now been twice deceived and had allowed myself to be led so far afield, I took the bait a third time when he showed me letters he had received from Moscow which (he said) offered him high military office; or so he interpreted them to me, boasting loudly of good and regular pay. As he set out with wife and child I thought he could not well be going on a wild-goose chase. So I accompanied him hopefully, the more so as I saw no means or opportunity of an early return to Germany. Yet when we crossed the Russian frontier and met numbers of discharged German soldiers— most of them officers—I became alarmed and said to my colonel: 'What the devil are we doing? We leave a country at war and go to one where peace reigns and soldiers are discharged and discarded!' But he calmed my doubts, saying I should leave it all to him, for he knew better how to manage than these fellows, who were, in any case, of little account.

When we arrived in Moscow I saw at once that I had again been deceived, for though my colonel conversed daily with men of importance, it was with bishops rather than Boyars. This gave me much food for thought, though I could not imagine what his intention might be. Finally, he informed me that war was out and that his conscience drove him to embrace the Greek Orthodox faith. His sincere advice to me was that I should follow his example, since in any case he could no longer keep his promise to help me. His Majesty the Czar, he said, already had good accounts of my character and ability and would be graciously pleased, if I were agreeable, to make me a knight and endow me with a fine estate and many serfs. Such an offer, he said, should be accepted the more readily, since it was better to have so powerful a monarch for a gracious lord rather than an offended prince.

I was so dumbfounded at this that I did not know what to

reply, and had I been elsewhere, I would have let the colonel feel my answer rather than hear it. But now I must play my cards differently and bear in mind that I was little short of a prisoner in this place. So I held my tongue until I had well considered my answer. At last I told him that I had come to Moscow in order to serve His Majesty the Czar as a soldier, to which he—the colonel—had himself persuaded me. If my services in this capacity were not required I could not help it; nor indeed could I blame the Czar that I had undertaken so long a journey for his sake, for he had not summoned me. His Majesty's graciousness in wanting to bestow so high an honour on me was something of which I would be proud to boast to all the world. Yet I neither deserved it nor did I feel myself able to accept it. I was not at present prepared to change my religion, but wished myself back on my farm in the Black Forest, causing neither concern nor offence to any man. To this the colonel replied: 'Sir, you may do as you please, though I should have thought that if God and fortune smiled on a man he had cause for gratitude. If, however, you will accept no help and do not wish to live like a prince I hope you will at any rate bear witness that I have spared no pains to help you to the best of my ability.' With that he made me a deep reverence and swept out of the room, leaving me standing and not even permitting me to escort him to the door.

There I was, in deep perplexity, considering my situation, when I heard two Russian carriages outside our lodgings and, looking out of the window, saw my fine colonel with his sons step into one and his wife with her daughters into the other. The carriages and liveries were those of the Grand-duke, and several priests were among the retinue, who waited upon the family and showed them great courtesy and respect.

CHAPTER XI

Simplex is trapped; it falls to his lot
To make for the Russians powder and shot.

FROM this time on I was watched—not openly, but secretly and so that I did not perceive it—by soldiers of the Imperial household guard. I never saw my colonel or his family, nor did I know what had become of them. As the reader may imagine, it was a time of much anxious thought and many grey hairs for me. I sought out Germans who lived in Moscow as traders and craftsmen and told them of my predicament and how I had been deceived. They gave me comfort and advice how I might seize a favourable chance to return to Germany, but the moment they got wind of the Czar's intention to keep me in Russia, and that he was pressing me to consent, they all fell silent towards me and began to avoid me, so that I was hard put to it even to find lodgings. I had already sold my horse, complete with saddle and bridle, to keep myself alive, and now I was prising one ducat after another from the lining of my coat, where I had wisely sewn a supply before we set out. In the end I even began to sell my rings and jewels, in the hope of keeping myself until an opportunity occurred to return to Germany. Meanwhile three months went by, at the end of which my colonel and his household were baptized and admitted into the Orthodox Church, and received a fine nobleman's estate and many serfs.

At that time there was issued a decree that on pain of severe punishment no idlers, either natives or foreigners, should be allowed to batten on the working people. Any foreigner who would not work must leave the city within twenty-four hours and the country within a month. So some fifty of us banded together with the intention of making our way, with God's help, through Poland to Germany. But we had not been gone from the city more than two hours when a troop of Russian horsemen caught up with us. They gave us to understand that His Majesty the Czar was much displeased at our wickedly daring to gather in such numbers and traversing his country at will without a passport. They added that His Majesty had half a mind to punish our audacity by sending us to Siberia.

On our way back I learned how my affairs stood, for the leader of the troop told me in so many words that the Czar would not let me leave the country. His sincere advice was that I should submit to His Majesty's most gracious pleasure, adopt the Russian faith, and, like the colonel, accept a handsome country estate. He assured me that if I rejected the offer and refused to live among them as a lord, I would be held against my will and forced to live among them like a serf. Nor could the Czar be blamed for his reluctance to let out of the country so able and experienced a man as my colonel had made me out. Thereupon I began to belittle my abilities, saying that perhaps the colonel had endowed me with more knowledge, virtue and art, than I possessed. It was true that I had come to Russia to serve the Czar and the great Russian nation against their enemies—even at the risk of my life—but that I should change my religion was not part of the bargain. If, however, there was any way in which I could serve His Majesty without doing violence to my conscience I would do so to the utmost of my ability.

After this I was separated from my companions and lodged with a merchant, where I was now openly under guard, but at the same time provided with the most lavish food and choicest wines from the Imperial kitchens and cellars. I also had visitors every day who talked to me and sometimes invited me out. There was one in particular (a clever man), no doubt specially assigned to me, who entertained me daily with friendly conversation (for I was already fairly fluent in Russian). This man discussed all manner of mechanical matters with me, such as engines of war, the science of fortifications, and gunnery. In the end, when he had sounded me out repeatedly whether I would not, after all, submit to the Czar's wishes and found me adamant in my refusal, he suggested that I might, to honour the Czar, impart and communicate to his nation something of my knowledge, even if I did not want to become a Russian. The Czar, he said, would requite my compliance with high and royal favours. I retorted that my desire

238

had always been most humbly to serve His Majesty, since this was, after all, the reason for my coming to Russia, and that this was still my wish, even though I knew I was being held a prisoner. 'Not so, sir!' said he, 'you are by no means a prisoner. It is simply that His Majesty loves you so much that he cannot bear to part with you.' 'In that case,' I said, 'why am I being guarded?' 'Because His Majesty fears you might come to harm,' he replied.

Now that he knew my mind he told me that the Czar was graciously considering digging for saltpetre in his country and making gunpowder. As there was no one in Russia who knew anything about the business, I would be doing the Czar a most acceptable service if I were to undertake it. I would be lavishly supplied with men and materials, and his personal view was that I would be most unwise to refuse this very gracious request, because they already knew that I was excellently qualified to do it. So I answered: 'Sir, I can only repeat what I have already told you: if there is anything in which I can serve His Majesty, provided only he will be graciously pleased to leave me my religion, he shall never find me remiss.' The Russian, who was a Boyar of the highest rank, was highly delighted at this and toasted me more often and more copiously even than a German.

Next day two Boyars came with an interpreter to conclude the agreement and bring me a costly Russian robe as a present from the Czar; and only a few days later I began searching for saltpetre and instructing the Russians assigned to me in the art of separating it from the soil and refining it. Then I drew up plans for a powder-mill and taught others to burn charcoal, so that quite soon we had a fair supply of powder both for muskets and heavy artillery. I had men aplenty for the task, and also my personal servants, who were supposedly to wait on me and minister to my comforts, but whose real task it was to guard and watch me.

When I was well launched my erstwhile colonel came to visit me, magnificently attired in Russian robes and surrounded by a retinue of serfs—in order, no doubt, to persuade me with this show of splendour to follow his example and change my religion. But I knew very well that his robes came from the

Czar's wardrobe and had been lent out for the occasion to make my mouth water, this being a very common custom at the Russian Court.

To give the reader an inkling of how this is commonly arranged I will take a personal example. One day I was busy at the powder-mill I had built on the river outside Moscow, assigning to my men their tasks for that day and the next, when there was a sudden alarm that the Tartars, 100,000 horse strong, were no more than fifteen miles away, laying waste the land and advancing steadily. So I and my men were ordered to go to the palace, where we were fitted out from the Czar's armoury and stables. For me there was a quilted silk breast-plate for armour which might perhaps have been proof against arrows but would have stopped no bullets; boots, spurs, and a truly princely head-dress with heron's plumes; as well as a sabre that would split a hair, its solid gold pommel set with jewels. Of the Czar's horses one was put under me the like of which I had never seen—far less ridden—in my life. The horse's harness and I glittered with gold, silver, jewels, and pearls. At my side hung a steel mace, polished as bright as a mirror, so well made and heavy that it would easily have smashed the skull of any man I struck with it. All in all, the Czar himself could not have set out more splendidly caparisoned. Behind me rode a man carrying a white banner with a double eagle, to which people flocked from every side, so that in less than two hours we were 40,000 horse strong and in four hours 60,000 with which to advance against the Tartars. Every quarter of an hour I received new orders from the Czar by messenger, but their gist never varied, and amounted to no more than exhortations to show myself this day as good a soldier as my reputation made me out. Our army grew apace as single men and groups arrived to swell it, but in the little time I had I could discover no one who might have commanded this host or disposed it for battle.

I will be brief, for my story is not much concerned with this encounter. We met the Tartars, weary and burdened with spoils, quite suddenly in a valley or dip in the ground when they least expected it, and rode at them so furiously from all sides that our very first charge broke their ranks. As I went into the assault I said in Russian to my retinue: 'Follow me, and let each man do as I do!' This word they passed on among themselves as I galloped at full tilt towards the enemy and struck the first man I met—a Mirza—such a blow that I split his skull and his brain stuck to my steel mace. The Russians followed my heroic example, so that the Tartars could not withstand their assault, but turned and fled.

As for me, I behaved like one demented or one who in desperation seeks death but cannot find it. I struck down whoever crossed my path, Tartar and Russian alike, and those who had been set by the Czar to watch me followed so close behind that my back was always perfectly guarded. Arrows flew as thick as swarming bees, and one of them struck me in the arm, for I had rolled back my sleeves in order to wield my mace and sabre the more freely and murderously. Before I received this wound my heart laughed within me at such bloodshed, but when I saw my own blood my laughter turned to mad fury. At last, when these fierce enemies had been routed, several Boyars commanded me, on behalf of the Czar, to render His Majesty an account of our victory over the Tartars.

So I turned back with about a hundred horsemen as my retinue. I rode through the city to the Czar's palace and was hailed and cheered by the multitude as their saviour. But as soon as I had made my report to the Czar (who had already had a full account of the battle), I was made to divest myself of my princely trappings, which were carefully returned to the Czar's wardrobe, although they and the horse's harness were so stained and spattered with blood and spoilt that I had fully expected to be allowed to keep them and my horse as part reward for my brave bearing in this encounter.

So I knew well enough what to think of my colonel's splendid attire, which doubtless was no more than borrowed finery and belonged, like all things else in Russia, to the Czar in person.

CHAPTER XII

Simplex tells of the long journey he had
Before he returned at last to his dad.

As long as it took my wounds to heal I was indeed treated like a prince. I went about in a sheepskin fur, braided with gold and lined with sable, though my hurt was neither fatal nor even serious; and never in my life have I eaten more richly than I did then. But this was the only profit I had from my labours, save for the Czar's praise, which the envy of some of the Boyars quickly turned to gall.

When I was quite restored I was sent down the Volga by boat to Astrakhan, to set up a powder-mill there like the one I had built in Moscow. For the Czar found it impossible regularly to provision his frontier fortresses in those distant parts with fresh and suitable powder from Moscow, whence it must travel the long and perilous journey by water. I went the more readily, since the Czar had promised me that when I had finished he would send me back to Holland with a reward appropriate to his exalted rank and the value of my services. But alas, whenever we feel most secure in our hopes and plans an envious gust of wind comes unawares and blows away the flimsy shelter we have been so long a-building.

The Governor of Astrakhan treated me as if I were the Czar in person, and I soon had everything on a good footing. His badly stored ammunition, spoilt, ruined, and quite useless, I refounded (like a tinker makes new tin spoons from old); which was something so unheard-of in the Russia of those days that some took me for a magician and others for a new saint or prophet.

But when I was hard at work and spending my nights outside the fortress at my powder-mill I was seized and kidnapped by a troop of Tartars, who took me and my companions so far into the interior of their country that I was able not only to see the herb Barometz—or sheep-plant—growing but even had it to eat. The Tartars who had captured me bartered me to other Tartars from Niuchi in exchange for some Chinese

242

merchandise, and these in their turn made a present of me to the King of Korea, with whom they had just concluded an armistice. There I was held in high esteem, for I proved a better fencer than any they had in their country and taught the king how, with his musket over his shoulder and his back to the target, he could still hit the bull's-eye. As a reward, and at my humble request, he granted me my freedom and sent me by way of Japan to the Portuguese in Macao, but there I found myself of little account. I went about among them like a sheep that has strayed from the fold, until in the end I was captured by Turkish pirates, who carried me about with them for a year or more among the strange peoples who inhabit the islands of the East Indies before selling me to some Egyptian merchants in Alexandria. These took me with their merchandise to Constantinople, but because the Turkish emperor just then was fitting out galleys against the Venetians and needed rowers, many Turkish merchants had to surrender their Christian slaves—though against payment in cash—and I, being a young and vigorous fellow, found myself among them. So I had to learn to row, but this heavy labour lasted no more than two months, at the end of which our galley was boarded and seized by the Venetians in the Levant, and I and all my fellows delivered from Turkish bondage. When the galley reached Venice, loaded with spoils and several important Turkish prisoners, I was set at liberty, having declared my intention of making a pilgrimage to Rome and Loretto, to see these places and to thank God for my deliverance. I had no difficulty in obtaining a pass for the journey as well as a fair sum of money from several generous people, especially Germans, so that I was able to fit myself out with a long pilgrim's cloak and depart on my journey.

I made straight for Rome, where I did very well, for I got many alms by begging from great and small. When I had stayed there for some six weeks I set out for Loretto with other pilgrims, among them some Germans and more Swiss on their way home. Thence I travelled over the St Gotthard pass and through Switzerland, until I reached the Black Forest and my Dad, who had been keeping my farm for me and managing it to my great profit. Yet the only thing of note

I brought back with me from all these travels was a beard I had grown in the course of them.

I had been away three years and some months, during which I had crossed several oceans and seen many different peoples, at whose hands I had commonly experienced more evil than good, and it would take a large book to give a full account of it all. Meanwhile, the Peace of Westphalia had been concluded, so that I could live contentedly and securely with my Dad. I left him to manage the farm and household, while I returned to my books, which were once my work and my delight.

CHAPTER XIII

Simplex reflects on his sinful ways;
Resolves as a hermit to end his days.

I ONCE read what the Delphic oracle replied to the emissaries from Rome who asked it what they must do to rule their subjects in peace. 'Nosce teipsum,' it said; that is: Let every man know himself! This led me to reflect, since I had little else to do, and to render unto myself an account of the life I had led. Then I said to myself: Your life has been no life, but a death; your days a heavy shadow, your years a nightmare, your lusts mortal sins, your youth an illusion, and your happiness an alchemist's treasure which vanishes up the chimney and is gone before you know it is there. You have followed war through many perils and had much good as well as ill fortune from it. It has made you by turns exalted and humble, great and small, rich and poor, merry and sad, popular and hated, honoured and despised. But at the last, oh my poor soul, what profit have you had from this long pilgrimage? This is the reckoning: I am poor in worldly goods, my heart is burdened with cares, to all good impulses am I unresponsive, lazy, and spoilt; worst of all, my conscience is heavy and vexed, and you, my soul, are overwhelmed with manifold sins and horribly defiled. The body is weary, the understanding bemused, innocence vanished, the best part of my youth gone and precious time wasted; there is nothing in which I take pleasure, and in the end I have come to hate even myself. When I stepped out into the world after my saintly father's death I was simple in heart and pure, upright and honest, truthful, humble, discreet, modest, temperate, chaste, pious and devout. But soon I became malicious, false, deceitful, haughty, restless, and above all entirely godless, learning all these vices entirely without benefit of tutor. Not for its own sake did I guard my honour, but only for my personal advancement. Not to use it well for my soul's salvation did I heed time, but for the pleasures of the flesh. Often have I risked my life, yet never attempted to improve it in order that I might die comforted and blessed. I looked only to the present and to my worldly profit, without once giving thought to the future or to the account I would one day have to give of myself before God.

With such thoughts did I torment myself daily, and they pierced my heart, so that I left the world and became a hermit once more. To this end I retired to a wilderness where I began anew the life which once I led in the Spessart; but whether I shall, like my father of blessed memory, persevere in it to the end I do not know.

God grant us all His grace
That we may all obtain
from him what we stand
most in need of:
a blessed
END!

POSTSCRIPT

VERY little is known about Hans Jacob Christoffel von Grimmelshausen. He was born in or near the town of Gelnhausen, at the foot of the Spessart mountains in Western Germany, probably some time between 1621 and 1625; that is, towards the beginning of the Thirty Years War. In 1634 the town was sacked by Croats, and Grimmelshausen, separated from his family, found himself with the army. He probably spent the winter of 1634/35 in the fortress of Hanau, not far away, and in 1636 served with the Imperial Forces before Magdeburg. Some three years later he became secretary to Count von Schaumburg, who was commandant of Offenburg in Baden, in Southern Germany, at the foot of the Black Forest. Except for another spell of active service about 1647—towards the very end of the war—he appears to have spent the rest of his life in this part of the world; first, employed by the Schaumburg family in various capacities (including that of host of a tavern they owned), and then in the service of the Bishop of Strasbourg, in which he became mayor of the village of Renchen. He died in 1676, and the church register records that all his sons were present at his death-bed.

Grimmelshausen was probably less than thirty years old when he finally settled down in the Black Forest, but had presumably experienced enough adventures by then to last a lifetime. The second half of his life, in settled but not onerous employment, must have left him plenty of leisure to write his books. The most notable of these are the so-called 'Simplician Writings', of which *Simplicius Simplicissimus* is the best known.

One of the reasons why so little is known about Grimmelshausen's life is that he never wrote under his own name, but under a bewildering array of pseudonyms, all of them anagrams of his real name. Here are a few samples: Melchior Sternfels von Fugshaim, Philarchus Grossus von Trommenheim, Signeur Messmahl, Simon Lengfrisch von Hartenfels, Erich Stainfels von Grufensholm, and there are a number of others. Why he did this

247

no one knows. Some say it was because literature in those days was held in abject contempt in Germany; others, because he was describing contemporary events and some of the protagonists featuring in his books were still alive. Neither explanation seems very convincing. Other authors, far less talented and successful than Grimmelshausen, had no scruples about writing under their own names at the time; and Grimmelshausen himself wrote several completely conventional works of fiction, featuring no recognizable contemporary, yet still used a pseudonym on the title page. Perhaps it was simply his peculiar sense of humour, of which his books provide plenty of examples.

Be that as it may, for more than a century after his death men of letters were still attributing his books to imaginary authors, and when they finally stumbled on the truth many clues to Grimmelshausen's life had vanished for ever.

In the case of *Simplicius Simplicissimus*, Grimmelshausen succeeded in making confusion virtually complete. The first edition named the author as German Schleifheim von Sulsfort, but to the second edition a sixth and somewhat unrelated book was added which contained a note to the reader, supposedly by von Sulsfort, stating that the whole was the work of one Samuel Greiffensohn von Hirschfeld. So Samuel Greiffensohn von Hirschfeld was accepted as the author until well into the nineteenth century. Finally, writing the story in the first person singular, Grimmelshausen used one of his other pen-names, Melchior Sternfels von Fugshaim, as the real name of Simplicius, so that in effect no fewer than three of his pseudonyms are associated with the book and serve to confuse the issue.

There is no doubt that many of Simplicius' adventures are autobiographical, or at least based largely on Grimmelshausen's own experiences. The birthplace, the winter's stay in Hanau, the siege of Magdeburg, the exploits in Westphalia, and the eventual retirement in the Black Forest all closely correspond with what we know of the author's life. Many of the characters in the book, too, are authentic, such as Commandant Ramsay of Hanau, de Saint André of Lippstadt, and the Generals von Mansfeld, Banér, Wahl, and Götz. So also are the battles.

Grimmelshausen has also paid close attention to the chronology of events. Simplicius was born at the Battle of Höchst, in 1622, left the forest after the Battle of Nördlingen, in 1634, when he was twelve years old, and spent the following winter in Hanau. The siege of Magdeburg was in 1636. He was active as Huntsman of Soest in 1637, at the age of fifteen, and spent the winter of 1637/38 in Lippstadt. His adventures in France occupied no more than the spring of 1638, for he was back in Germany for the Battle of Wittenweier in July of that year and took part in the siege of Breisach the following winter. The later adventures, being more obviously imaginary, are less well documented.

The book was an instant success when it was published in 1669. It was the first German novel to deal with contemporary events in everyday language, and a complete break with the tradition of Romances and Tales of Chivalry which were the standard works of fiction of Grimmelshausen's age. Grimmelshausen, in fact, did for the German novel what Defoe did for the English. The only difference was that he remained an isolated phenomenon in German literature and had no successors. *Simplicius Simplicissimus*, however, did have successors. Seeing how well his book was received, Grimmelshausen wrote a whole series of others in a similar vein, all featuring the original hero and one or other of his friends and associates. One of these books tells the story of an uninhibited and resourceful camp-follower by the name of Courage from which, in our day, Berthold Brecht drew the idea and the title for his play *Mother Courage*.

As for *The Adventures of Simplicius Simplicissimus* itself, the first edition was followed by at least two others within a year. These contained a sixth book, tacked on somewhat loosely to the original five, in which Simplicius sails to a desert island, where he finds rest and contentment at last. This sixth book, which is not part of the original work, has been left out of the present translation, and the remainder somewhat shortened to bring it within the compass of a single volume. The cuts have been made in such a way as to preserve the continuity of the story, omitting mainly a highly fantastical journey to the centre of the earth, a certain amount of moralizing, and a peroration near the end which Grimmelshausen lifted bodily—with due acknowledgements—from the Spanish divine Guevara.

W. WALLICH